Hollow Minds

COOLEY

Copyright © 2017 by Adrian Cooley
Printed and Bound in the United States of America

Published and Distributed By
The Big Storyteller Publishing
rockywaters@comcast.net

Cover and Interior Design by TWASolutions.com

ISBN: 9780692422953

For inquires, contact the publisher.

MY ANGER

MY ANGER makes me want to react

From years of hatred and racism, skin tone black

MY ANGER makes it hard for me to worry

About the right here and right now, attitude is to hurry

MY ANGER could destroy my American dream

Disrespecting the one they call an African Queen

MY ANGER leads me to kill

And seeing blood spill became more than just a thrill

MY ANGER makes me want to hustle and be in the game

Even clapping on a nigga for wanting my fame

MY ANGER has no future in my eyes

The right here and right now is how I stay alive

MY ANGER needs to fall back and let me see

That this is a disease that's killing me

MY ANGER was built on years of oppression

Being cursed for my color is a valid lesson

MY ANGER is the reason that I'm losing my blessing

Is the mighty dollar my God, now that's a logical question

MY ANGER is the reason why I'm second-guessing

To leave the streets alone or continue stressing

MY ANGER won't let me see tomorrow

Which leaves the thoughts in my mind to always remain hollow

—Raymond Cobbs aka Chance

CHAPTER 1

The Hit

In total darkness, a deep, thunderous voice roared, demanding answers. Logic wasn't the only man in the room blindfolded and tied to a hard, metal chair. Surge and Buttons were with him, the three oddballs commonly known as the Geek Squad. The voice was cold and his only concern was their stash. Desperation laced his tone, it was a hit and they knew it. There was no turning back now and the voice wasn't leaving until he got what he wanted. These well-known computer hackers hadn't been in the game long enough to protect their interests or themselves. They spent the majority of their time indoors, robbing people around the world for their hard-earned cash. No one knew them on the streets, a well-kept, secret criminal enterprise, which was the best part. A rumor that the computer geeks hacked into various accounts to get their paper was all these thieves needed to run down on them. The three geeks robbed everyone who owned a computer and kept the cash somewhere in this house and these thieves were willing to kill for it.

It was Pemont and his soldiers who found out and knew where to make the hit. Taking their stash would be easy. The room was quiet and there was only one voice heard. No one person singled out. The question was toward all three men, but no one talked. The cold voice was getting impatient and ready to make an example out of one of them. The young hackers could tell they were in the basement of the house because of the wet smell in the air of mold and mildew. It was cold and the hard, dirty surface crackling beneath their feet was all the proof they needed, besides the sudden push down the hard wooden stairs from the first floor. An echo followed each time the young killer spoke. No one was giving up any answers and tension was building. Suddenly, there was a click, followed by a loud boom. It seemed like an eternity before it ended with a hard thud on the concrete floor. The room went silent, causing one of the geeks to panic and give up the secret location of their stash, which was a built-in safe in the basement wall. After the voice got what he was looking for, he had his goons place duct tape over the geeks' mouths and left them there.

After what seemed to be a long wait, Logic was able to loosen the duct tape from his mouth. He called out to his friends and all were present. *So, who got popped?* Buttons eventually broke free and untied everyone. They removed their blindfolds to an empty chair lying sideways on the floor, which matched the empty safe in the wall. There was no blood or body. They got played and had no clue of who had done it. It was obvious they were saving them for future hits. This was their livelihood, they would find another way to get their stash back up and the young robbers were counting on it.

...

Pemont and his crew couldn't believe how easy it was to pull off, and couldn't stop laughing. They were all young killers who wouldn't have a problem ending the lives of all three of those so-called hackers, if the plan didn't work. But, why kill those clowns for being stupid enough to get robbed? Pemont let them breathe. If they were dumb enough to get caught slipping the first time, then they'd be foolish enough to get caught twice. It was easy money for the crew, but Pemont wasn't after the money. He wanted to play the game to master their craft. He knew it would come in handy in due time.

CHAPTER 2

Clouds of Smoke

Chance was conducting a meeting with the Young Hitters, making sure everyone got their cut. It was enough to put a smile on everyone's faces. Business was slow with Pitch mourning the loss of his little sister, Fatima. Others were starting to lose their loyalty and it showed in their actions. They barely put in work and started to question the lieutenants and captains, who made it seem as though it was in the form of a challenge. Some of his workers started doing business with Polo the Don across the bridge in Philadelphia, Pennsylvania.

Tuck was returning from the Dominican Republic soon with Chaos, who hooked him up with his new connect in Santo Domingo. As soon as Tuck returned from his trip, he would have Chance pick him up to take care of some business elsewhere.

While counting the money they stole from the Geek Squad, Chance scanned his crew of young killers.

"You guys did a great job tonight. We were able to hit it off with no problems." Chance looked upon his crew like a proud father. They were true, loyal soldiers who knew how to follow rules.

"Shit, I was hoping one of those muhfuckas would do some dumb shit, so I could set it off in that muhfucka." Dundy stretched his arm out with one eye closed, pretending to pull the trigger of an imaginary gun. Pemont and Syphee shook their heads, while he jumped up and down, laughing at the thought of it. Dundy was very hyper and unstable.

"Well, I'm glad it didn't come to that, and Dundy, I see you still need some work. That attitude is gon' get one of us killed. Now let that shit marinate." Chance paused to let it soak in. "Tomorrow, I got a meeting with this duck ass nigga who killed my peoples, Willy. I want this nigga outlined in chalk by sunrise." Chance was spitting venom.

"Just point us in the right direction and we'll handle it," Pemont responded with eagerness.

"Now we talkin' my language." Dundy was punching his fist in his hand with excitement.

"What's this dude's name?" Syphee asked. He appeared more focused, as if he were taking in every detail of their next mission. This was a hit; they looked up to Chance and were willing to prove their loyalty. Without Chance and Tuck, there's no telling where they would be and how their lives would have turned out. All three had nothing and started at the bottom. They were getting desperate and desperate times called for desperate measures. The Young Hitters were heading down the path of destruction. Chance looked them over, once again, before announcing his next assignment and the intended target. Just as he started to speak, both front and back doors exploded as the feds came pouring through, with their badges and guns drawn.

"Police, everyone on the ground!" a voice yelled, as a black cloud spilled through the door.

Men dressed in police uniforms, with "task force" written on the back of their Kevlar vests and black helmets with protective lenses, rushed in. Long barrel weapons with a red beam of light danced on the young thugs' heads and chests. Shooting their way out would be foolish. Suicide by cop ran through Chance's head, but that's not how he wanted to go out. He had to weigh out his options first.

Before the Young Hitters had a chance to reach for their weapons, the feds tackled them hard to the floor and handcuffed them. Now Chance was standing alone, looking like a red disco light. There was a ton of cash for him to do some serious time behind bars, but having cash wasn't illegal and there were no drugs around. They would probably come after him for tax evasion, if he couldn't explain where the money came from and if he paid his taxes with it. He could get a good lawyer to get him out of this jam, so there was no need in him trying to shoot his way out. He slowly raised his arms in submission. The swarm of officers looked like black smoke. It was dark and he was unable to make out the gang of shadows that blocked not only his means of escape, but smothered the little light that came from the small lamps on the corner tables. Chance stood silently, waiting for the officer to give his next command.

Then a figure advanced toward him. He could only make out the rage in the masked officer's red eyes. The officer had his rifle raised and the butt of the gun aimed at him. He held the weapon with two hands as it rested on his right shoulder. Chance was waiting for the angry officer to read him his rights, but before that could happen, everything went black.

CHAPTER 3

Misty Faces

Chance slowly opened his eyes. The room was dark and his eyes burned. He wanted to wipe away the stinging sensation, but was unable to move his arms.

He looked to see what was holding him down. He was on his belly, tied down by a rope. His flesh burned with each turn of his wrists. Surrounded by a silhouette of misty faces, he had to blink hard to clear his vision. A look of familiarity drenched his face, as Cat Daddy's goons surrounded him. Pitch was standing above him with an evil grin. Chance could tell he was lying on a hard surface above ground. Some sort of table. It was very uncomfortable and hard. It was a pool table. He could tell by the green felt and the empty holes on the left and right corners and on the sides. A lone light hung above. The casting shadow on Pitch's face made him look menacing. A cold draft made the hairs on Chance's arms rise and gave him goose bumps. He was nude, body shivering from an unseen breeze that chilled him. He was in a fucked up situation and he knew there was no getting out of it.

Tuck wasn't around. He was out of the country, making moves. The few goons left were out on the corners, getting money. The Young Hitters stood before him with a look of confusion. This was like a scene from the movie *In Too Deep*. They had no weapons and were outnumbered ten-to-one. All the other goons were still wearing tactical police uniforms. Chance should have known better; from a well-trained eye, one could tell they weren't real police officers from their stance and...the way they moved...very lazy and laid-back. There was no need to question the money taken from the Geek Squad. Chance knew that Pitch kept it for his own personal use.

"Wake the fuck up, nigga!" Pitch hollered, smacking him hard across the back while circling the pool table. The loud smacking sound was hard enough to make everyone in the room cringe.

"Yo, this shit ain't cool, Pitch!" Chance roared, trying to hold on to what little dignity he had left.

"It ain't cool," Pitch reiterated. "I'ma tell you what ain't cool. You fuckin' Cat's girl, while he's on ice." He motioned, coming to a full stop in front of Chance who saw the shocked look on the Young Hitters' faces. They couldn't believe one of Cat Daddy's soldiers was stretched out on a pool table in such a manner, or maybe it was hearing that Chance disrespecting Cat Daddy like that, or maybe it was a combination of both.

"Man, yous out yo cotton pickin' mind. I don't know what the fuck you talkin' 'bout," Chance murmured.

"You don't know what I'm talkin' 'bout. I knew you would say some dumb shit like that." Pitch pulled out his cell phone and showed him a video of Crystal walking into Cat Daddy's auto body shop and having sex in one of the vehicles in the back of the shop. The video was distorted. It was hard to make out the shadow figures, but it was obvious they were having sex. It wasn't hard for him to tell because of the aggressive bumping of flesh. The figure fucking her could have been anyone. The only clear part of the video was Crystal entering and exiting the shop in her white Mercedes Benz. Her license plates were also on that video.

CHAPTER 4

I've Got a Story to Tell

"Fuck outta here. That shit ain't me and you know it. You best go 'head and kick rocks," Chance argued.

"Yes, it is you and I do have more proof." His cocky grin was annoying.

Chance frowned. "Proof? What proof?"

"You, out of everybody here, kept talkin' 'bout how you gon' fuck the shit outta her and didn't give a fuck 'bout Cat. You even said it in front of everybody here in this room," Pitch said, with outstretched arms, "that you would be the one to lay him down if he tried to step to you the wrong way."

"I was jus' talkin' shit. I didn't mean any of that shit," Chance tried to explain.

"Pussy, don't try to cop a plea now. You been caught on many occasions, talkin' secretly to her. Explain that, muhfucka," Pitch scowled.

"That don't mean shit. You freestylin'. You never liked me from the rip and this is your way of takin' me out. Let's get it over wit'." Chance was a roughneck and not afraid to die. He knew his life was short. Opening his eyes each morning to see another day was a major plus and a blessing.

"No, you pretty muhfucka. It ain't gon' be that easy. I'm gonna make you beg and plead for your life. You fucked Cat's bitch, while he was on ice and somebody killed my little sister. Since you're a dead man already, maybe you'd give me something and I might jus' make it quick."

Pitch pulled out a small package and slammed it on the pool table. He opened the package, exposing surgical instruments.

Everyone stood around, watching in silence. Pitch was giving them a sample of his madness. Fear resonated on their faces.

...

Pitch was sweating and breathing hard. He tortured Chance for over an hour and Chance was a bloody mess, fucked up beyond recognition. He was missing teeth and his left eye was swollen shut. Pitch decided to give him the opportunity to speak his peace before taking him out of his misery. Chance spat out a bloody tooth before telling him the story. He didn't like Pitch and was planning to take him out, but Pitch beat him to the punch. He looked on the floor, with his good eye and saw a bloody ear. *Whose ear is it?* He knew the answer to that question because of the throbbing sensation on the left side of his head.

Chance had to catch his breath for he knew Pitch was going to end his life right then. In front of his goons who were too afraid to move. This was what Pitch wanted, for all to see the extent of his madness and to fear the man that would be running the streets. This was Chance's opportunity to explain what was really going down, so his young followers saw the truth about the man they proudly called boss. He had their undivided attention.

CHAPTER 5

Six Months Earlier

The redevelopment had begun. Townhomes replaced demolished, project homes. In order to reside in the new development, residents must adhere to the rules or risk eviction. The new blueprints made it harder for drug dealers to set up shop in and around the area. The rules were strict and enforced. Any occupants not on the list would face eviction. Upon monthly inspection, unkempt property was cause for eviction. If occupants were arrested for selling drugs, they were evicted. If their bank accounts exceeded the maximum amount allowed, they were evicted. There was no moving forward, as this plan was to hold the community down and dependent.

Tuck and Chance sat at the bar at Off Broadway, trying to drown their sorrows. Their entire day consisted of Willy's passing. Willy was that third connection with the tight bond they shared. After having a son, Willy decided to go the straight and narrow. Cat Daddy made him the head manager of his auto body shop and everything seemed to have been heading in the right direction. Now, he was suddenly gone after a drug overdose that somehow sparked a fire in an abandoned warehouse.

"Yo, man, that was fucked up how Willy went out like that," Tuck said, as they sipped on cold Budweiser's.

"I ain't even know the nigga was on drugs." Chance was hurt and angered.

"I don't know. He said he would never touch the shit after seeing what it did to Mom Dukes."

Chance's eyes lit up. "You don't think he was set up, do you?"

"Don't know. Shit ain't adding up right." Silence lingered

between them as they sat in deep thought. The music was pumping and bar patrons were having a good time drinking, but no one was dancing.

"Did you holla at Mel yet?" Chance asked, finishing off his first beer and ordering another.

"Naw, man. I don't know what to say," Tuck uttered, twirling his empty bottle on the bar top.

"Yeah, I feel ya on that. I'm stuck like fuckin' Chuck." Chance was now analyzing his empty beer bottle.

"I'ma send one of the hitters over to drop some paper off. She gon' need it," Tuck said, as the bartender handed him another cold one.

"You know we gon' have to show love," Chance reminded him.

"I know. My schedule's tight. I'll swing by later this week, but I'ma make sure to call her celly before then."

More people entered the bar, giving Tuck and Chance love, as if they were celebrities.

"I'm ready to bounce; my head's all fucked up." Tuck slammed his empty bottle down. He pulled out a wad of cash and dropped it on the bar top. Chance knew it was time to leave before the alcohol brought out the Hulk.

CHAPTER 6

Looking for Answers

Tony got to the hospital as quickly as he could, with Mark and Dave alongside him. Tony was upset and very emotional. He needed someone by his side to help him in time of need. Even though they liked to play and joke around, this was serious and they were there to have his back. The place was busy with concerned loved ones gathering in the lobby. Tony made his way to the counter to sign them in. The receptionist pointed them in the right direction, after handing them their visitors' passes. The hospital smelled as if they mopped the floors with peroxide and penicillin. Everything in the hospital was white: the floors, walls, curtains, sheets and blankets. It was like preparing for heaven, so it felt.

When they entered the room, there were tubes running from Frank Debartello's body to a bunch of monitors. He was unresponsive and bandaged up. A man everyone looked up to, the boss of all bosses, a man feared by many; now reduced to a frail-looking old man with nothing left to give.

The sight was too much for him to bear. Tony stood frozen. He wanted to call out to his father, but his brain couldn't get his mouth to respond. He wanted to run over to him and wake him from his slumber, but he couldn't move his legs. All he could do was stand there, staring at his father lying in a comatose state.

"Hi and may I help you, gentlemen?" The nurse asked, as she entered the room, snapping him out of his trance.

"Yes, I want to know what happened to my father." Desperation laced Tony's voice. His brain was working now.

She checked his vitals then began to type on her computer. "According to this report, there was a massive explosion that destroyed his home. The firefighters found your father lying in the bushes a few yards from the home. Your father is a very lucky man to survive such an explosion of that magnitude. Right now, we induced him into a coma, because of the seriousness of his wounds. He did suffer second and third-degree burns to his legs and back. The back of his head also suffered severe burns that did some massive tissue damage. He'd never grow hair in the back, but other than that, he'd be fine."

Tony stared at his father in his weakened condition. He was reduced to a shell of a man, dead to the world. *Who gave the order?* Now that was the big question. It clearly had a mob hit written all over it. Someone was going to pay for this shit and Tony was going to make sure of it.

CHAPTER 7

Talking In Code

Clean, in a Giorgio Armani suit, with a fresh haircut, looking like a true don, Pitch sat in the visitor's room at the Camden City Jail. Cat Daddy entered the room on the opposite side of the glass partition and took a seat. With a quick nod, they both picked up their receivers and held them up to their ears.

"Yo, Cat, what up, homie? How's things holdin' up?" Pitch tried to soften up Cat Daddy's hardened expression, sported a red jumpsuit, which was one of three different colors the inmate population wore. Orange jumpsuits were for minimum status inmates who had to do a short stay for minor charges, mainly child support and traffic violations. Blue jumpsuits were for medium status inmates who had to do a little time, but could expect release in five years or less. Red jumpsuits were for maximum status inmates who would have to get comfortable for a long stay with inmates who had king pin and murder charges.

Cat Daddy gave his condolences on the loss of his sister, Fatima and felt bad he couldn't attend her funeral.

"I've been hearing some things and it ain't all good." He paused.

"So talk to me. Whatchu been hearin'?" Anticipation laced Pitch's voice. Since it wasn't all bad that meant he was hearing some good things as well.

A scowl grew on his face. "Fuck you think I been hearin'? You got a fuckin' big mouth. That mouthpiece gon' get you in lots of trouble. You got the streets callin' you the new HNIC. Now that I'm on ice, you think you gon' take over my whole operation like

I'm dead."

"Yo, Cat, man, it ain't like that."

"Oh yeah, then how is it? You tell me," Cat Daddy barked.

There was a long pause before they both burst into laughter.

"So that's how you gon' do that movie you been talkin' 'bout?" Pitch asked, but he knew where Cat Daddy was taking it. The phones were bugged and they had to talk in codes to throw the feds off. "Movie" meant the line was hot and they were the center of attention. Cat Daddy was aware of it; he just lost his cool for a moment.

"Yeah, I've been workin' on it for a while now. I see you still remember it."

"Why wouldn't I, you read it to me 'bout thirty-six million times," Pitch said, telling Cat Daddy he was able to save up thirty-six million dollars in cash.

"Well, I'm ready to get the fuck outta here and I'm gon' leave that up to you to get me out." Cat Daddy was telling him he wanted out the business.

"So what you want to do when you get out?"

"I want to go to that barber spot in Camden so he could give me a brand new haircut." Cat was telling Pitch to get his crew together to get him out and take him to a surgeon in Cherry Hill, New Jersey, for a face-lift.

"Then what we gon' do?" Pitch asked.

A woman in the visiting room was trying to get Pitch's attention once she recognized him. Pitch ignored her and continued with Cat Daddy's plan. The woman's man, who sat across from her behind the glass partition, was going off. She was trying to calm him down before the guards kicked him out. If Pitch or Cat Daddy gave into her flirtatious lure, then there would have been problems with the man trying to prove himself to the other inmates.

"I want to party all night long with no end." Cat Daddy was out the business and now passing the torch to Pitch. The thirty-six million dollars were enough for him to live comfortably. Once Pitch was in charge, that would make Tuck his second in command, but Pitch had other ideas and wasn't feeling Tuck enough to hold that position. Now it was time for Pitch to put this shit in motion.

CHAPTER 8

He Was Ready to Snap

After leaving the hospital, Dave drove with Mark seated next to him in the passenger seat and Tony in the back seat, staring into space. So many questions filled his head. *Who did this shit and why?* However, those questions didn't matter. His father was seriously hurt and someone was going to pay. It was up to him to put a stop to this and rebuild his family. Dave and Mark saw the concern in his eyes and knew they had to choose their words wisely. Tony looked like he was ready to snap at any moment. The longer he sat in deep thought, the more wrinkles formed on his forehead. Mark decided to break the silence.

"Hey Tone...are you gon' be a'ight?" His words were shaky.

Tony's eyes darted to the back of his head as if he had asked him an insane question. For a moment, it was as if he were looking at a complete stranger. His face finally softened once he realized he was overreacting. "Ah, yeah... I'm good."

The air grew silent, as if no one knew what to say next, but Dave decided to speak up.

"Yo, Tone, you wanna get a few drinks?"

"Naw, I need to make some moves to get some answers. I can't afford to cloud my judgement. There was a hit on my dad and I need to take care of that before they strike again." Tony dropped his head in the palm of his hands and squeezed. His head felt like it was about to explode. There was so much to do with so little time. Tony was making some money on the side with his illegal rental property scam, but that wasn't enough for what he had planned. Now that his father was out of commission, he needed to make more money to pay for his hospital bills and hold all his father's business and finances down. Tony needed a team of players he could trust. Ever since Nicolas died, Tony began hanging with his friends, Dave and Mark. Getting drunk at the hangout spots started to build a close bond between the three of them. If Tony could trust anyone, it would be Mark and Dave. The three of them had two things in common: pussy and money. Now that they were both working for him, one question lingered. Would they have his back in time of need?

CHAPTER 9

Haunted by Her Actions

Crystal's head was all fucked up. She wondered how Fatima got a video of her and Willy fucking at the shop. Crystal wasn't slow. She knew Fatima had a big mouth and couldn't keep any secrets. But, how much did she know and who did she tell? The way Pitch looked at her before handing her Fatima's iPad at her funeral said he knew. Now Crystal had to cover her tracks and handle anyone with that information. She decided to start from the top and step to her man, Cat Daddy, first. He was the last person she wanted to have that information. That would be a death sentence for her. Maybe he did know and had the hitman take Willy out first and she was next. To be safe, she had shooters around her on this trip. But, for now, they had to wait outside. There was no way they were getting into the building heavily armed. She was at the jail, paying her man a visit. Crystal was dressed to kill in a gold, fitted Chanel dress, six-inch Alexander McQueen heels and sporting Michael Kors' shades. All eyes were on her, as she entered the place. Security abandoned their post to get a good look at her. Crystal was a dime piece and she knew it. As she waited for the first group of visitors to exit the visiting room, Pitch was the last person to exit. Their eyes met. Crystal's heart dropped, but she maintained a calm exterior. Pitch smiled when he noticed her, but kept undressing her with his eyes. To him, she was more of an object than a person.

"Hey, Queen Pin, good to see ya." His tone was laced with cockiness.

"Good to see you, too, Pitch." She wondered why he was there and why he was smiling so hard. "Who you come to see?"

"I had to update Cat on what's goin' on while he's on lockdown." He cheesed. "Who you come to see?" He already knew the answer.

"I'm here to see Cat, why?" She snapped. Now her heart was racing. *What did this snake ass nigga tell him?*

"Oh, jus' askin'. Okay, I don't want to hold you up. I'll holla at'cha later." He looked her over once again before spinning off. The whole conversation just gave her the creeps. There was always something behind his ugly grin. To make up for the fucked up grill he was cursed with, he lusted for power. She entered the visiting room to see Cat Daddy seated behind the glass partition, with a big smile on his face. That was a good sign. She smiled back, walking over to him with an extra sway in her hips.

CHAPTER 10

Time to Make Moves

Pitch had an emergency meeting with all his captains. He was looking clean in a navy blue Tom Ford suit and black Louis Vuitton dress shoes. Six months went by and still no word on who killed his little sister, Fatima. The longer it took to find his sister's murderer, the harder it would be to have a peace of mind. The bounty for her killer's head was raised from one hundred thousand dollars to two hundred thousand dollars. The captain's job was to spread the news.

After the meeting, everyone dispersed. Tuck and Chance went to the bathroom to use the urinal.

"I'm headin' over to the Dominican Republic wit' Chaos to handle some business in Santa Domingo. I need you to hold shit down while I'm gone and keep that shit airtight. Only you and the youngins know 'bout this," Tuck said, taking a leak next to Chance. His business trip was a secret.

"No prob, fam. How long you think you'd be out?" Worry filled Chance's voice.

"Don't know. Depend on the outcome of our agreement." Tuck wasn't too comfortable with making moves without backup. This was unsafe and very dangerous, but the outcome was too big to pass up.

"So, when did Chaos get out and you think you can trust him?"

"He got out last week. Him and Willy had everything set up before he got out and the answer to your question is no. I don't trust him. So if anything ever happens to me, I expect you to handle it."

"You already know I'ma make sure that nigga gets a one-way ticket to hell. Even if I have to take the ride wit' him. Then we both can spend eternity beatin' his dumb ass." Chance giggled; tickled by the thought of it. Death to him was a part of life and he had no problem accepting it with open arms.

"If all goes well, we gone be swimmin' in mad dough." Tuck couldn't contain his devilish grin.

"I like how that sound. You takin' the Young Hitters wit'chu."

"Naw. I'ma keep them wit'cha. I have to do this solo. A lot is ridin' on this. Keep your celly up in case I need to reach'chu."

"Gotcha, I got some work for those lil' niggas. Money's tight and we gone have to do things the old fashion way." Chance was now talking about stealing from the rich to feed his own needs.

"Just don't get caught slippin.'" It rolled off Tuck's tongue like a direct order.

"You already know how I's gets down." Chance raised his hand as if pulling the trigger a few times with an imaginary gun. This was his way of letting Tuck know that if the cops tried to arrest him there would be a problem.

"No doubt." Tuck chuckled in agreement.

"Yo, Pitch is on some Scarface shit," Chance complained.

"I agree, but you can't blame him though. I'd do the same shit if that was my little sistah," Tuck said, now washing his hands at the sink.

"I'd probably do the same shit, too. I just wish Cat was here. Shit would run a lot smoother though," Chance uttered, pulling up his zipper.

"Yeah, I'm feelin' ya on that," Tuck agreed, drying off his hands.

"Plus, I love how Crystal walks through with her fine lookin' ass and shut shit down." Chance was staring at the ceiling with a big Kool-Aid smile.

"Now, there you go again. I'm startin' to believe that you's on some stalker type shit. Don't let her catch you outside her crib. You know she gone blow yo fuckin' head off."

"And that's exactly what I want her to do to me," Chance said, washing his hands, while smiling at his reflection in the mirror.

"Don't think that I won't hesitate to cut yo fuckin' tongue out when Cat finds out you talkin' 'bout his bitch," Pitch growled, now standing by the doorway.

CHAPTER 11

Extra Protection

Last night felt like the longest night of Tony's life. If he had gotten any sleep, he couldn't tell. It was as if he changed overnight. Someone brought trouble to his front doorstep and his father almost paid the ultimate price. Putting three armed security guards on his father was the first thing he did before leaving the hospital: one in the room and two outside his door. Taking his father out wouldn't be easy with three guns at his bedside. There was no need putting his goons on him. They were not registered and that would bring heat to his operation. Instead, he hired Celebrity Security Detail, the best security company money could buy. This was the security top celebrities would hire for protection. He also gave a few nursing staff members some extra cash to keep an extra eye on his dad. No amount was too much for his father. The expression the nurse's faces showed meant they were pleased with his kind gesture and willing to do their part.

Tony got up two hours earlier than normal to start his day. He had a lot of work to do before heading to work. Once he got himself together, he paid a visit to a few people that knew what was going down before it happened. Tony wasn't able to get much out of them, but that didn't stop him. Someone knew who ordered that hit and for the right price, he was going to get his answer. Law enforcement wasn't getting any answers from any one because that was a sure sign of a rat. A two-faced snitch. Anyone telling the law anything that could help their case was only signing their own death wish, but cash, on the other hand, was more powerful. As long as it wasn't from the cops, it was acceptable and Tony had plenty of hard cash to create a whole football team of snitches. There was one guy by the name of Paulie. Cash was his weakness and Tony knew this. If anyone had any solid information, Paulie was that guy to go to. Paulie kept all his answer general and Tony had to read between the lines. If any of what Paulie was saying got back to him, he was a dead man. Tony promised not to say anything and played it off as if he worked for another crime family. He gave Paulie empty promises of hooking him up with his boss in a moneymaking scam Paulie was interested in. Lies and money was all it took to get the information needed to know who was behind all this. Paulie was unaware that Tony was Frank Debartello's son. All Tony had to do now is prove what Paulie was saying before making any moves. After paying for the information needed to get his answers, he headed to work, as if nothing happened.

CHAPTER 12

Verbal Tennis

"Hey, Daddy, how you holdin' on?" Crystal spoke in her provocative voice, knowing how much it turned Cat Daddy on.

"I'm still strong... I miss that pussy, though. My dick feels like concrete," he whined. It's been a while since a woman pleasured him and now his manhood was working overtime. Losing his freedom was the worst thing that could have ever happened to him.

"Don't worry 'bout it, Daddy, I'll make sure to keep it nice and wet when you get out," she teased, with a seductive look.

Cat Daddy paused, eyes hooded as his lips formed a straight line. "You ain't been sharin' that pussy wit' nobody, have ya?"

Crystal had to think fast, unaware of how much information he had on her. "Why, was someone telling you shit?" She came at him hard and caught herself. She tried to play it off with a giggle.

Cat Daddy leaned back and chuckled. "Woah there, babe. No need to get all defensive. I was just askin'."

That raised a flag. She should have known better. Cat Daddy didn't last this long in the game on stupidity. He was throwing out some bait and she snagged it.

With a smile, she said, "I'm sorry, Daddy. I thought someone was trying to play me out."

"No need to get defensive on me, babe. I'm stuck in here and can only go by what you tell me."

"Then the answer to that is no. My pussy stays wet and fresh for you, Daddy and you only." She moved around seductively in her chair to turn him on. Every time she moved, it seemed to attract wandering eyes.

Cat Daddy wasn't slow. He knew she was out there getting hers in. Somewhat like a man would do every time he got that itch, but he knew it would be in due time when he caught her slipping. So, for now, he'd play dumb and wait it out. He needed her company to help the time move at a faster pace.

Crystal could tell he knew something. As long as he played dumb, she would play along with him. Cat Daddy was a dog who was addicted to new pussy. He couldn't live without it. She turned a deaf ear to his cheating ways, but this time he got a project girl pregnant and she wasn't turning a blind eye to that. Once she found out that the girl had Cat Daddy's son, she had to get back at him by fucking that girl's man. Now someone had him murdered and it had the Hitman written all over it. But, the big question was, who hired him to make that hit? The only person she could think of was Cat Daddy because he couldn't get to him from behind bars and didn't have the patience to wait.

Cat Daddy leaned into the glass, giving Crystal a hard gaze. This is how he could tell if she were lying.

"Now, all I'm askin' you is to keep it one hunnit wit' me. Who you been fuckin'?" His voice was hard and deep. No matter how many women Cat Daddy slept with, he was refusing to share Crystal with anyone and his jealous tone revealed as much.

For him to ask meant he had no answer. So Crystal chanced it, keeping her game face on. "There's only one of us that enjoys gettin' attention outside this relationship. Need I say more?" she asked, which was more rhetorical.

Cat Daddy held his gaze for a moment and then sat back. The bitch was lying and he knew it, but Crystal was the best connect he had while on lockdown. She was the only one who made power moves. Going off on her now wouldn't do him any good. He needed her. He played it off and spoke softly during the short visit. She could tell he knew more than he claimed he did. It was time for her to make her own moves to protect her own neck.

She needed a man who was strong in his spot and didn't fear Cat Daddy. A killer for hire would serve as the perfect bodyguard. She wasn't sure who that person would be, so it was time to start the wheels turning.

CHAPTER 13

Finally Given In

Tony entered the Home Realtor Association building, looking sharp as ever, but without the added smile. He was not in the mood for socializing, as he gave everyone a quick nod and stormed toward his office. It was hard to concentrate on work. He reclined in his big leather chair and closed his eyes. The first thing he had to do was clear his mind. *Who the fuck did this and why*? That question continued to haunt his every thought. No one was talking and right now, he had no real concrete answers. If he didn't get any answers soon he'd start taking shit out sacrilegiously. The little information he got from Paulie would have to do for now, but could Tony really believe what he was telling him. For all Tony knew, Paulie could be pulling his leg just to get into the made-up scam business. A soft knock at the door interrupted his thoughts.

"Come in." He refused to adjust himself.

"This is not you at all. I could tell that something's bothering you by the way you stormed into your office. What's the matter?" Kim entered his office, with a soothing voice that seemed to calm him a bit. Her sweet perfume entered his nostrils. That was enough to cause his eyes to open. For a moment, he was lost in her seductive eyes and edible lips. She looked as if she were ready to do a Cover Girl commercial, with the hair pulled back in a ponytail and dressed like an attorney ready to win a case. Her body was screaming for attention. She couldn't hide that Coke bottle physique. Her hips were too big and waist too small. The perfect woman that would give any man bragging rights. In comparison, it was like looking at Serena Williams.

Once Tony realized he had lost himself, he went right back to moping.

"My dad was in a serious accident and now he's in a coma at Cooper Hospital. All I was told is that there was a real bad explosion, but I don't think so." Pain showed in his eyes, as hot tears started to form. He turned away.

Kim's face fell, now covered with worry. "Oh, Tony, I'm so sorry to hear that. Is there anything I could do?"

Tony looked up, fighting back the smirk trying to force its way out when the dirty thoughts entered his mind.

Yeah, you can come to my spot after work and give me some sympathy pussy or better yet, I would gladly accept a good blowjob right here.

Instead, he said, "Naw, that's okay. I'll be all right. I hired a security team to keep a watch over him twenty-four-seven." Tony caught himself. He was saying a little too much around Kim. He wasn't in the mood for her detective skills.

Kim leaned forward. "Tony, listen, you've been a good co-worker and a really good friend to me. I really hate to see you like this. I know it's hard because you still haven't gotten over Nicolas and your brother's passing. I don't want to see you hurt like this. So if there's anything I could do, please let me know." *Shocker! She didn't question the explosion or the security team I hired.* Usually known for questioning everyone's actions, today Kim's concern for Tony must have thrown her game off.

Tony gave her a hard gaze. This wasn't like Kim to be so sensitive to his needs. *What angle is she going with this?* He wasn't sure if this was the friend he could lean on with a listening ear or if she was finally ready to give in to him. The invite was there; no need in turning a blind eye.

"Well, since you offered, it will make me feel better if you at least let me take you out. That would make the perfect distraction and I promise you I'd be on my best behavior." He gave her the puppy dog eyes. She knew how he felt about her for quite some time now and for him to come out his face with that request shouldn't have come as a surprise to her. Now the ball was in her court and the clock was still ticking.

Kim paused, looking him in the eyes. She waved a finger at him. "I don't think so. Not after the last time you tried to take me out. You are not to be trusted. Better luck next time, Tony." She sauntered toward the door. He didn't respond. The hurt look on his face spoke for itself.

Tony reclined in his chair, looking like a little kid who just had his bike stolen. Her turning away when he needed her the most felt worse than a swift kick in the testicles. It was as if she lured him in just to slam the door in his face.

Kim stopped halfway out the door. "You know what? I'm going to take you up on that offer as long as you promise me that you'd be on your best behavior." Her conscience must have gotten to her.

Tony couldn't control the big smile that grew across his lips. "I'll do better than that. I promise to be the perfect gentleman."

"I knew that would put a smile on your face. Just don't have me waiting." She walked out the door.

"Yeah, I promise not to fuck this one up, with your fine ass," Tony mumbled to himself.

CHAPTER 14

Ready to Die For It

"Yo, my nig, you needs to stop that stupid shit you be doin'," Tuck said, driving his vehicle with Chance in the passenger seat. The cloud of smoke filled the air as they rolled more weed for enjoyment. This seemed like the best way to calm their nerves after the loss of their best friend, Willy.

"I know. I can't help how bad I want that sexy ass bitch." Chance slid into his seat, as if he were melting. His eyes rolled in the back of his head for added effect.

"You know that bitch is crazy. You forgot what Willy said about her." Tuck tried to warn him, but his actions only revealed how desperate he was.

"I know. That's why I want her so bad." He clutched both hands into fists with enthusiasm.

Tuck could hear the excitement in his tone. He had never seen Chance drool over a woman like this before. Chance was feeling her so much it was scary. His obsession for her was only going to lead him into deep waters.

"Man, ain't no bitch worth my life," Tuck protested. His love for money was stronger than anything else. His obsession for it was more of an addiction.

"Well, I'm ready to lose mine, 'cause I'm dying to get that pussy," Chance emphasized.

He laughed it off as if it was okay, but his lustful intentions were becoming well known throughout the crew. Chance was taking Pitch's threats too lightly, but Tuck knew better. Pitch was a snake in thug gear. He only cared about his needs and everyone else was secondary.

Still locked up in the City Jail, Cat Daddy patiently awaited release. His attorney, Charles Hunt, was working hard on his case. If it didn't work and Cat Daddy was going to face serious time for this, he was ready to get out the game by any means necessary. The body shop was under investigation. He owned the shop under an alias and now he owed close to a million dollars in taxes. Now they were pinning him to different murders and the body count kept growing. Pitch was now in charge, but the new leadership was going to his head. He thought he was the president and was surely acting like one. He kept hitters around him and had a parade of SUVs, with tinted glass, escorting him through the city. Unbeknownst to him, this was creating unwanted attention from the feds. They were now aware of his operation and were gathering evidence on him and everyone in his organization. They wanted to make sure they had enough dirt on him to bring the entire operation down to its knees, putting it away for good with no fighting chance of a victory. Pitch wanted to be the black Scarface and even started getting high off his product. This only affected his mood swings and judgement in the worst way. It was as if the shit was causing him to lose his mind.

CHAPTER 15

Protecting What's Left

Tony slowly started to feel more like himself. Kim's presence seemed to erase all the stress that was weighing him down. After his date with Kim, he'd shot over to the hospital and check on his father. Their relationship wasn't that close, but he was still his father—the one who got his mother out the projects, bought her a nice home in Voorhees and got him a good education and nice job at his firm. He was always around to make sure Tony was straight. With that, Tony felt obligated to take care of him. Even though his mother had nothing to do with him. Tony knew Frank still had a special place in her heart. For now, Tony had to keep his head straight. Whoever was trying to take his father out was trying to erase his entire bloodline. If they knew he was his son, would they come after him next? The thought continued to plague his mind. Tony made sure he kept a gun on his side just in case. He wasn't going out slipping. As for his father, there was no report of them finding a body. Tony paid a lot of money to keep it a secret. This was only for his protection. After making sure his father was okay, Tony headed back to his office to sort through some paperwork.

Just then, there was a knock at the door. "Come in!" Tony yelled.

His uncle, Big Bill, entered the room. "Hello, Tony, how are you doing?"

"I'm good so far, just trying to make it day by day." Tony drummed his fingers on his oak desk.

"I'm sorry about what happened to your father. Your mother called me last night with the news. Plus, there was a big meeting with all the bosses this morning in the conference room. Is there anything I could do for you?" Tony's mother was Bill's younger sister and Frank was the co-owner of the firm.

Those words were like sweet music to his ears. If there were a better time to take advantage of that offer, today would be a good day to do so.

"Well, I'm not feeling too good. Is it possible that I could take a few days off to make sure my dad is okay?" Tony asked. It really didn't take that much effort, because the feeling was genuine.

Bill paused for a moment as if he were trying to read his facial expression. Tony was very good at trying to find ways of getting out of work, but today was different and Bill didn't like seeing his nephew this way. "Go right ahead and take as much time as you need. Like I always say, family comes first. I just hope you don't make me regret those words." He waved a finger.

"Uncle Bill, I promise I won't and thank you so much." Tony grabbed his things and rushed out the office. He gave Kim a quick bye and told her he'd meet up with her after work.

Kim gave him a puzzled look, with a hand on her hip, as if she knew he was going to stand her up.

CHAPTER 16

Flexing his Power

It was nightfall and Pitch was riding around like the President, in a black GMC Yukon with limo tints, seated in the back with two goons, one on each side. Tuck and Chance were up front with Tuck behind the wheel. He was about to have an important meeting with Polo the Don and anything could happen.

Whatever this meeting was about, it didn't feel right. No one informed Cat Daddy about it. While being on lockdown, he only spoke with Pitch about business and Crystal who kept his family updated on his situation. Cat Daddy didn't want to make any mistakes. So, he kept his circle of interest small. Pitch had Cat Daddy believing everything he would tell him. This is what Pitch needed to under mind him.

"So what we got goin' down?" Tuck asked, glimpsing at him through the rearview mirror.

"Don't worry 'bout what's goin' down. All I need you to do is have my back," Pitch snarled. Tuck could tell by his tone he wasn't in the mood for small talk. Something sneaky was going down and he wanted to keep it a secret.

"You already know my shit's on point," Tuck replied with confidence.

"Now that's the shit I want to hear." Pitch directed his attention to Chance. "So, Chance, you still be fantasizing 'bout Cat Daddy's bitch while dickin' those project hoes down?" Sarcasm drenched his tone.

Chance peeped how Pitch was trying to throw him under the bus in front of everyone. "Naw, I'm good. I got that shit out my system a long time ago," he said sarcastically, knowing it wasn't true.

"Good, now that's the shit I want to hear."

After that, silence lingered. Pitch had made his point. Chance and Tuck saw now he was flexing his leadership. The facial expression on the two goons in the back seat showed that they were very uncomfortable with the way Pitch was abusing his newfound power. They continued to drive in silence, focusing straight ahead. It was time to put their game faces on.

CHAPTER 17

The Bill Collectors

Dave and Mark were driving around, collecting rent for the first of the month, while Tony was out on his first date with Kim. Tony gave Dave and Mark the head's up about her and they promised not to bother him while they collected his money.

"Yo, Dave, man, why you keep eatin' up my shit every time I put somethin' in the frig?" Mark complained, as Dave drove.

"My bad. I be thinkin' it's my shit." Dave tried laughing it off.

"Listen, man, I'm tired of talkin'. Eat my shit again and see what happens," Mark threatened. From his tone, Dave could tell that it bothered him.

"Oh, now you want to get violent over food, right?" Dave teased, not taking him serious enough. They exited the vehicle and approached one of the townhomes.

"Nah, I ain't gon' get violent over the shit, that's petty. I'm just lettin' you know I got somethin' for you," Mark said, as they knocked on Gary Holland's door, a tenant who was late with a payment. A car drove by with loud music playing through the speakers. It was hard to make out the song through the cheap speakers, but the driver got what he was looking for and that's their attention.

Before Dave had a chance to respond, a loud, booming voice interrupted him.

"Who the fuck is it?"

They were on the North side of Camden. The row homes on that block looked shitty and needed some serious remodeling.

"The bill collector. Your rent is overdue," Mark yelled back.

"Yo, I told Tony I was goin' through somethin' and I was gonna hit him up as soon as I got back on track."

"Only thing that nigga's goin' through is a few crack bags," Dave joked with Mark. They both giggled like little kids before Mark put his game face back on.

"Well, we're here to let you know that it's been a year now and you still comin' up empty. You got twenty-four hours to come up wit' somethin' or we gonna have to evict you." Mark continued to yell at the closed door.

"Then you gon' have to do whatchu gotta do then." The voice hollered.

Dave and Mark walked off to continue their rounds before reporting to Tony. Tony was so excited about this first date with Kim that he didn't even worry about Gary Holland not coming up with the rent. He was on cloud nine and all he could talk about was how much he enjoyed being with Kim and being the perfect gentlemen.

"Man, how the hell you pussy whipped and you ain't even get the pussy yet?" Dave yelled into the phone. He had Tony on speaker so Mark could join in on the conversation.

"Naw, he ain't pussy whipped, yet. That's just puppy love," Mark stated.

"Now you're Doctor Phil and shit," Dave barked at Mark.

"You two can call it what you want, but from where I stand, I can detect some jealousy. It's all good though. Someday, you'll find the right girl, if you work hard enough at it," Tony said, laughing through the speakers.

"Yo, I'm good. As long as it's a snow bunny," Dave vocalized as if he were trying hard to convince them.

"Man, you don't know what you want. Every week you change up. Last week you were into big girls and the week before that you were into skinny girl. What's it gon' be next week, older women?" Mark cracked.

"It doesn't matter what I'm into next week as long as I have the freedom to do so. You all tied down and shit with your ready-made family," Dave snapped, knowing how bad Mark wanted that luxury.

"Okay, fellas, before you two end up taking each other's heads off, I'm on my way to your spot to collect the cash. I should be there in fifteen minutes."

CHAPTER 18

Thinking Like Detectives

Tuck and Chance were relaxing in the living room, smoking weed and drinking alcohol. Silence loomed as they thought about the loss of their right-hand man, Willy. They had a history together, but the autopsy report stated he died in a house fire from a drug overdose.

"Died in a house fire? That shit was an abandoned buildin' and my nigga wasn't no crackhead," Chance voiced, breaking the silence. His boy's death was unacceptable. The more they talked about it, the more pissed off they became. It was as if the investigators accepted his fate and swept the rest under the rug. His death was nothing more than an added number to all the casualties that haunted Camden's streets.

"That fire was deliberate and someone purposely made it look like a drug overdose," Tuck said, sounding like a detective trying to solve a case. He wanted answers and the truth was nothing more than a witch-hunt. The only person who knew the whole story was Willy and he wasn't around to tell it.

"One thing's fo' sho', my boy ain't no crackhead. His mom was a crackhead. Even his daddy was a crackhead, but he wanted no parts of that shit," Chance stated with anger.

"Then who did the shit and why?" Tuck questioned with meaning. Selling drugs was one thing, but using it was even harder to believe. They all grew up together and knew each other's habits all too well. Drug habits were very hard to hide and there would have been a sign.

"Fuck if I know. Maybe that bitch had something to do wit' it. He did say that she was crazy and would take him out if he broke it off." As crazy as it sounded, Chance was finally making sense. Willy was having a secret affair with Crystal and maybe she was covering her tracks.

"You know what? I don't know how truthful that shit is, but that bitch would be a good start." Tuck was already plotting on taking her ass out, even if it meant getting in her head. Even if it meant getting in her pants.

"Fuck, if she had anything to do wit' it, I'll personally take her ass out so my manz can whoop that ass on the other side." As bad as Chance wanted to fuck her, he was willing to kill her if she had something to do with Willy's death. Thoughts of taking the pussy before doing so did enter his mind.

"True that," Tuck agreed with a hard fist bump.

They were starting to put something together. Wasting their time drinking and moping over his death was getting them nowhere. It was time to put in some work.

CHAPTER 19

Business Minded

Tony and Kim walked the boardwalk in Atlantic City. The cool breeze from the ocean waves felt good as it glided across his skin. Getting the business started was harder than he thought. The money and the manpower weren't there yet and getting started and covering his tracks was the hardest part. He had to be on point when doing this. The feds were on everything and the slightest little glitch would cost him dearly. Trying to hire the right man for the job seemed impossible. The Geek Squad was the only reliable source he had, but they weren't interested in doing business with him.

"Tony, are you okay? I'm right here, hello," Kim said, breaking his mental planning.

"Yes, why you ask?" He gazed into her eyes seductively. She had his full attention now.

"Okay, there you are. You seem distracted like you're in deep thought about something. What's bothering you?" Her caring tone was soothing enough to make him open up.

"I'm sorry. I'm just worried about my father. It kills me to see him lying up in that hospital bed helpless and weak. I wish there was more I could do about it." Tony wanted to tell her about the business. To build a good relationship, he wanted to tell her everything and not hold back, but it was illegal and he didn't want to get her involved. Tony knew going into this would destroy her trust factor once it leaked out. The key was to do his best at keeping a lid on it.

Kim slid her arms around his midsection and lightly squeezed while still making eye contact. "It's going to be okay. From looking at you, I can tell that your father is a strong man and I know he'd pull through."

This is what he needed. Her positive words of guidance. Kim wasn't sure if that was the right speech to give him in his time of need, but unbeknownst to her it was all he needed to move forward. When his father did make it through, he'd be well established to help him get back on his feet.

A few aggressive seagulls swooped down, looking for food, startling them for a brief second. They both laughed it off.

"You know what? You're absolutely right. There's no need in me getting upset over something I can't change. Only time would tell."

Tony wrapped his arms around Kim as they embraced each other against the cold metal railing of the boardwalk. Kim felt so good in his arms. All he could do then was enjoy the cool breeze with her and hope she'd give him what he worked so hard for and that's reaping the benefits of wishful desires.

CHAPTER 20

The Secret Meeting

They pulled up to the warehouse on Broadway Street and Morgan Boulevard. Pitch made sure everyone was in position. Three of the goons hidden up high in the ceilings were Army-trained snipers. Two more snipers posted up outside—one on the roof of the warehouse and the second in the bush about a hundred yards away. The rest of his goons were spread out in clear eyesight. Once in position, they all waited patiently.

Polo the Don drove up with four cars loaded with goons.

The sniper on the rooftop radioed in to the other snipers inside, through an earpiece.

"Yo, head's up. They here," one of the snipers yelled down from the ceiling.

"Shit is on and poppin," Pitch cheered, rubbing his hands together with Chance and Tuck beside him. Even though they didn't get along so well, Tuck and Chance were his best shooters. Pitch wouldn't trade them two for just anybody.

Polo the Don walked in with his goons, fifteen deep. The other four were standing outside. One posted at each vehicle. Pitch didn't sweat it at all. If his hitters couldn't protect him, his snipers would definitely come through for him. Pitch and Polo the Don were looking like *GQ* models in their expensive suits.

"I'm glad you could make it and on time," Pitch said, as they embraced.

Everyone else stood with blank facial expressions.

Melody's little brother, Tucan, was standing next to Polo the Don with his hand tucked in the pocket of his hoodie. It was obvious he was concealing a weapon.

Tuck noticed the goon that bumped into Pitch at the club in Philly when they were having a good time. Even though that was a while ago, Tuck was still feeling some type of way. His name was Eziel, Tucan's right-hand man and partner-in-crime. Tuck kept his cold eyes locked on him. If any shit were to spark off, he would be the first goon to take out.

"I don't play around when it comes to business. Now that I'm here, may we talk somewhere a little more private?" Polo the Don smiled.

With a nod, Pitch took Polo the Don in the back of his private room that looked like it used to be an office space. Everyone stood around in silence, waiting for something to happen. It just ended up being a hard stare competition, but no one was losing this game.

An hour later, Polo the Don and Pitch finally exited the room.

"It was good doin' business with you. Until next time, have a good night," Polo the Don said, as he and Pitch embraced again.

Pitch watched Polo the Don and his crew hop in their vehicles and drive off.

CHAPTER 21

Unwanted Guest

Crystal got home after visiting Cat Daddy. She was nervous about the look Pitch had given her. *What is he up to?* Pitch was slimy and always had tricks up his sleeves. If he had seen the video, then what was he waiting for? He definitely wanted something or else something would have happened to her by now.

Deep in thought, the doorbell startled her. She pressed a button on her remote control that displayed an image of Pitch at her door. She talked into the remote.

"Yes, may I help you?" She asked with an attitude.

Pitch looked up at the camera. "Yeah, you can start by lettin' me the hell in," he demanded. This was not like him to talk to her disrespectfully. That could only mean he had something on her and felt free enough to come at her in such a way. Besides, he didn't have his goons. Something was up and she did not like this picture.

"What you need, Pitch? You know you can't come up in here unannounced." She tried to punch out a hard tone.

"Well, I'm here and I know you ain't gon' leave me hangin.'" The look on his face showed that of a man that had something on her and was there to make a deal. Crystal knew this and was ready to put him out his misery. She first had to see where his head was and if he knew anything about his sister, Fatima's death.

"Just give me a minute," she said, changing into something more comfortable, but not too revealing. She didn't want to turn his nasty ass on in any way and put extra thoughts in his head.

She then opened the door with a straight look, blocking his entry.

"So, you gon' let me in or do I have to let the entire neighborhood hear our conversation?" Pitch said, with a raised voice, looking up and down the street. Crystal opened the door wider. Pitch stepped halfway in, checking out the interior. "Nice spot you got here."

"Make it quick. I don't want you getting comfortable and shit." She took a seat on her cream-colored sofa, making sure to cover any exposed flesh.

"Ah, okay then. I know you're aware of why I'm here, so let me just get down to business. You've seen the video that was on that iPad I gave you, right?" This was where the bullshit started. She should have known by the way he was talking proper. Pitch only put his words together professionally when it came to business or something very slimy that only benefitted him. This is what scared Crystal the most.

"Yeah, and what about it?" She bit off her words. The temptation of cursing him out crossed her mind a few times. It was a struggle to maintain her composure.

"Well, the guy that was on that video was not Cat Daddy, right?"

"And what about it?" She repeated, head rocking side to side with a hand on her hip. This was not a typical question, but more of an interrogation.

"Who was it?"

Crystal was losing her patience. "None of your damn business. So what, you turning snitch on me now?" Crystal was now standing in an aggressive manner. She knew he was after something, but the prolonged questioning meant he was slowly working his way to it. The anticipation was driving her crazy. Maintaining a cool disposition was becoming a struggle.

"Watch your fuckin' mouth. The fact that you're Cat's bitch is the only reason why you still breathin'." He was talking reckless with clenched teeth. Pitch was overstepping his boundaries. Either he was on a suicide mission or overly confident he had some good shit on her.

"So now you think it's okay to disrespect me?" She reached for her banger, but Pitch already had his weapon aimed at her.

"I already know how you get down. So don't test my patience." He took her weapon and tucked it away in his pants. There was no taking any chances with Crystal. She was a killer. His harsh choice of words would cause her to do what she's known for—committing murder.

"Now you're holding the gun. Get to the point of why you're here, so I can get back to what I was doing," she barked as if she still had the upper hand.

He dropped his gun to his side, still keeping a finger on the trigger.

"That right there is what I'm talkin' 'bout. You really are gangsta." He chuckled while still maintaining a stone face. "So, I'ma cut to the chase. The reason I'm here is 'cause I got some serious information. The type of information that could jam you the fuck up and cause you to lose your position as Cat's main bitch." He paced around the room. "And knowing my man, Cat, he gone off yo dumb ass wit' no hesitation. Plus, the nigga you fuckin' and everyone that's close to you to keep that shit you did on lock. The last thing he wants is everyone finding out that his main bitch can't keep her fuckin' legs close long enough for my man to get accustomed to his new surroundings. So I'm gonna ask you this one last time. Who you been sharing that pussy wit'?"

Crystal put a twisted hand on her hip and with a bobbling head said, "That's for me to know and you to find the fuck out. I don't kiss and tell, so now what?" She challenged.

Pitch chuckled at her comment. "So now what? That's how you want to play this? Okay, I'ma play and then I'll holla at Cat to see how he wants to handle this." He walked away, leaving her front door wide open. At that moment, Pitch was the only person with her secret now that Fatima and Willy were dead. If he were to tell Cat, he would probably have her thrown out and lose her status as Queen Pin or have her head blown off and made as an example to the next bitch that tried to play him out. Either way, she was fucked; she couldn't let Pitch get away.

"Pitch...wait a minute!" She yelled out to him before he got into his whip.

Pitch turned with a smirk on his face. "Now that's the shit I'm talkin' 'bout." The ball was in his court and he was flexing it hard.

Crystal didn't say a word. She just held the door open, allowing him to enter. She then closed the door behind him.

CHAPTER 22

Putting a Lid on It

Tony enjoyed the few days off getting his thoughts together. He spent most of his time by his father's bedside every day, hoping he would come through and open his eyes. Frank was looking like a mummy, wrapped up like King Tut. Tony was also putting more time into his business adventures. He was so tied up; he never had a chance to focus all his attention on Kim. He really enjoyed spending time with her on their first date, but his father's condition was weighing heavily on his heart. Kim didn't like seeing him this way. He was so zoned out he didn't notice her presence, but she made sure to remind him every time he pass by her.

When Tony got to work the next day, he had a lot of explaining to do to Bill about a complaint he received from Gary Holland, who said if Tony came at his neck the wrong way again, he was going to the police. This was the third complaint Bill received from a customer he did not know. There was no paperwork with his name on it. So why were they mailing their complaints to his office?

"I don't know what that guy's talking about," Tony lied.

For now, Bill couldn't argue with him until he found out what was really going on.

"Get out!" Bill shouted, excusing Tony from his office.

Tony practically ran out his office. Gary Holland was about to go into snitch mode. It was time to hit him up hard and shut him the fuck up. Back in the day, he was that dude to go to whenever you needed that good shit. It didn't matter whether it was legal or illegal; Gary Holland had no problem getting his hands on it.

But, then he got locked up and not seeing his kids was killing him. His baby momma left him and he had to pay child support. Upon his release, he got a job to pay bills and child support, but he was also hooked on cocaine and wasn't making enough to pay bills and support his drug habit. So, he made an executive decision and decided to support his drug habit.

Kim entered Tony's office to tell him how much she enjoyed herself at his expense. Tony laughed and told her he had no problem making himself available for her.

"That sounds good. So what are you doing tonight?" She asked. Kim was never the aggressive type, except for the time when she forced herself on Nicolas Coles when he first started. Her being the aggressor toward Tony was turning him on and she started to notice it.

"I was going to handle some business, but for you I'd put that off for another day. It could definitely wait." He stroked his chin.

"Then I want you to pick me up at my place after work and surprise me." She smiled a beautiful smile that no man could resist, as he offered a smile in return. The shit was contagious. Lately, Tony seemed different. He was more mature and showed Kim respect. His new laid-back attitude caused Kim to check him out and notice his *GQ* style. Tony was nervous around her. Kim was the only woman that could do that to him. The two of them having sex would never happen, Tony thought, so he had a "fuck it" attitude and moved on. He was more himself around her and didn't do extra. He gave her full eye contact and a listening ear. He never forgot her birthday or holidays. He always got her a card with a gift and flowers always brought a smile to her face. The gift cards would be for her favorite stores, restaurants, or tickets for a big concert or flight somewhere nice. He made sure it was always two tickets for her and one of her girlfriends. He was hoping it would be him she invited and not another man. Even though he thought nothing would happen between them, he never stopped trying with the hopes of there being a possibility.

Kim was looking so good. Everything about her was perfect. Her hair neatly cut short, revealing her long sexy neck. Lips, full and juicy. Her lip-gloss shined from the room lighting. Her bedroom eyes seemed to snatch his breath away. Tony had to keep his cool. That's what attracted her to him in the first place. *Wasn't it?* Unbeknownst to her, he had every date planned out for a while now. Before she even looked at him in that way, he kept a list of things to do with her. Tony always paid attention to what she liked and what turned her on.

After Kim left Tony, he called Mark and Dave to take care of Gary Holland. He had something else important to take care of. They got the rundown of what Tony wanted them to do to Gary before disconnecting the call.

CHAPTER 23

Snake in the Grass

"For one, give me back the piece, and two, what is it that you want to keep your fucking mouth shut?" Crystal leaned on the door, refusing to let Pitch leave. Deep down, she knew she would regret giving him that much power over her.

"Uh, look at you all gangsta wit' it. That shit does nothin' but turn me the fuck on. So, on that note, you take care of my physical needs and I'll keep my fuckin' mouth shut. We can consider this as a one-night-stand if that would help you feel better." He palmed his half-swollen manhood. Yeah, she should have killed him when she had the chance and tried to clean up the mess she made on her own, but that would have been too risky.

"So that's what you want?" She placed both hands on her hips like Wonder Woman. What he was asking for was a death sentence if Cat Daddy found out.

"Most def." He looked her up and down with lustful eyes.

"How you know I ain't gonna set you up and blow your goddamn head off?" She questioned, knowing that was the plan from the start. She just wanted to hear what he did to protect himself.

"'Cause you ain't stupid. Plus, I'm covered full circle. If anything—and I mean anything—happens to me, you gon' be in hell joinin' me before my dick goes soft." He looked at Crystal for a response, but she just dropped her clothes and looked for a reaction. There was no hesitation or shame in her game. When it came down to doing whatever it took to get what she wanted, she was about that life. She knew she had to find a way to get out the mess she was in, but for now, she'd go along with his demands. Pitch's eyes nearly popped out his head. Her body had him stunned for a minute and speechless.

"All right, snap the fuck out of it and get the shit over with," Crystal barked, removing her bra and string bikini panties. She turned around, walked over to the sofa, before bending over with her ass tooted up, to avoid seeing his face. Pitch didn't hesitate to remove his clothes. His excitement was more like a horny felon that did ten years in prison and was yearning for pussy. He placed both his gun and hers on the coffee table, out of her reach.

"That thugged out gangsta shit be turnin' me the fuck on." His dick was rock solid, craving for relief.

Crystal stopped him as he walked up on her and handed him a condom. Pitch looked at her as if she was crazy. He desperately wanted to get a good feel of that sweet pussy…raw.

"It ain't going down without protection," she said with an attitude. It was bad enough she was submitting to his demands.

"I gotcha."

When Crystal looked away, he quickly ripped the condom wrapper at the tip and rolled it down his shaft like it was a rubber band. He mounted her and the excitement caused him to thrust his hard dick inside her with force. Crystal arched her back from the sudden pain with a slight whimper. Her pussy was wet as if she was playing with herself before answering the door. Pitch didn't go light and kept ramming his dick inside her until his entire dick was wet. Crystal reached over to make sure he still had the condom on. She felt the part that was rolled back on his shaft and assumed it was still on. She knew Pitch wanted that pussy bad and figured she'd speed up his orgasm by talking dirty to him.

"You like that pussy, don't you?" She arched her back with her heart shaped ass in the air.

"Fuck…yeah," he grunted in a lustful trance. Her small waist and ass cheeks spread open kept his dick hard as a rock. Her cream color skin was smooth and flawless, causing his loins to fill. He was ready to bust inside her. Pitch knew she couldn't get pregnant from the stories Cat Daddy told him about how hard they would try and nothing would happen. Pitch wanted that ass the day he first laid eyes on it and tonight was going to be the biggest nut of his life. Crystal kept talking to encourage his orgasm.

"That's right nigga, beat that pussy up. Make me feel that hot cum." She spoke as Pitch rammed all twelve inches of raw dick in her.

"Oh yeah, you gon' feel this cum, bitch." He spoke softly in short breaths.

"Oh, I'm ya bitch, huh?" she said, ready to go off on him for disrespecting her, but instead she just wanted to get it over with. "Then let me feel you cum for this bitch. Go ahead, nigga, pump that seed out that big, hard dick." His bareback shaft was hard as a brick with excitement.

He had never seen this freaky side of her before, and the shit turned him on even more. He couldn't hold back. He wanted to know when it was coming so he could force his whole dick in, down to the balls, but it came to quick and prematurely shot out. Suddenly, the room started spinning and his body felt like clay. The sudden orgasm caused his knees to buckle. He felt like Superman receiving a big dose of kryptonite. He then pushed his rod deep inside as far as it could go so she could get all that dick juice. The room kept spinning like he was high off some good shit. Pitch never came so hard in his life. He tried to stand up to pull his pants up, but lost his balance. He was too weak to protect himself if she decided to attack him. He stood there for a moment to maintain his composure. Crystal got up and headed for the bathroom to clean herself.

"All right, we're done here. Get the fuck out and close the door behind you," she said, not looking at him. Pitch pulled the so-called condom band off his dick and tossed it in her front yard as he stumbled out the door. He jumped in the car and laid-back in pure ecstasy. That was the best pussy he ever had. The pussy could have been good or maybe it was mental. Whatever it was, he had to have it again. He was not going to let it be a one-night-stand. There was a change in plans. He was still holding the key to her submission. He started to drift off in deep thought until he heard Crystal scream through the bathroom window. He knew what it was. Crystal discovered she was more than just wet. She discovered his semen found a way to enter her body by busting through the condom, or he didn't have one on. Either way, he came inside her and now she was worried about being pregnant, but no, she couldn't get pregnant. She tried many times with Cat Daddy and the test they took said so. Maybe she was afraid of contracting an STD, maybe one that's incurable. Pitch wasn't waiting around to found out, as the squealing of his departure ripped through the still night sky.

CHAPTER 24
Searching for Answers

Tony was on his way home after a long day's work. He noticed the unmarked unit parked next to his vehicle with two plain-clothes officers behind the wheel. They both got out of the unit, as Tony approached them. It was Detectives Stewart and Morris looking for shit, like always. Tony remembered Morris from the time him and Willy went up to the police station to file a complaint on one of their officers for being racists, but he didn't know who his partner was.

"Mr. Satario, may we have a quick word with you?" Detective Andy Morris said, as both he and Stewart flashed their shiny, metal badges.

"How may I help you, officers?" Tony responded so willingly in a calm and collective tone with so much professionalism that it was hard to detect his nervousness. They were on to him and his illegal property business. He was sure to be cuffed and sent to jail, but their approach was non-aggressive and that alone meant they were looking for answers. Tony's heart felt like it was about to crack his chest cavity. It was beating so heard it hurt, but he managed to keep a laid-back exterior.

"Yes, we have a few questions about Willy Mays' death," Stewart said.

So, this was not about his illegal business. Tony was relieved, as the fear he had for the property scam was now replaced with Willy's death. How was he tied to it and where were they getting their information? This shit was much more serious and came with a much longer prison sentence.

"And, what about it?" Tony was eager to hear the question, as they took their time, testing his tolerance. They were seeing if he would fold under pressure. This act would determine whether he's guilty by their standards.

"Well, you were the last one seen with him before his untimely death, according to his baby momma." Stewart spoke with sarcasm.

"Yes, I stopped by to talk to him about a few things and then I left," he admitted. Reacting to Stewart's sarcasm would surely give him probable cause.

"And what did you have to talk about?" Stewart questioned, but he seemed to be the one with the attitude.

"Him wanting to buy a home for his family," Tony explained.

"At three-something in the morning?" Stewart blurted out loudly. This only made him appear very unstable and unpredictable.

"I take my business seriously. Is that a crime?" Tony asked, trying to stay as calm as possible

"Only if you kill your clients off for not buying," Stewart barked. His sarcastic remarks were starting to become very irritating.

"Besides the fact that I stopped by to check on him doesn't mean that I killed him. What was the motive and what other proof do you have?" Tony questioned. These officers were doing nothing, but raising his blood pressure.

"I have a witness and that's all I need for now," Stewart ranted.

"So why we here talking?" Tony's attitude changed and he was now more angered than defensive.

"Good question, but this is how we work. We slowly gather up all the information that's needed and when we feel as though it's enough to take you in, make sure you got your lawyer on speed dial and some clean underwear," Morris responded in a more aggressive manner. They both looked as though they were looking for any excuse to lock him up. *Whatever happened to good cop, bad cop rule?*

"Look, Detective Morris," Tony said, looking for anything that had Stewart's name on it. "And whatever you said your name was."

"Stewart, and don't you forget it," he voiced out.

"It doesn't matter, because my lawyer is going to eat this case for dinner. Are we done here? I have somewhere important to be." These cops were digging and their sense of direction was only wasting his time.

"By all means... feel free." Morris stepped to the side to let him pass.

Tony jumped in his vehicle and drove off.

CHAPTER 25
Catching Feelings

Tuck and his goons were in an abandoned building, counting money. It was attached to Linda Myers' house and the only way in was through her front door. The back door was sealed shut. No one was getting in. Linda Myers made a living off the child support of her three kids. She ended up losing them in a custody battle, and now ordered to pay. She refused to work and the drug money was an easy source of income. The house was paid for, but to look abandoned. They were in there counting money, which was the day's pay. Pitch would walk in to check on things and make sure it was running smoothly. The way the house was setup, if the cops broke in, it came with secret doors and escape routes. An underground tunnel led eight blocks away to another abandoned house next to Kia Redd's house that also came equipped with secret doors. Kia was Pitch's cousin. She knew Pitch was all about the money and couldn't be trusted, but her addiction to the product made her a slave. Tuck would pop up every now and then whenever he had free time and today he was making sure everything was running smoothly. The money was now counted and ready for pickup. They were relaxing, waiting for Pitch's arrival. Pitch walked in on Chance talking about how he would fuck the shit out of Crystal before he got there.

"You know if Cat finds out about you talkin' 'bout Queen Pin, he gon' slice yo dick the fuck off," Pitch said, entering the room with an attitude.

"I'm just sayin' what the rest of you muhfuckas scared to say. I ain't committin' no crime. Freedom of speech, right?" He said, making light of the situation.

"You can say whatever the fuck you want to say, but it's the consequences that follow is what you need to be worried 'bout, nigga," Pitch retorted.

"Damn, my nig, you sound like you feel some type of way 'bout the shit," Chance stated.

There was a long pause and hard stare before Pitch forced a smile and said, "Nah, I'm good, jus' breakin' balls. So put that bread in the whip so I can get the fuck outta here." Pitch was starting to feel some type of way when Chance spoke of Crystal. He was whipped by that good pussy and he didn't even know it, but for a brief moment, he was tempted to pop a few slugs in Chance's dome with no remorse, and that alone was a pure sign of someone who was pussy whipped. Pitch had to calm down and catch himself before the rest of the crew caught on to his sudden mood swing. There was no need in getting physical. His legs were still wobbly from the big orgasm he had fucking her.

They took all the money and placed it in the tinted SUV. Bones was posted outside as a lookout. There was a grey, tinted Nissan Maximum and a black, tinted Chevy Impala filled with armed thugs to make sure the stash got to its destination safely. They all came equipped with secret storage compartments in case they had to stash their weapons.

CHAPTER 26

This is a Warning

Dealing with Rolisha was becoming a big ass headache. Mark massaged his forehead as he drove from New York to New Jersey where he stayed to get away from her and to clear his head. She constantly nagged him about spending more time in New Jersey than with her and her ready-made family. He was beginning to have second thoughts about the whole relationship. Rolisha was wearing out her welcome. It was time for her and her kids to pack their shit, and head back to South Carolina where they came from.

After the long drive, Mark stopped at Brother's Kitchen in Lindenwold and ordered a soul food platter before heading to Dave's house and placing it in the refrigerator for later. He wanted to take care of Gary Holland and his big mouth, New York style, and then fuck that platter up later. He knew what he had in store for Gary Holland would build his appetite.

After hooking up with Dave, they waited outside the house for Gary to return from work. He worked at Aluminum Shapes and he should have clocked out by now. Gary was out of the game and wanted to provide for his family with a real job, but it wasn't enough to pay the rent and support his family. Plus, he had to pay child support for three other kids. With the money he gave Tony, the house was paid for according to his calculations, but he never added in the twenty percent interest rate. Gary was behind and late on all his bills and payments. His added coke addiction wasn't helping either.

Mark and Dave talked about their current situation and how much they missed their boy, Nick. Everything seemed fucked up now he was gone. Nick was good at keeping everything together. He was a stickler for keeping order. They didn't believe he killed himself in that jail cell and knew his death came from the hands of someone else. All they could do was keep their ears to the streets and knew it wouldn't be long before it started talking. Their conversation came to an abrupt end when they spotted Gary Holland getting out his car. They waited for him to walk up toward their vehicle and that's when they jumped out. Gary was ready to run, but they both lifted their shirts to flash the handle of their weapons and Gary froze.

"Is this how Tony's doing this now?" He huffed and his shoulders dropped easily, giving up without a fight.

Dave told him about his big mouth before Mark gripped him up and tossed him in the nearby alley like a pimp did his whores. They both walked over and gave him the beating of his life. Then they threatened to go camping if he doesn't cough up the rent money he owed. This meant they would burn the house down with or without him in it. They also threatened to take him out of his misery if he opened his big mouth again. Mark and Dave weren't killers, but they had to make Gary believe so. Deep down they knew it would come to them taking a life. The money was good and if they had to choose, they both believed they wouldn't hesitate to pull the trigger.

They talked about it on the way home. Before getting out the car, Mark's cell phone rang. It was Rolisha yelling on the other end. She was hot and Mark's face was filled with fear. Dave got out the car and told him to holler at him if he needed him. Mark nodded and took off speeding down the road.

Once inside the house, Dave made a beeline to the kitchen for something to eat. There was nothing in the refrigerator to eat, except Mark's platter being the only thing edible inside it. Dave was starving after beating Gary Holland down. The physical exertion worked up an appetite. That took a lot out of him and now his stomach was grumbling. He knew how Mark felt about him eating his food, but the temptation was hard to resist. Cooking up something would have taken some time and he wasn't patient enough to do so. Dave said, "Fuck it," and made the soul food platter his next meal.

CHAPTER 27
Keep Him Coming

Crystal was in the tub soaking for hours. She wanted to wash every bit of Pitch off her skin. She scrubbed hard until she got sore. The suds from her rage started to build with each passing moment. She couldn't believe she slipped up and now she was paying for it in the worst way, making her feel more like a whore…a slut…a cheap hooker. Sacrificing her body to appease a man was something she never thought she would stoop to doing. Now this excuse for a boss is going to run with it. She shouldn't have tried to make him cum by talking shit to him. That only helped him to enjoy it a little too much, which would only make him come back for more. She had to make moves. She needed every piece of evidence he had on her.

She should have tried to milk him for it, but then she would look too desperate and he'd take advantage of that. Pitch was an opportunist. There was no way he was going to give her all the evidence he had on her. His snake ass would have a backup copy stored somewhere for safekeeping. Whenever he felt the need to fuck her again, he could always pull it out and wave it in her face. There would have to be a better way of getting it and protecting herself from anyone else who may want to use the shit to their advantage. Pitch was a low-down dirty dog. A wolf in sheep's clothing. Everyone looked at him as if he was a leader, but a close enough look would expose the weasel he is. She would work on getting back at him, but for now, she'd play along. The more he enjoyed the pussy, the more time she would have to work on clearing this mess. It wouldn't be easy and she would have to think it through. Crystal would need to seduce someone with status. Someone that wanted her bad enough he would take his own life. He would have to be more than just the bodyguard she planned to seek out. It would have to be someone that had no fear of Pitch. Someone that posed a threat. A cold-blooded killer with no problem committing murder. For now, she'd look around until she found the one she could make herself his arm candy. Someone she could breakdown and rebuild as her own personnel puppet.

CHAPTER 28
The Right Moment

Tony pulled up to see Kim waiting for him in her car. She jumped out and hopped in his.

"I thought you wanted me to pick you up from your house," he said, staring at the well-manicured townhomes, uniformly connected together.

"I'm not going to make it that easy for you, silly." She playfully smacked his shoulder.

"Okay, I can accept that. So you ready to hang?" He smiled, leaning back in his seat for her response.

"You know I'm ready. So let's see if you can impress me three days in a row." She giggled.

Tony adjusted himself before throwing the gearshift in drive. Kim was looking good in her sexy, tight fitting, baby blue Guess dress and white high heel stilettos. She wore a white button up blouse over it.

"I'll make sure to do my best." He smiled with his chest out.

"So what were those detectives talking about?" She threw out with no hesitation.

"You don't miss a thing, do you?" Tony's surprised look was humorous.

"I wanted to make sure it was safe before I stepped out. So what was that all about?" She pressed, determined to get answers.

"One of my clients was found dead after an overdose, so they were out looking for answers." He was trying to make light of the situation.

"Oh, sorry to hear that." The conversation was killing the mode. It was time to get moving while he was on a roll. The music on the radio would be a good distraction while he worked his magic.

Tony took Kim to the movies first. He figured it would be a good topic to discuss over dinner. Something he already planned years in advance. After the movies, they ate at Ristorante Pesto in Philadelphia, Pennsylvania. The place was nice and the atmosphere was very romantic. They talked about the movie. What they liked and disliked. It killed fifteen minutes before the food arrived and then they discussed future plans. Kim was more open and relaxed. It was as if she couldn't keep her eyes off him. Maybe she was feeling him after all. Maybe he was getting to her. Only question that plagued his thoughts was if he had a chance of getting to home base.

The conversation drifted off to total silence. They were gazing into each other's eyes. Tony felt it and he knew Kim was feeling it, too. Something was drawing him toward her. Maybe it was her eyes. This was the perfect opportunity for him to do or say something. To let her know how he really felt about her. This was the right moment for him to open up. He started with telling her how nice she looked and how beautiful she was. Suddenly, his cell phone went off, breaking the mood. Tony looked at the screen. It was Dave.

CHAPTER 29

Heads Up

Pitch and Polo the Don started to have private meetings at the warehouse two to three times a month. Tuck and Chance knew whatever was going down wasn't in Cat Daddy's best interest. Pitch was grimy and couldn't be trusted. Tuck and Chance weren't the only ones to notice this. From the look on the faces of the crew, they could tell they were feeling the same way. Someone had to inform Cat Daddy of these secret meetings, but he would only talk to Pitch and Crystal. His life was being monitored under a microscope. Now they had to put their heads together and come up with a plan. Tuck would have to set it up for Crystal to attend a meeting so she could see what's going on and inform Cat Daddy before his whole operation blew up in his face.

The plan was simple. Tuck and Chance would have to catch Crystal leaving the gym. This was the best time to catch her by herself. If anyone from the crew found out, they would run to Pitch with the information and there's no telling how Pitch would react. Tuck and Chance drove out to LA Fitness in Cherry Hill. They found her white Benz in the parking lot and parked right next to it. They sat in the car and waited patiently. Drake was pumping through the speakers. As much as they loved the song, it was only good for soothing the tension they felt. They were so focused that the music barely registered in their brains. Then Crystal finally exited the gym, wearing a black spandex bottom, white tank top, and white Reebok sneakers. Her skin glistened from perspiration. She was looking sexy, like an exotic dancer. Tuck and Chance jumped out the car as she approached.

"Queen Pin, sorry to bother you, but we need to holla at'cha," Tuck said, blocking her way to her vehicle.

Crystal hesitated before responding. She slowly slid her hand in her gym bag. It was obvious she was reaching for her weapon. Now that Cat Daddy was behind bars, Crystal was more on edge lately. Tuck and Chance were Pitch's mean hitters. For all she knew, they could have gotten the order to take her out. Tuck and Chance threw their hands in the air to let her know that they came in peace.

"Yeah, what is it?" She barked with a straight face. She sounded as if she had somewhere important to be and they were holding her up. If they were trying to use the video of her fucking at the shop to blackmail her into having sex like Pitch did, then they had another thing coming. Pitch was the only one person she had to deal with. With more members of the crew coming at her would only lead to her going on a killing spree, starting with Pitch.

Chance gave her a friendly wave, but she just ignored him. They knew behind that beautiful exterior was a cold-blooded killer. Crystal had a past that was more than just being Cat Daddy's girl. It wasn't hard for her to get close to Cat Daddy's enemies before striking. Her beauty and youthfulness was nonthreatening. When questioned by the detectives, she would always have an alibi and a tight story. This was why she was so paranoid. Crystal knew too much about his past and his operation. If the police found out about their history of how their operation got so big, they would both end up behind bars for the rest of their lives. Cat Daddy wasn't willing to breakup with Crystal like a regular relationship. He was willing to get rid of her to keep her mouth shut…permanently.

"I'm here to talk about Pitch and his secret meetin's wit' Polo the Don. What's goin' on and does Cat know about this?" Tuck announced with bass in his tone.

Crystal gazed at him with a shocked expression. "I have no idea of what you're talking about."

Tuck's and Chance's eyes met for a brief moment before turning their gaze back at her. "Something's big about to go down. Pitch been handin' Polo duffle bags full of bread. We can't holla at Cat and you're the only one that's able to give him the heads up on this shit."

"Thanks for the pull up. I'll give him the heads up next time I see him, but I want to know when the next meeting goes down first." They both pulled out their cell phones and exchanged numbers.

"You need me to holla if Tuck can't reach you, right?" Chance said with a big smile. Crystal's only response was the rolling of her eyes. Chance kept smiling as they continued their conversation. She must have known he was feeling her or she couldn't stand the pretty boy look as if he were expecting her to fall all over him like he was a celebrity. After everything was said and done, Tuck stepped to the side and allowed Crystal to enter her vehicle. They waited for her to drive off before they took off in their own vehicle.

"Yo, what was that shit about?" Tuck asked, noticing Crystal rolling her eyes at Chance.

"I don't know. Lately, all she do is give me cold stares." Chance was concerned.

"It probably got back to her, all that shit you been talkin' 'bout hittin' that," Tuck said. If this were true and Cat Daddy found out, he might as well consider himself a dead man walking.

"I hope not," Chance whispered loud enough for Tuck's ears.

Tuck noticed the nervous tone. "Don't worry 'bout that, my nig, I ain't gon' let shit happen to you."

"You best not. 'Cause you knows I's already got yo back and that's real talk."

CHAPTER 30

Peanut Attack

Tony and Kim entered the hospital room with Dave laid up in the bed with his face swollen. It took Tony a moment to recognize him. Mark was at the foot of the bed taking pictures of him on his cell phone. If it wasn't for Mark being there, Tony and Kim would have walked passed him.

"Dave, what happened?" Tony questioned as he entered the room.

"This black Grizzly Bear Adams looking muhfucka tried to kill me," Dave barked. He still had jokes and that was a good think. Tony knew he would be all right despite the disfigured features of his hands and face.

"Whaddayah mean, tried to kill you? What happened?" Tony's voice was laced with concern.

"He knows I'm allergic to peanuts, but yet instead he puts the shit in his food knowin' I was gonna eat the shit," yelled Dave in protest.

"Told this apple-pie-face-lookin' muhfucka not to eat my shit. Now this shit is goin' viral on YouTube," Mark said, now recording everything.

Tony stared at Dave's round swollen face and dropped his head in a silent laughter.

"Yo, Tone, I know you ain't laughin' at this shit. I could have died from the shit," Dave complained in a spoiled pout.

Tony tried to erase the smile now plastered on his face. "I'm sorry, Dave, but the shit is funny." He struggled to hold back his laughter. Kim stood there with a blank expression.

"Oh yes, this right here is Kim and Kim this is Dave and Mark." Tony introduced them when he noticed them staring at her. He saw the admiration displayed on both their faces.

"Hey, fellas." She waved.

"Uh um," they both responded, unable to form a word or sentence. It sounded as though they were clearing their throats. They were so worked up they didn't even notice Kim's presence until the last minute. Even Tony was so caught up in the moment he forgot to introduce her.

"I can see how she got y'all converting back to the Stone Age. She had me dumbfounded like a caveman when she first started on the job. So I think it's best we leave now before y'all find your voices and talk our ears off. I'll call you guys later," Tony said.

"Nice meeting you guys." Kim waved with a bright smile.

Mark and Dave were still stuck on stupid.

CHAPTER 31

His Personnel Sex Slave

Crystal was desperate and needed some dirt on Pitch. Fucking her became a daily ritual for him. It was supposed to be a one-night-stand and he'd leave her alone, but the sex was banging and he couldn't get enough of that sweet pussy. Maybe it was the fact he was taking it against her will and it turned him on. Majority of it was at her place and the others were at random locations, including the warehouse and at his crib. Only when his girl was in New York with her mom. Pitch would start an argument with his main girl, which led to her staying at her mother's house for a few days. Pitch didn't care, because Crystal had that banging pussy. He was never giving up the tape of her fucking at Cat Daddy's shop. This was his meal ticket to fuck her as much as he wanted. There were times when he forced himself on her in his office after a meeting. It got to the point that he stopped using condoms and didn't care. He would constantly cum inside her as if he was trying to get her pregnant. What could she do at this point? Her life was in his hands.

Crystal had become his personnel sex slave to do as he pleased. Not only was this unacceptable, but it was a pure demonstration of the lack of respect Pitch had for Cat Daddy. Crystal hated him for that and gave him silence. Something needed to be done. She couldn't wait for Tuck to give her a head's up on the next meeting and if he does, she would be ready.

Pitch wanted to hear her talk shit as she did the first time they had intercourse, but she refused. Crystal didn't know he would abuse it the way he was doing. So he would manhandle her to try to get a buzz out of her. It got to the point he started disrespecting her in public. Pitch was now taking it too far, and she was recording each act with her iPhone.

This would be her defense when the shit hit the fan. She would act afraid of him as he roughed her up. Pitch was so at ease and loving how he broke the Queen Pin down. This was never going to end until he got tired of the pussy and that was no time soon.

It was a young boy. The newest member of the crew and he didn't get a chance to meet everyone from the team, but he knew Crystal was Cat Daddy's main squeeze. The Queen Pin of this organization. That's all she needed to know before stepping to him. The young thug's name was Bones. He was an eighteen-year-old killer with no conscience. He was a hitter with a short fuse. Without Cat Daddy around to discipline him, he was more of a liability to the crew if one of them were to try to test him. Pitch didn't care. He admired the cold-blooded killer and gave him free reign to run wild. Bones was Pitch's favorite goon, because he was young and hungry. Everything he did was to please Pitch like he was his son. So, he kept the kid near to teach him and raise him into his one-man enforcer. He was the one Crystal would manipulate and her pussy would be her bargaining chip. She had to wait for the right time to strike, and today would be the perfect moment.

CHAPTER 32

Getting to Know You

After arriving to Kim's home, Tony and Kim sat in the car for a while. Time seemed to fly when they were together. It seemed as though there weren't enough minutes in one day for them to know more about each other. Kim was so interesting and Tony couldn't get enough of her. He wanted to know so much about her life that seemed so amazing to him. He could also tell that she was feeling the same way.

Somehow, Tony playfully talked himself into walking her home. If he found her house, she would probably let him in and he was up to the challenge. Tony ended up finding the house on his own and Kim did let him in. With today's technology, finding a person's information came so easy. Everyone's name, address, phone number, and place of employment are public knowledge these days. This source of knowledge became very helpful for stalkers, robbers, and scam artists, but yet the government still allowed it. The whole thought of it was a scary one.

Once they got inside, they talked some more. Sitting in the living room, they opened up more about their past, how they felt about life. Kim talked of her complex about her weight, and growing up in the streets of North Philadelphia as the fat girl on the block. They would tell her she had a pretty face, but was too fat to date any of the boys around the way. She got so tired of it that she decided to do something about it. Kim got a membership at the gym and worked out every day until she lost all the extra weight. Being obsessed with the results, she continued her workout with the same schedule to this day. The new look created a new life. Men were willing to do anything to please her. Her opening up to Tony felt good. He was that open ear she needed. Kim never opened up like this, because she feared that exposing her weakness would somehow be used against her. Tony had been so cool and she knew him for so long that it was like having a conversation with a best friend.

Tony gave her a brief background on himself. He explained how his father was a mob boss and how hard he tried to keep him on the straight and narrow. Hearing this gave Kim a newfound respect for Tony. The entire time she believed whatever he was doing out there, which would cause him to come to work late and leave early, had to be illegal. The customized vehicles he owned that looked as though he spent a mint on them didn't help either. Him going the straight and narrow was what he wanted her to believe. Tony knew if she learned he was doing anything illegal, she would have nothing to do with him at all. Making her believe his illegal affairs were nonexistent was the hardest part of getting with her.

CHAPTER 33
Baiting Him In

Bones entered the Chinese carryout on Broadway Street for shrimp fried rice and a chicken wing platter. The place was empty with a Chinese woman behind the shielded glass counter. He paid for his order and waited patiently for his meal. Crystal, dressed in the finest material, walked in, looking so good in her outfit. She caught Bones' eye, but his youthfulness caused him to look away quickly, hoping she didn't notice. Crystal saw his shyness and inexperience with women underneath his thug gear, but she redirected her focus on the woman behind the counter. She ordered a pack of gum and bottled water. Crystal never liked Chinese food, but had to put on a front to get the youngster's attention. Bones silently checked her out when she wasn't looking. Crystal saw his reflection through the thick Plexiglas. After paying for the gum and small bottle of water, she placed it in her Prada bag before leaving. Crystal pretended not to notice his presence and bumped into him on her way out.

"Excuse me. I didn't see you standing there." She softly placed her hand on his frail chest. His chest was small, but hard to the touch. Sliding her fingers downward, she could tell it wasn't his chest at all, but his rib cage. The hard ripples were a dead giveaway.

"No problem, ma," he said, giving way.

There was something about a man calling her by ghetto slang. To her it was degrading, a form of disrespect. She gazed into his eyes without even knowing she gave him a hard stare.

"Oh, Queen Pin. Whatchu doin' out here solo? You good?" He asked, as if she came from Mars.

Crystal's hard face softened. "I'm good. I needed something to quench my thirst." She tried to play it off. There was a pause as if Bones was her thirst quencher.

"Jus' checkin'! Sorry 'bout the way I came off earlier. I didn't know it was you." He apologized as if he knew his words offended her.

Crystal smiled and playfully smacked his shoulders. "It's okay. I'm not mad at you." She gave him a knowing look. "Hey, I know you. You're Pitch's youngin'...Bones."

Bones blushed with a big smile. "That be me." He flared out his boney chest and gave her a puzzled look. "How you know my name?"

"I just told you. I've seen you with Pitch. I make sure I know the names of all the hitters," she said, but the bold-faced kid's expression told her he didn't believe her story. When it came to the crew, he was nothing more than a pawn in the game of chess. Too new for any recognition. That's why Pitch placed him under his wing.

"Oh, okay," was his only response.

Crystal broke down laughing. "Nah, I'm lying. I really don't know how to tell you. It's so embarrassing." She covered her face with her free hand while holding her Prada bag in the other. She was going for an award-winning performance. "I had my eye on you for a while now. Don't you find me attractive?" She dropped her hand and started pushing up on him. Bones never backed off. He stood like a strong soldier.

"You a'ight," he said, nonchalantly.

"'A'ight'? That's all you can say?" She barked as if offended by his response.

"But you's Cat's bit—" He caught himself and corrected it with "girl." Still keeping a stone look.

"I'm still a woman. You don't like what you see?"

Bones looked around nervously. "Yeah, you all good and all that, but you still belong to Cat."

"You make it sound like he owns me." Her head dropped, eyes scanning the floor now.

"Real talk, he do."

She slowly looked up as their eyes connected. "I thought you were a real soldier with some balls, but you straight pussy." She backed up and was ready to walk off. It was a fifty-two fake out to lure him in. Bones reached out, grabbing her arm. The plan was working. Crystal looked at his hand as if he was crazy for putting it on her.

"Hold up. What? You tryna play me?" He roared, now ready for the challenge.

"No, I'm just making sure you're strong in your spot." She was insulting his ego.

"Yo, I'm strong in my spot. So whatchu tryna say then?" That's what she needed to hear. He was hungry and still needed something to prove. Crystal realized the young thug was a cold-blooded killer. A killer for her to manipulate. She knew she had him from the way he kept sneaking glances at her when she wasn't looking. It wasn't the *way* he looked at her, but *how* he looked at her that alarmed Crystal. Bones gazed at Crystal as if she was a stack of buttermilk pancakes and he wanted to be all over her like hot syrup. Before she knew it, he was writing his number on a napkin. After he handed her his number, she told him this incident was between the two of them. Their little secret. Bones zipped his fingers across his lips and walked off as if she didn't exist. Yeah, he was perfect for what she had in stored.

CHAPTER 34
Going for the Prize

Tony froze when their eyes met. All sounds around them seem muted. A chill ran through his spine. It was as if he was an elementary school kid with a hard crush. He couldn't move nor gather the words from his mouth to form a complete sentence. The clock was ticking, but yet it was like time and space no longer existed. Tony had to do something fast, because the silent treatment was getting boring.

Tony reached out and pulled Kim near. There was no reaction or any resistance. Kim kept her gaze on Tony like a deer in headlights. Tony then seized the moment and began kissing her on the collarbone. Then he worked his way to her neck. Kim's moans were low, but loud enough to encourage him to continue. Tony worked his way to her soft pink lips. They tasted like cherries. Only because of the flavored chewing gum she was eating.

Their lips locked as he removed her clothes, starting with her blouse. The object was to be smooth, no pulling and no tugging. The clothes were to fall off her. Tony did so as his eyes nearly popped out his head at the size of her nipples, like two light switches sticking out. She was definitely turned on. Tony followed his line of sight and went straight for her nipples. He sucked on them like a baby starving for fresh milk. Kim grabbed the back of his head and held it tight. She then took her free hand, unbuckled his pants and reached in to feel what he was working with. Tony stood still, accepting her touch. She suddenly gripped his dick hard with excitement and started stroking it and before Tony knew it, he was all over her. The house was nicely decorated and Kim had taste. The sweet smell of passion fruit brought excitement to his love muscle. Tony finally got what he was wishing for, at last. A fantasy come true. The way she gyrated her hips only meant she was hot and ready. So, Tony was willing and able to answer her calling.

As Tony started to remove the lower half of her clothing, he was stopped by a chop to the chest. Nothing was said, as she held her hand there, but it was like he could read her mind or as if she was using some sort of hypnosis to control his thoughts. He was like putty in her hands, as she pushed him off her and positioned him on the living room floor. Giving no fight, as she removed his pants and underwear, leaving him lying there butt ass naked. Kim then stood to her feet and removed all her garments, except for her Kate Spade six-inch heels. Tony's dick stayed at attention as she stood over him legs apart. Kim then climbed on top of him and inserted his dick inside her love box. Tony lay still as she gyrated, working his dick with her wet pussy. Tony was still in a lustful gaze, stuck. He was enjoying the moment, hoping not to cum too soon. Kim was doing all the fucking. She was the man and he was the bitch. His dick was bringing the beast out of her. Kim was a freak by nature. She was aggressive, slamming her pussy up and down on his concrete shaft.

Suddenly she came to an abrupt stop. Her entire body started to shake as if she was going through a severe nervous condition, but this was more orgasmic. Tony felt her hard breaths as she breathed heavily in his left ear. She came and it was hard. Then her body went limp and just like a dude with his first big orgasm, she was done. Now it was Tony's time to take over. He gently rolled her over on her back and slowly penetrated her sensitive walls. Tony knew he had to take it slow or it would ruin the moment. With soft kisses to the neck, he slowly stroked his love muscle in and out. It felt so good that he could feel his loins building with hot juice. He stopped for a few seconds with each stroke, trying not to explode, even though he wanted to so badly, but this right here was for pleasure and not for baby making. Kim started moaning. She was coming back to life. Her voice was like sweet music to his ears. Tony was so lost in his sexual fantasy that he forgot about pleasing Kim. He was just pleasing himself. That's when it snuck up on him. Tony knew what that feeling was before it was followed by his rod exploding with pleasure. Tony then pulled his dick out and jerked it off, over her. His love juice started shooting from his hard pole like a water gun. Cum was squirting all over her. To his surprise, she welcomed it with her eyes closed and beautiful smile. Tony then rubbed it on her skin like lotion. Tony loved every minute of it. They then went upstairs and got into the shower together.

Early that morning, Tony woke up happy and refreshed. They ended up going for round two before taking another shower. Afterward, they went out for breakfast at IHOP restaurant. They were running late for work and didn't care. Tony told her not to worry; he'd handle it when they got there. Kim wanted to know how Tony ended up being friends with Mark and Dave. Tony told her they met through Nicolas Coles. After hanging out together a few times, they just happened to grow on each other. They talked a little more and Kim brought up Nicolas Coles, wanting to see how much information Tony had on her. Tony played it off as if he didn't know she gave Nicolas some pussy at the workplace. Tony wasn't sweating that at all. He really didn't care too much about her past. If she were so concerned about it, then why would she wait until after the fact to question it? She wasn't going to get the answers she was looking for and Tony wasn't fucking this one up. He was only interest in building a future with her. She could have been a hooker for all he cared. The prize for him was experiencing her body and he loved it. Now that he accomplished that goal, the question was, how does he feel right now and where do they go from here?

CHAPTER 35
Interrupting a Meeting

Pitch and Polo the Don were conducting another secret meeting in the back room of the warehouse. The two became so acquainted there was no need to bring the whole squad for protection. Maybe they partnered with each other and there was no need to roll deep or maybe, just maybe, they didn't want too many ears and eyes on their private mission. Pitch only brought Tuck and Chance, and Polo the Don brought Tucan and Eziel. Eziel and Tucan were Polo the Don's best hitters. Eziel was in charge of all Polo the Don's soldiers in Philly and Tucan was in charge of the rest of his soldiers in Camden and Trenton. All four of them sat there mean mugging each other.

"Man, this is some bullshit," Tuck roared.

"Man, who you tellin'? Did you make that call yet or what?" Chance whispered.

"Yeah, my nig. I'm all about my business."

"You should give me that number so I can make sure she's still comin'." Chance threw out in desperation, but the way he said it made him sound more like a pervert.

"You's got a death wish or somethin'?" Tuck frowned, as if Chance was losing his mind.

"Naw, I just like the challenge. I can't believe she turned all this down." Chance paraded around in circles, aims spread out.

Not knowing what their conversation was about, Tucan and Eziel held a cold stare.

"Fool, get the fuck outta here." They shared a laugh, as Polo the Don's goons maintained their stone expressions.

Suddenly, there was a hard knock at the door. All guns aimed in that direction. They all looked at each other as if they were hallucinating. Then there was a second knock on the door. This one was harder than the last.

"Don't just stand there, this is y'all spot. Answer the fuckin' door." Tucan frowned at Chance and Tuck with his weapon aimed at the door.

With a silent nod, Chance slowly approached the door. He threw his back against the wall with his gun pointed in the air. No one knew what to expect, but the nervous tension in the air was strong.

"Who the fuck is it?" Chance yelled, ready to let the slugs fly.

There was a long pause. "It's me, Queen Pin, open up." Her voice boomed from the other side.

Chance slid the peephole open. It was Crystal dressed in black as if she just came from a funeral. With a quick nod from Chance, everyone concealed their weapons and waited in anticipation. He opened the heavy metal door to let her in. Tucan and Eziel stared at her like she was food and so was Chance. She ignored them and approached Tuck.

"Where is he?" Her serious look showed she wasn't for any games.

"In the back room," Chance volunteered, knowing she wasn't speaking to him. Even Tucan and Eziel noticed the desperate move.

Crystal looked at him and rolled her eyes as she headed for the back room. Tuck made sure to give Chance a hard nudge for speaking out like a geek. Chance stumble to the side, losing his balance before gathering himself. He then ran up and knocked on the door.

"Fuck is it?" Pitch's voice boomed. Chance opened the door and allowed Crystal to enter the room.

It was the look in Pitch's eyes when Chance did so. He gave Chance a hard look to tell him that he'd deal with him later. Chance remained cool, calm, and collected. All the other soldiers would have backed off and let Pitch do his thing, but what he was doing was sneaky and Cat Daddy needed to be told.

Pitch stared at Crystal, thinking about the video of her fucking in the back of Cat Daddy's shop. He thought it was Willy at first, but Willy was too geeked up to hit that and his status was too weak. Willy wasn't a killer nor was he a soldier. He only worked on cars, which made him no more than a grease monkey. So it had to be Chance. He was a killer and a pretty boy. Crystal was getting tired of Pitch coming at her neck recklessly. He told her it was a one-night-stand, but she knew Pitch wasn't hearing it. Crystal had that comeback pussy and he was hooked. The thing puzzling to Pitch was how she knew he was conducting a meeting with Polo the Don. There was a snitch amongst them and all fingers were now pointing in Chance's direction.

CHAPTER 36

Angered to the Max

Tony and Kim headed to work in separate vehicles. This was the best time they had together, he thought. For a very long time, Tony and his older brother, Frankie junior, both tried their hardest to get with her. If only his brother was here, he would have been bragging and rubbing it in his face. He finally got that ass and it felt good, but Frankie wasn't here. His life cut short because he dated a girl whose father stopped at nothing to break them up. Tony looked at Kim and knew if Nicolas were around, he would have held on to their dirty little secret as long as he could. With Nicolas's life cut short, was Kim his sloppy seconds? If so, was he wrong for fucking the woman that was with Nicolas even though he's not around?

They both parked next to each other and walked in the front door of the building late. Tony walked Kim to her office and, before he walked in...

"Tony!" Bill yelled across the hall, motioning him to his office. He gave Tony a hard gaze, totally ignoring Kim.

"Uh oh, it looks like you're in trouble again, mister." Kim laughed.

"Don't worry; I know how to calm the savage beast," Tony joked, heading toward the office. Kim shook her head and closed the office door behind her. Bill was his uncle and she knew Tony would have no problem taking care of whatever was wrong.

Tony entered Bill's office to find him pacing behind his desk with his arms crossed.

"What's going on, Unc?" Tony closed the door behind him.

"What's going on, you ask me?" Bill tossed the folded daily newspaper across the room, falling on the floor at Tony's feet. In big bold letters, Gary Holland was suing Home Realty with assault and battery with claims of bullying a tenant. Tony picked it up off the floor and read it. It was a full front-page article with graphic details of what appeared to be an illegal operation. The business was being run under mob rules.

"The shit's on the front page. Tell me what the fuck is going on and cut the bullshit, Tony?" Bill was cursing now. There was no memory of Bill using profanity before, and for him to go there he had to be pissed off to the max.

Tony saw the anger in his eyes. If he didn't take his words seriously, Bill would leap across that big desk of his and choke the living shit out of him. He couldn't laugh his way out of this one.

Tony straightened himself out, looking studious before speaking. "Look, Unc, don't get yourself all worked up over this. I'll call Charles Hunt to straighten this whole mess out."

Bill huffed, coming to an abrupt stop with his head down. He raised his head with his hard gaze on Tony, swinging arms for added effect. "That's the problem, Tony. You think that all the shit that you do, Hunt would get you out of it. Well, I'm sorry to tell you this, but I have to let you go." Tony's eyes widened and mouth dropped open. "Charles Hunt can't help you with this one."

"But why?" Tony fell into the nearest chair. It was like his legs gave out.

"You see, Tony. The shit you have gotten this company into made headlines. Your father gave me the responsibility to take care of this company and you seem to find a way to bring it down. I can't keep holding your hand. You're a grown man. If this guy presses the issue, we'll all be out of business. What you did was illegal and inexcusable. I can't believe that you had the nerve to use this company's name for your illegal bullshit. This would ruin the company's name. I'm sorry, Tony, but you're on your own with this. I need you to clean out your office." Tony had his face buried in his hands. "I have to make some calls to try to save this company."

Bill placed his hand on Tony's shoulder. "Whatever happen to family comes first?"

Tony yelled before jumping up and storming out the office, swinging the door open with force and slamming it so hard that one of Bill's plaques fell from the wall. Kim rushed out her office hearing the commotion. She tried calling out to Tony as he stormed out the building.

CHAPTER 37

Wrong Choice of Words

After Chance closed the door behind Crystal, Tucan blurted out, "Damn, that's a bad ass bitch," as he gave his partner some dap.

Tuck gave him a cold stare. "Watch yo mouth." His tone was hard and aggressive.

"Don't need to. These do all my talkin'." Tucan raised his shirt, exposing the handles of two hidden oozies.

Tuck wanted to say more, but the loud voices in the back room distracted him. Everyone's focus was on the yelling coming from the back room. No one knew what to make of it. Should they run in to make sure everything was okay or do they stand guard out there and wait it out? The decision seemed like a daunting task. Suddenly, the door swung open and the loud noise spilled out. The words were more understandable now.

"I can't believe this. Wait 'til Cat hears about this," Crystal barked, storming out the room. Pitch stormed out behind her.

"Bitch, you best watch yo mouth when you come up here," Pitch thundered.

Crystal turned, pulling out her weapon. She aimed it between his eyes. Tuck and Chance froze. They didn't know what to do. Crystal belonged to their boss, which made her untouchable, but with Cat Daddy locked up made Pitch the head nigga in charge. It was like watching a horror flick. Pitch saw hate and pain in her eyes. He knew she wanted to pull the trigger after what he had done to her, but she held back, letting him know she had a conscience and it had to be preaching a sermon. Tucan and Eziel watched like spectators with big smiles on their faces. Pitch then stepped forward daring her to do it.

"Go 'head, squeeze that shit and see what the fuck happens to yo stupid ass." His teeth were exposed, his face wrinkled with anger.

This was madness at its fullest extent. Pitch was stepping to Crystal with a gun to his head. Everyone in the room knew that a foolish attempt like that would cost him dearly. This was considered straight suicide. She couldn't tear her hard gaze from him as hot tears ran down her cheek. Tuck got between the two and tried to calm her with soft-spoken words as he gently removed the gun from her grasp. Chance then stepped in and wrapped his arm around her to escort her away from Pitch. Crystal then broke down. She couldn't help it. Chance tried to calm her down, but she refused to listen to him. No one had ever gotten her this upset and lived to tell about it. Tuck then stepped in Pitch's face as Pitch continued to talk shit to her. Tucan and Eziel was enjoying every minute of it. All they needed was some popcorn. Polo the Don was standing by the doorway with a blank expression.

"Fuck's wrong witchu? You know Cat would have yo head cut the fuck off for disrespectin' his woman like that," Tuck growled.

"So I take it that you'd gladly honor that wish," Pitch quizzed. Now he was starting shit with Tuck.

Tuck only responded with a cold stare and a slight tilt of the head.

"Oh yeah, it's like that," Pitch roared. "Oh, okay, then let me be the first to say fuck you then. Everybody get the fuck outta here, meetin's over." Pitch looked over and saw Chance still trying to comfort Crystal.

"Yo, Chance, why you all over her like that? What, y'all fuckin' and shit?"

Crystal's mouth dropped. She couldn't believe how reckless Pitch was talking to her. She pushed Chance away and approached Pitch with a raised finger.

"How dare you speak to me that way?" She snatched her gun from Tuck and stormed out the building.

Her words went right through Pitch. He lost all concern in Crystal and his newfound interest was Chance. Pitch's look could burn a hole straight through him. The kind of look that could kill without a second thought. Chance knew that gaze all too well. That look was enough for him to keep his guard up and his mouth shut from that point on. Tuck got Crystal to her car and waited outside until she drove off. Then he watched as Polo the Don and his crew got into their vehicles and pulled off. Now Tuck was getting himself ready to enter the warehouse to receive an ear load of Pitch's bickering.

CHAPTER 38
Maintaining Calm

After storming out of Bill's office, Tony hopped in his whip. He was ready to let the burning rubber display his anger. Suddenly, an unmarked unit pulled up in front of him. It was Detectives Morris and Stewart getting out of the car and heading over to him. Tony rolled the windows down as Detective Stewart leaned into the passenger window and Morris leaned into the driver side window.

"Just when I was about to give up on you, guess what just happen to fall in my lap?" Morris said.

"I don't know, detective, enlighten me," Tony replied sarcastically.

Stewart dropped the newspaper article on the passenger seat for Tony to read, but Tony ignored it and kept his eyes on him.

"A news article with your name in big bold letters. You are a very interesting young man. Every time I turn around you seem to be in something and for that I'm going to be all over you like a tick." Morris said this as if it was personal.

"So let me guess, you're going for blood." Tony was trying to play it off, but inside he was nervous enough to step on the gas pedal and head straight for the boarder. If it weren't for their unmarked vehicles blocking his path, he probably would have taking the risk.

Stewart jumped in. "Look, smart ass, you may find this shit cute and funny, but once you find yourself stuck behind bars you'd be singing a whole different tone."

Tony knew they had a hard-on for him and was looking for anything to jam him up. It was time for a Plan B. Tony had to come up with something to cover his ass and clear his name. Once he got rid of these clowns, he'd set up a meeting with Dave and Mark.

"Morris, you need to cut to the chase and keep it real. You didn't like me ever since my boy, Willy, killed one of your officers and now you're looking for a reason to put me away for good. It's all-good. I'll have my attorney file harassment charges if you think that you're going to keep coming up to my place of work harassing me for some dumb shit. That shit in the paper is filed by someone with no credibility. He's digging, thinking that this is a goldmine."

"So that's what you want to believe, then so be it. I'm not going to play this game with you." Morris waved him off.

"You're a fucking scumbag who belongs behind bars," Stewart scowled. He was itching to throw him in jail.

"Listen, gentlemen, I don't have time for all this right now. I have important business to attend to."

"Don't worry, Tony Satario, in due time. It won't be long before you end up having all the time in the world for us. So we'll leave for now and let you enjoy the little bit of freedom that you have before we take it away," Morris growled, before he and his partner hopped in their unit and drove off. They both had a strong hatred toward Tony and that's all the motivation they needed to take away his freedom.

CHAPTER 39

Eager to Tell

The next day, Crystal headed to the City Jail to tell Cat Daddy about Pitch and his secret meeting with Polo the Don. Whatever this meeting was about, Cat Daddy was not added into the equation. Crystal was so upset that she got up there without her goons to protect her. She would make sure her gear was right and her makeup and nails were flawless, but this was important and she didn't have time to prepare herself. If Pitch was doing some slimy shit behind Cat Daddy's back then he would give her the order to take him out of his misery and Crystal would have no problem with doing so.

This would be one mission she would gladly take care of herself. Crystal never did like Pitch and tried to warn Cat Daddy on many occasions, but he wouldn't listen. She couldn't wait to rub this in his face.

Crystal entered the facility in a gray Nike sweat suit and white Nike sneakers. This was not her every day look. This was something she threw on. Even in the sweat suit, she couldn't hide her shapely physique.

Cat Daddy was at the glass, waiting patiently for her arrival. Crystal sat behind the thick glass and pressed the receiver to her ear. She couldn't wait to give him an earful of all the dumb shit Pitch was doing behind his back. Then, she started thinking about the video that showed her fucking Willy in Cat Daddy's shop, and how Pitch threatened to release it to him if she breached their agreement. She knew it was a death wish if she opened her mouth. Pitch had her where he wanted her. Crystal was supposed to be there for her man in time of need and now she felt useless.

For all she knew, Pitch had this whole thing set up all along. Her cheating on him with another man gave Pitch that open-door policy he was waiting for to do as he pleased. It was killing two birds with one stone. With Pitch and Crystal being the only two people on the outside that could communicate with Cat Daddy, Pitch could secretly undermine Cat Daddy with his business deal with Polo the Don and fuck his woman without him knowing. Cat Daddy was being screwed over twice and the only person benefitting was Pitch.

Cat Daddy saw that something was wrong and he wanted to know, but Crystal put on a fake smile and pretended she missed him and couldn't wait to see him. Tears ran down her face as she could do nothing, but sit back and watch Cat Daddy's downfall. This visit became one of the hardest lies she had ever told to protect herself.

CHAPTER 40
What We Gon' Do?

Tony met up with Dave and Mark at their spot in Camden. They were sitting on the couch watching Tony pace. He was in deep thought and seemed very agitated.

"Now go over this with me again. What did you do when you stepped to Gary?" Tony's arms were crossed so tight that it started to wrinkle his Prada shirt.

"We did like you told us. Step to him about runnin' his fuckin' mouth and make sure we tenderize his ass a little. Why, what's going on?" Mark inquired.

"Well, that pussy filed a lawsuit on the firm and once they find out that I was working my own business, they'll be coming after my ass...hard."

This couldn't have been happening, not now. There was so much needing to be done. His father was still in the hospital recovering from his wounds. He was defenseless without him. Tony was still paying the security company to protect his father. He was still in his induced coma with the hitman out there looking for him, for all he knew. As for his Uncle Bill firing him from the company, Tony wasn't worried about that for now. Once he cleared his name, there should be no problem getting back in. Then there was Kim. He worked so hard at getting with her. This would definitely ruin their relationship.

"So whatchu gon' do?" Mark asked. He was worried. The pay was good and he was making enough to take care of Rolisha and still have spending money.

Tony closed his eyes, taking a deep breath. "I don't know, but I'm open for suggestions." He flopped down on the love seat.

"I say we run up in his crib and murk the nigga. That should automatically close the case and you could still keep it moving," Mark said. He was desperate and it showed.

"No, I can't do that. It's too risky. Doing some shit like that, it would be open season for every municipality," Tony explained, even though the thought of it was tempting.

"Why can't you sale your rental business and let someone else take the heat? Then use the money to shut him the fuck up. He's a crackhead. Just throw the bait out. His bitch ass would surely bite," Dave recommended. The money was good, but it wasn't worth their freedom. With Tony being a paper chaser, they knew it wouldn't take him long to get them back on track.

Tony paused, letting the words soak into his brain. Dave was well known for making jokes out of any situation. So for him to come up with something that made sense, everyone would have to analyze it before responding. "You know what? That sounds like a plan."

CHAPTER 41
Working Her Magic

Crystal was sneaking around with the young thug, fucking his brains out. She would have Bones meet her in different hotels in and around Philadelphia. Messing around in New Jersey was too risky. Crystal would play dress up and change into a new disguise before leaving the house. The windows of her white Benz were tinted so no one would see her from the outside. She would book a suite on the top floor at the most expensive hotels. This would make it hard for anyone to notice her, because spending money on expensive hotels was unheard of in the hood. The popular spots were the cheap motels. None of Pitch's goons had it like that. Business was slow and Pitch was starving them out until he found out who killed his little sister Fatima. Plus, the rooms were the perfect spots for blowing this young thug's mind away. Her extravagant lifestyle was a new experience for him. Once she got to her destination, she would wait for Bones to come in, do his thing and leave.

Crystal made sure to fulfill his every lustful desire. Except threesomes, because it was only the two of them in this game of sexcapades. It was what he wanted, what he needed. She would give him the best blowjobs he had ever experienced. She would even swallow his seeds and now and then she'd let him fuck her in the ass, but his favorite was her on her back, talking dirty in his ear with her sexy voice as he beat that pussy up. The eighteen-year-old kid wasn't in her league. She made it hard for him to keep up with her skills. Everything she did to him was new. He was like a three-year-old kid having fun at Chuck E. Cheese's. Going two to three rounds with no long breaks in between. Sometimes he would cum without her even knowing, because he would never miss a beat. He would hit that until he got his second or third nut and then be out. This was perfect. He would get what he wanted and so would she and they would be on their way to do their daily chores.

Then he started taking his time leaving as if he wanted to stay. She saw he was catching feelings and emotions. The plan was to turn him out and have his head all fucked up. From the looks of it, it was working. Good...everything was going according to plan. Pitch was abusing his shit; thought he couldn't make it through the week without getting some of that pussy. She felt like a prisoner, his personal sex slave. The shit was tiring her out. Satisfying two men on the regular made her feel more like a porn star. She was ready to blow Pitch's head off, but couldn't afford to take the risk. This was her freedom on the line, but her freedom came with a cost. She would have to speed up the process. Just then, her doorbell rang, destroying her thought process. *Who could it be?* She checked her monitor. It was Pitch looking into the camera, smiling. Yeah, she definitely needed to speed up the process.

CHAPTER 42

The Hook-up

Mark was getting pissed off, but Dave was his boy and he made sure to have his back. That night they were to meet up with Tuck under the Ben Franklin Bridge in Camden, New Jersey, but Tony was taking too long to show up. The main topic was Pitch. He was cocky, moving like the President. He was bringing all types of attention to himself. With Cat Daddy on lock-down, he was in charge, which meant Tuck was second in command. Pitch didn't like that at all. He was putting salt in the game, talking all kinds of negative shit about Tuck. This caused a separation amongst the crew, which wasn't good at all. With the division, Polo the Don was strong enough to hit up half the crew with no problem, but the crew as a whole would be a force to reckon with. All Pitch needed to do was to get Polo the Don to join forces with him and he would be untouchable.

Dave and Mark never experienced the feeling of taking a man's life, let alone pulling a trigger to do so. The closest the two came to justifying a murder was setting a few mousetraps around the house and killing a few insects. Now this time the shit was real. There was no telling how this meeting was going to turn out. They were hoping it didn't turn deadly.

"Where the fuck is this pasta-eatin' muhfucka at?" Mark barked. He was getting agitated about Tony's tardiness. Tony had a bad habit of showing up late and a bad excuse to go with it.

"Be easy, dawg. If the nigga said he gon' be here, then he's gon' be here. All we have to do is be patient."

Mark looked at Dave with a frown. "Now how much sense does that shit make? 'If he said he gon' be here, then he's gon' be here.' Do you ever listen to the shit that comes out your mouth?"

"There you go. You protein-juice-drinkin' muhfucka. They say liftin' too much weight will make you stupid. You just dumb and strong. A fuckin' meat stick with muscles," Dave cracked.

"Now that's the dumb shit I'm talkin' about. How does liftin' weights have anything to do with my IQ?"

"The lack of blood and oxygen affects the brain. You kill thousands of brain cells each time you work out. It won't be long before you start walkin' around here like a caveman." Dave was on a roll and running with it.

"You fuckin' idiot. You dumber than I thought," Mark yelled.

Dave was good at getting him pissed off. This tactic eased his mind enough to remain focused on the meeting before Tuck and his crew showed up.

Tony finally pulled up in his custom vehicle. He was dressed in business attire, looking like money.

"What took you so long?" Mark fussed. He was still worked up.

"I had to take care of a few things before I got here."

"Man, if we had a quarter for every time you used that line, I'd have a full tank of gas," Dave complained.

"As long as I got here before they did then it's all-good." Tony adjusted his suit as if he was preparing for a job interview.

Tuck pulled up and parked his ride in front of them. They were at least fifty feet away and they saw he brought his goons with him.

Tony looked Mark and Dave over to make sure they were straight and with a quick nod, "Okay, fellas, it's show time."

CHAPTER 43
Making a Deal

Pitch didn't know how to command his troops and would abuse his shit. Tuck would show his crew love and was always there when they needed him most. Tony heard what was going down, but he didn't know how serious it was until he saw how everything looked like it was about to come crashing down on the whole organization. A light went off in Tony's head. This was what Tony needed so his father could see that he was well organized and responsible enough to be part of his crime family. Tony wanted to set up a meeting with Tuck. He needed the muscle to get shit started right. Tuck told him he would set everything up and he'd wait for his call. So that's what led them here.

Tony approached Tuck and his young killers, while Dave and Mark stood silently, watching. They spoke privately. Tuck wanted in with the Geek Squad and together they would supply the protection they needed to run their business. They knew it wouldn't be long before they got robbed. They were easy targets for those that were looking to rundown on them. Tony explained his plans to Tuck and what he needed from them. Tony wanted them on his team as well. In the end, there would be enough money to spread around. He heard about the beef between Pitch and Tuck and how Pitch was starving them out. Tuck was dipping in his own savings account to keep them from starving to death. The deal was one they couldn't turn down. Tuck had his three young guns he wanted to bring along and Tony told him the more the merrier. However, Tony was still trying to get the Geek Squad on their team. Tuck opened his own chop shop and had Chaos running it. Chaos had a hook-up with his uncle with the crooked car deal. Tuck would be making a killing in stealing cars since Pitch cut him off from the drug supply. This would be a temporary hustle, because it wouldn't take long before the feds got a whiff of it. So the plan was to hit hard and run. This would help restart the drug game. The money Tuck would make off the car scam business would help him buy a boatload of pure coke from a new connection in the Dominican Republic. Chaos was the only one who still had that reach. The connect was his uncle, Jose Fernandez.

CHAPTER 44
Taking Control

Kim was at Maggiano's Little Italy in Philadelphia, waiting at the table for Tony's arrival. Maggiano's, an Italian place with private rooms and dimmed lighting, was very romantic with the smell of tomato sauce, garlic and pasta in the air. Tony finally arrived and gave her a big hug.

"Sorry I'm late. I had to take care of a few things," he said, taking a seat on the opposite side of the table. Tony had studied Kim during the time they worked together, making her his main science project. He knew what she liked, places she loved to go, favorite restaurants, malls drinks, movies, etc. He was eager to know everything about her, even her blood type.

"It's okay, I wasn't waiting long," Kim admitted, adjusting her clothing.

"Good!" Tony looked her over again. "You look so lovely tonight."

"Thanks. It's nothing. Just something I threw on," she lied. Tony was so into the shit that happened earlier that he lost himself in a trance-like state. Making a big deal like this with Tuck and his crew was a big risk he was taking. If everything worked out right, he'd be straight, but if it didn't, it would cost him everything he worked so hard for, which would make this one of the biggest gambles Tony had ever taken. With the Geek Squad turning down all his offers, he would have to press harder and find a better way for them to listen.

"Tony, I'm right here." Kim snapped her fingers. "Am I boring already?"

Tony coughed up a laugh. "Naw, not at all. I'm so sorry. I just can't stop thinking about my dad's condition. I hate to see him all laid up in that bed, dead to the world," he lied. Larry still walking the streets was making him very uncomfortable. For all he knew, Larry could have been out trying to hunt him down, but Frank Debartello being his father was a deep secret to the world around him. Only a hand full of people knew of this and they weren't telling.

After enjoying their meal, Tony decided to take Kim to Cooper River Park. The view was perfect for Tony to unwind and clear his head. They sat and talked for a few minutes. Tony told Kim how he wished his father were there to raise him, be proud of him as his son and not have him living a secret life. Kim told him how she always wanted to take a vacation trip with her mother somewhere on a cruise with palm trees, nice sandy beaches and clear water. Jamaica would be the dream spot, but her mother doesn't want her paying those high prices to do so.

With everything that was going on, his judgement was starting to cloud. Tony needed to be focused in order to not get caught slipping. Devising a plan took time and strategy. Tony wanted to be well prepared when the shit hit the fan.

Tony must have drifted off in deep thought again, because he didn't notice Kim making her way on top of him until she was on his lap sucking on his neck. Tony didn't react. He just moaned and allowed her to do her thing with him. While sucking on his neck, she pulled out his hard penis and inserted it into her love box. It was soft and wet. Kim was a freak and taking what she wanted only increased his arousal. Tony watched in a lustful gaze as Kim rode up and down on his hard pole. He couldn't take his gaze off her bedroom eyes. Thank goodness, he made sure the windows had extra limo tints installed.

Her beauty and sex appeal was too much for him to handle. Without notice, everything started to spin out of control. Then his body started to jerk uncontrollably. Only one thing could describe this feeling. Tony ended up having a big orgasm. He could not recall ever having one this hard before. His entire body collapsed, as he sat there weak and exhausted from doing nothing but just sitting there. Maybe it was physical and she had some good pussy, or maybe it was mental and he'd been craving it for so long or maybe it was a combination of both. Whatever it was, it was enough to drain him of all his energy.

Kim climbed off him and readjusted his pants. Tony didn't know which way was up. Her panties were still wrapped around her left leg so she slipped her right leg in and pulled them up. This was the best part of wearing a miniskirt, easy access.

CHAPTER 45
Across the Blue

Chance took Tuck to the Philadelphia International Airport. Tuck was catching a flight to the Dominican Republic with Chaos to meet up with his uncle, Jose Fernandez, in Santa Domingo. He had a big organization that dealt with stealing high-end vehicles in Florida and selling it for one-third its price value. The titles for the vehicles were good enough to fool motor vehicles. He was a big drug lord with multiple illegal operations. If it was fast cash, he was in on it. The United States government couldn't touch him with the law protecting his rights in the Dominican Republic, but for him to have free reign cost him. He paid the government a lot of money to look the other way.

"I just got us hooked up with a new connect while you were out last night chasing some tail. Good thing the youngin's were around to have my back. Why didn't you answer my call?" Tuck argued.

"Man, I was all up in some pussy last night, fuckin' Erika and forgot I had my phone off. Stupid ass bitch couldn't follow instructions and ended up gettin' locked the fuck up. I'm done with that bitch. So who's the connect?"

"Some Italian dude that Cat hooked me up with. I'll fill you in on it when I get back. Hopefully you could get pussy off your mind long enough for me to introduce you to him."

"Man, I ain't that bad." Chance waved him off.

"Yeah, let you tell it." Tuck chuckled.

"I still think that you shoulda brought me witcha." Chance pouted.

"Naw, someone still gotta stay here to hold shit down. We can't be in two places at the same time. Plus, I'ma need you to keep an eye on that weasel, Pitch."

"You right, 'cause when Cat makes that call to air that nigga out, I'ma be the first nigga to rock his ass to sleep. Then I'ma piss on his fuckin' corpse." Chance giggled.

Tuck then gave him a hard gaze. "Just remember if anyone ask, I took a flight to Atlanta for a family reunion."

"Don't worry; I gots yo back, my nig." Chance beamed.

"And keep the Queen Pin off yo tongue. You see how Pitch was lookin' at'cha," he warned Chance, but that was one task that would be hard for him to do.

"I ain't worried 'bout his ass. He'll be all right. Jus' make sure you holla soon as you touch down."

"I will and make sure you stay away from Mel. She's vulnerable and I know your track record." He knew Chance all too well and was hoping he would, for once, listen to him.

Chance gave him a shocked look with his mouth open. "Ah, that's really fucked up. I'm not that greasy."

"Yeah, let you tell it." Tuck smirked.

They both showed love and went their separate ways.

CHAPTER 46

Overlooking Him

K im had a good time with Tony and for the first time, she saw another side to him. A side she found to be very attractive. Tony did have his head on straight and mapped out his goals, step by step. Tony had a master plan to get rich. Kim started weighing the pros and cons on Tony without him even knowing and, so far, the pros were holding all the weight.

To Kim's surprise, Tony was the perfect gentleman. He never came at her sexually. He was more concerned with her mental than her physical. This was different from the Tony she knew at work. The Tony she knew was very immature and playful. He took his job lightly and was always late for work. Whenever Bill would tell him to do something, he never did it. He would always pass it on to someone else. Bill was the boss, but he was also Tony's uncle and, for that, Tony was able to get away with anything. Now the new Tony was totally different in every way. Maybe he was mature now and was ready to be a man and take on all the responsibilities a real man does. This is what Kim was starting to see in him.

Every guy she dated would start off as if they're interested in her mind and before the date ended, they were trying to get her in bed. Tony was old fashion. He always kept eye contact during conversation. Opening doors and walking on the outside of the curb seemed natural. All the small things she thought Tony would need to be taught, he already knew. That was a major plus on her "man scale."

That is why she threw herself on him. Something about a hardworking man turned her on. These traits would make a good man for her and a good father if they were to build a family out of this relationship. His curly hair, sexy physique and a face like the younger version of Enrique Iglesias only made it that much easier.

With Tony's ingenious plan of success would have worked if he had decided to follow it through, but the whole process would have taken some time. The paperwork and constant transfer cash from this company to the next was time consuming and stressful. The workload in general would have been too much for him to handle on his own. By the time he reached rich boy status, he would be too old to enjoy it. This was not what he intended and he lacked the patience to do so. The real plan was to take the money that he made off his illegal rental properties to start his funeral business. Once he got his funeral home started, then everything else would surely fall in place.

CHAPTER 47
Funds are Low

Chance drove to Stanley Park to meet up with the Young Hitters. Stanley Park was in the Chelton Terrace Apartment section of Camden. It was an open field for concerts and baseball games in the summer. All the heavy drinkers hung at this park. There was a play area for the kids with a three story high rocket ship and a jungle gym play area. There was also a full basketball court with an additional two hoops on each side. They were already there playing basketball. Chance walked over and sat at a nearby bench. The young boys stopped playing and headed over to him. They all showed love and sat around him.

"Yo, what up, my nig? Where's Tuck at?" Syphee asked. He was the youngest of the three and usually the quietest.

"He's in the ATL for a family reunion," Chance said. They knew the drill and they were waiting for Chance to let them know what story to go by.

"So is that your final answer," Pemont teased. He was good at analyzing things.

"Yeah, that's what I'm stickin' wit'." Chance smirked. Kids played in the distance.

"Fuck all that. What's up wit' Pitch? Ever since his fat ass sister got aired out, he's been buggin'. Shit ain't the same," Dundy said. He was the hyper one out of the three. Each time he talked, he would swing his arms and punch his fist in his hand. He was filled with extra energy.

"Yeah, he's been letting Polo the Don bring his crew in and take a few positions. Niggas worked hard to hold them spots. Shit ain't right," Pemont voiced.

They were pissed off because the money wasn't right. They were starting to question their loyalty to Pitch, as well as Cat Daddy. They knew there was nothing Cat Daddy could do from a jail cell, but it didn't matter, they were starving for money and ready to do whatever it took to get that cash. Chance saw the hunger in their eyes.

"Tuck got hooked up with a new connect last night. Some rich-looking Italian dude. Where were you at?" Dundy asked, jumping up and down as if he was playing a game of Double Dutch.

"I was tryna hook up with another connect last night," Chance lied.

"Did it come with a fat ass and cute face?" Pemont teased.

"Damn, am I that obvious?"

"Yep." They all responded in unison, followed by fist bumps.

Chance was now thinking about reevaluating his thought process.

"Word on the street, there's these corny ass geeks makin' mad papah from some computer scam they got goin' on. They ain't holdin', so robbin' them fools would be easy," Dundy said, snatching the basketball from Syphee and twirling it on one finger.

Chance paused for a minute to let his words sink in. "Okay, fellas, it's time for practice," Chance said, letting them know it was time for an emergency meeting.

CHAPTER 48

The Rundown

Chance was at his spot with the Young Hitters. They sat around the kitchen table. At nine forty-five in the morning, all his neighbors would be sleep or at work. This was the best time for them to make moves before the nosey shift got started.

"The plan is simple. We run in, hit 'em hard and be out. Shit should take no more than thirty seconds." Chance said, with a breakdown of everything.

Pemont raised his hand and with a slight nod from Chance, he now had the floor. "That sounds good and all, but we all know they ain't gonna cough the shit up that easily. We talkin' some serious cash flow here."

Everyone nodded in agreement.

Chance put his elbows on the table and placed his face in his hands. The mental strain of planning each job felt just as bad as taking a state exam. He raised his head and looked over each one of his team members. They knew what they were talking about; they were experienced. Chance was pleased with them.

"Yeah, you right. I don't want none of these bitch-ass niggas gettin' aired out. It ain't that type of job. We just want to give them a chance to restock their bread and then we go at 'em again. This is going to be our money train, ya dig?" Chance explained.

"I get it. Just pump a little fear in 'em. I don't mind crackin' a few skulls while I'm at it," Dundy jumped in, punching his fist in his hand. He was looking for an excuse to burn energy.

"But you know the next time we try to hit 'em up, they gon' be strapped," Syphee said.

"Then we'll deal with that when the opportunity presents itself," Pemont responded.

Chance was proud to see how well the Young Hitters worked together like a real team. It was not that long ago when he took them under his wing. Pemont was the first to be recruited to his team. He was a loner that kept getting picked on by the school bully and his crew. Pemont was no follower and wasn't afraid to put in some work. Win or lose, he wasn't going out without a fight.

Syphee was quiet and kept to himself. His mother was dealing with a guy who couldn't keep his hands off her. One day he decided to put his hands on Syphee and that was the last straw. Syphee fought back, but was no match. That's when he pumped a few holes in him. The cops couldn't get shit from him so they had to let him go. The shit happened on the streets. So it was labeled as a deal that went bad since it happened in a high drug area. That's how he got the name The Silent Killer.

As for Dundy, he was a firecracker, wild and off the hook. All he needed was a little guidance to settle him down and that's when Tuck and Chance stepped in. They were young and dangerous, but with Tuck and Chance to look up to, made them the perfect soldiers.

Suddenly his hip started vibrating. Chance reached in his pocket and pulled out his cell phone. The name that appeared on the screen read Melody Reed.

CHAPTER 49
Rain Proof

Melody was standing at the doorway of her apartment, waiting on Chance as he pulled up. The weight of her worries displayed on her face. Her eyes were red and wet from so much crying. Her son, Carlton, was in her arms. From the way his head slumped on her shoulder and his lifeless arms dangled to the side, meant he was asleep.

Melody turned and walked inside to place the baby in the crib. Chance walked in behind her, closing the front door as he entered. Even in her depressed state, her killer physique had Chance staring at her fat ass wiggle while she walked. Suddenly he was overwhelmed with guilt. This was his boy's girl and even though he was no longer here, fucking her would be wrong in so many ways. Tuck told him to stay away from her until he got back. Chance was not to be trusted and he knew if the opportunity presented itself, he wouldn't hesitate to take advantage of it. Even though he wasn't there for that. Melody needed him and he wasn't going to turn his back on her.

"I'm sorry for bringing you here, but I needed someone I can trust with the information I have. I tried calling Tuck to get both of you guys down here, but he's not returning my calls. It just goes straight to voice mail."

Chance saw the urgency in her eyes. He wanted to tell her the truth of where Tuck was, but knew it wouldn't be a wise thing to do. What Tuck was doing was business and he couldn't afford to risk it. This type of business that could cost him his freedom. Even worse, his life. For Tuck, it was get rich or die trying.

"Yeah, he had bounced to the ATL for a family reunion. Don't know when he gon' get back," Chance lied. From the look in Melody's eyes, she could tell he was doing so. It didn't matter; she had to let him know what really went down on the night of Willy's death.

"Anyway, the night that Willy died in that abandoned house on Marlton Pike wasn't from him using drugs. I don't care what the autopsy say. Willy was murdered and that realtor, Tony, had something to do with it." Her voice cracked, trying to hold back the pain.

"Tony…who the fuck is Tony?" Chance barked. He was now in war mode.

"He works for that Home Realty Firm in Cherry Hill. He was the one that was going to hook us up with the crib in Merchantville."

Chance thought about it for a second. "Oh yeah, I remember him tellin' me 'bout that dude. He got that hook-up on properties."

"Well, what y'all didn't know was that Willy was working for the hitman, Larry something. He hung with Willy while they were locked up."

"Hitman? What hitman?" Confusion was written all over his face.

"The one that works for the mob boss, Frank Debartello. He was all over the news."

"Fuck was he doin' workin' for that guy?"

"From what he told me, that crooked cop in Merchantville name Rodeski kept harassing him. He was the same cop that locked him up the last time."

"Yeah, I remember him tellin' me 'bout that shit." Chance had disdain for that officer.

"Well, that same cop harassed that realtor, Tony. So Tony hired Willy and the hitman to take him out. The night that Tony showed up to pay Willy for taking that cop out, Willy left the crib with Tony and the next thing I remembered was Willy being on the news as being a crackhead, in so many words."

"Who would have known that Willy was a killah. My head's all fucked up now." Chance dropped his face into his hands. After gathering himself, he looked up, giving Melody his full attention. "Now fill me in on this realtor guy."

CHAPTER 50
Getting to Know Him

Chance looked at his cell phone screen to see if Tuck returned any of his calls. He wanted to tell Tuck about Willy being a killer when they thought he didn't have the heart to do so. There was no other way of getting in touch with him. Chance didn't believe in discussing business over the phone and decided to leave messages for him to return his calls, but Tuck never responded. Not hearing his voice was starting to worry him. Chance was on his own to try to handle things. He went as far as getting Tony's number to set up an appointment for one of his properties.

"Hello," Tony answered his cell phone.

"Yes, may I speak with Tony, please?" Chance tried to sound as polite as possible.

"Yes, this is Tony speaking." Tony sounded professional on the phone. His geeky mannerism made it hard for Chance to believe this was the same guy who killed his homie. It really didn't matter to Chance. His mind was already made up that this man was already dead. His boy, Willy, was dead and someone was going to pay. Innocent or not, murder was the only thing that would help ease his pain, even for the moment.

"Yeah, I'm lookin' to get a crib."

"And how did you get my information?" Even though he was using his professional tone, Chance could still hear the concern in his voice.

"From Cat. He told me to holla at'cha 'bout it a ways back," Chance lied. Melody gave him the information he needed to set it up.

"Good enough. When is the best time to meet up?" Tony was ready to do business.

"You tell me. I ain't doin' nuffin'." Chance was working his way into seeing him today, the sooner the better.

"How about two this afternoon." Tony perked up. Chance had him right where he wanted him.

"That sounds like a plan." Chance was excited to see the face of the man that took Willy's life.

"Just give me your name and address and I'll meet you there shortly."

CHAPTER 51
Show and Tell

In an empty parking lot at the River Front in Camden, New Jersey, Chance stood alone next to his ride. This was the address he had given Tony. He didn't want him to know where he lived. Chance patiently waited on Tony's arrival when he noticed an unrecognizable customized ride pulling up. The tint was too dark for him to see who was behind the wheel, let alone if there were more than one passenger that occupied the vehicle. Chance was strapped and ready to light Tony up, but now wouldn't be a good time. For one, he would need to be sure this joker was capable of doing such a thing. He would have to pick at his brain first. The slightest hint of deceit would justify his action.

The car door opened and Tony stepped out. His appearance did not fit the voice he spoke to earlier. He looked Hispanic or Italian with a rich golden tan. Nice physique, curly black hair and a face of a model or celebrity. His style of fashion and expensive car screamed *baller*.

"Raymond Cobbs, correct?" Tony said, with an extended hand. This was his government name and Chance knew Tony probably investigated his name first before coming down here. There was no need to spook him now. In order to pull this off, he had to build this man's trust.

"Yeah, so whatchu got?" Chance said, getting to the point, acting eager to get it over with.

"It depends on what you are interested in moving to. I have a few homes in Camden and many more outside of Camden."

Chance paused, thinking hard about the question. He never thought it through. This wasn't supposed to be a real meeting, but an execution. He only hesitated because he needed more to go by. Plus, there were too many cop cars present. He didn't plan an escape route. This move would be foolish and Chance was a smarter killer than that. There was no need to allow his emotions to guide his decisions.

"Cherry Hill would be a good start," Chance said. This way he could work out a better strategy.

"Before doing so, how much you working with?" Tony asked, as if this could be a waste of his time.

"How much I need?" Chance challenged.

"At least two hundred thousand cash." Tony looked at him, waiting for Chance to reconsider. This is what Tony was afraid of; this thug was nothing more than a waste of time. Chance's hard look turned into a devilish grin. He popped the trunk of his ride and inside were two huge duffle bags of money.

"There's over three hundred thousand there and I got a lot more to play with. So stop wastin' my time and show me whatchu got," Chance barked with a hard look.

Tony's eyes widened with surprise. "No problem. Follow me and I got something that will give you more bang for your buck," Tony bragged.

Chance jumped in his car and followed Tony. He was devising a plan to question him before taking him out. The money wasn't for his personnel use. Chance was to drop it off to Pitch, but Melody told him Tony wanted to see the cash up front before he does business with him. Holding on to the cash worked out great, so far. Chance's plan was to squeeze off a few rounds into Tony and leave his body there to rot. Not hiding it meant he wanted everyone to see his handy work. Multiple shoots to the head symbolized anger and hate. This action was commonly known as an act of revenge. He would then drop the money off and keep it moving, but then he ended up questioning his hasty decision.

CHAPTER 52

Making It Count

After a lengthy tour of a mansion Tony owned, they ended up in the foyer.

"So what do you think about it?" Tony asked, with his arms proudly extended.

"It's a'ight. I was expecting more." Chance pouted to show disappointment.

"I apologize if it's not towards your liking, but this is the biggest home I have available. Are you married, single, family?"

"Naw, I'm single with no kids."

"Then this would be the perfect house, if you like to party or impress the females. It all depends on how you get down." This was all game to get a quick sale.

"Man, I ain't wit' all that. I just need a place that's perfect to start a family." Chance wasn't focused on the property. He was thinking of a way to murder this guy. That is, if he was the one that took Willy out.

"Well, this is the place. Any woman you bring to this house will automatically fall in love. No woman would turn this down."

"Then I'll wait on it and think it through. If I happen to have a change of heart, I'll holla at'cha later."

"I could work with that." Tony extended his hand. Chance then gave him a firm handshake before leaving the home.

While heading toward their vehicles, Chance stopped and turned his attention to Tony with a finger waving at him. "I remember you now. You're that dude that was sellin' a crib to my boy, Willy, in Merchantville." Chance beamed to read his facial expression. Tony's eyes widened.

"Who? Oh yeah, Willy. How's he doing? He never returned any of my phone calls," Tony said, but his weak acting skills told on him. He was guilty in so many ways. He might not have been the one to kill Willy, but he certainly knew who did it.

"He's dead," Chance shot out.

"Oh, sorry to hear that," Tony said with sympathy, keeping it short and to the point, but it was too late. Chance had made up his mind to drop his ass right in the driveway.

"You wouldn't happen to know who killed him, would you?" Chance asked.

"No I wouldn't. Why you coming at me with this?" Tony growled with an attitude. His whole demeanor had changed. Chance was looking into the eyes of a killer, as he knew this look too well. It was like looking into a mirror.

"I'm just askin'. I don't want no problems." Chance gave him a confused look while throwing his hands up for added effect.

This was a test and Tony failed. His defensive behavior was enough to convince Chance he was guilty. There was no need in taking him out right there. All evidence would lead to Chance starting with the scheduled meeting under his government name for the viewing of the homes. Chance was good at what he did and knew he would get Tony later. Tony's face was beet red with anger.

"You know what? Fuck it! Lose the number," Tony said, hopping into his whip and peeling out of the driveway, the tire marks revealing his frustration. Tony was done doing business with him. Chance wasn't interested in the home in the first place. His mind was programmed to kill, with Tony as his prime target.

CHAPTER 53

Weak Stomach

Tony met up with Dave and Mark at the Purple Parrot in Cherry Hill, New Jersey. They were ready to unwind and party hard. Chance had Tony all worked up. Telling Dave and Mark wouldn't have been beneficiary. So a few drinks would have to do for now.

"Yo, Tony, what's up with your boy, Dave, here?" Mark asked, changing the subject after they had enough beers to calm his tension. Gary Holland had them all worked up over this lawsuit and they were depending on Tony to make this all go away.

"What he do now?" Tony asked, as if Dave was prone to trouble.

"This muhfucka been fuckin' nothin' but ugly bitches. I'm talkin' 'bout the ones that look like that bitch with the crossed eyes on *In Living Color* that Jamie Fox played." Mark laughed.

Tony winced at the thought of it. "No, get the fuck out of here." He chuckled.

Dave stood to demonstrate his reasons. "Let me explain so we can be on the same page here." He had the center stage. "The pretty bitches are hard to fuck. They just lay there lookin' at you like you're there to please them." He bounced up and down with a straight face, demonstrating a weak fuck, more so a dead zombie. "Fuck all that. Now the ugly bitches be puttin' in some work. They are there to please us. They want to feel wanted from being rejected by so many men all their lives. Now me, I like them black as hell. Like a scab that's formed on a wound. That extra crispy lookin' bitch with a natural looking hairstyle. I don't want her talkin' 'bout 'Don't mess up the hair' type shit either. I love it wild and nappy like she just got out the shower and let it air dry. I want her to have big swollen lips that look like a fist. The kind that look like they could knock a muhfucka out if she kisses him too hard. I want them shits to look like she could suck the sap out of a tree. You feel me?" Dave said, making sure Tony and Mark were paying attention.

"Yeah, yeah, yeah, keep goin'," Tony said, eager to hear the outcome of his crazy-ass philosophy he had going.

"Well anyway, they have to be ugly. I mean dogface ugly. That way my conscience won't get in the way when I'm fuckin' the shit out of them. Now she has to be cross-eyed as well. That's a major plus. What I would do is lay her on her back and stroke the shit out that pussy. You know how bitches make those ugly faces when you're fucking them right. An ugly face already looks like you fuckin' them right, the process of elimination. An ugly face looks like you tearing that pussy up, which is an ego boost. Then you tell her to open her eyes and when she looks at you, all cross-eyed and shit, makes it look like she's cummin'. Now that shit soups me up and makes me fuck her even harder. Now if she's layin' there, all quiet and shit, you take your thumbs and press them in her shoulder blades hard. She'd be pinned on her back tryna move your hands away, but she can't reach to remove them, because your arms are wrapped around her. That's when she starts screamin' loud as hell. That shit gives me the longest bust ever," Dave bragged with his chest out. Tony and Mark were laughing hard and falling on the floor.

"That is the dumbest shit I've ever hard, but funny as hell," Tony said, getting back up.

"But effective. You should try it," Dave offered.

"Nah, that's all right. Knowing my luck, she'd call the cops and have me locked up for rape," Tony said, holding his stomach, trying to catch his breath.

"Yeah, I'll pass on that, too. There's no telling what Rolisha would do if I tried that shit with her ass." Mark laughed, throwing back a nice cold one.

"Yeah, once you go asphalt black, you never go back," Tony sung, as he and Mark burst into laughter.

"You can't hide from that crazy ass female. She can sniff you out like a blood hound," Dave teased.

"Yeah, that shit is crazy," Mark agreed, thinking how Rolisha was good at tracking him down whenever he stayed out late. She would embarrass him in front of his boys. Mark wanted to curse her ass out and send her back home to South Carolina, but he was too afraid to do so and didn't know what Rolisha was capable of doing. She was unpredictable like a pit-bull.

CHAPTER 54

Drinking it Up

"Anyway, I'm tired of lookin' at you muhfuckas. Let's hit a club tonight. I want to fuck me another ugly bitch," Dave threw out to Tony, eager to leave the bar. They were still at the Purple Parrot, making jokes about the unattractive women that interested Dave.

"Now we're talkin'. I know a good spot in Deptford called Adelphia's," Tony said.

"What, in Philly or Jersey?" Dave asked. He must have heard of the place before.

"Jersey," Tony responded.

"What's that, an all-white club?" Mark asked.

"Majority white, but they got a mixed crowd," Tony said.

"It don't matter to me. I'll fuck a bitch in every color. Even avatar blue. Pussy's pussy to me," Dave said, jumping out his chair.

"Yo, I want me a snow bunny," Mark stated, pertaining to a white female.

"Now, Mark, we ain't gonna worry 'bout yo bitch, Rolisha, showin' up, spoilin' the night for us?" Dave words were unfiltered with the alcohol in his system.

"For one thing, you gon' stop callin' my girl a bitch. That's the mother of my seed," Mark said, with gritted teeth.

"So now you acceptin' the shit," Dave said, in a shocked tone.

"No, but if that is my seed she's carryin' then the disrespectful name callin' will stop," Mark demanded with emphases.

"My bad, fam. I can respect that, but if that ain't yo seed then it's back to callin' her every bitch in the book." Dave smiled from ear to ear.

"I can respect that. So let's do the damn thing. I want me some pussy. I couldn't fuck my girl with that big ass hump she calls a stomach, no matter how wonderful it is to create your own seed. I just can't get used to that shit. I think that my dick is hittin' the baby. What if it comes out with dents in its' head?" Mark complained.

"Man, it's a baby and it's too far up in her for your dick to reach," Tony explained.

"Yo, dawg, I got a python between these legs and it will reach," Mark bragged. "What if it's a boy and while I'm nuttin' all up in that he thinks it's a pacifier and starts sucking on it, drink my semen. Then comes out all gay and shit." His facial expression was one of curiosity.

"Say no more, 'cause you're talkin' that dumb shit. We can take my ride," Tony offered, walking away before Dave got started on Mark again.

CHAPTER 55
Visual Tricks

Tony, Mark, and Dave entered Adelphia's and sat at the bar, checking out the females. Dave and Mark were impressed with the beautifully designed building with pillars and status that aligned the place in and out. The water fountains that were in nicely decorated areas gave it a more serene feeling. This place looked more like a wedding reception hall.

"Yo, I'm feelin' this spot," Mark yelled in Tony's ear while getting his drink on. The music was loud and the place was packed. They came to the club with a buzz and now they were about to get fucked up and didn't even know it.

"Tony, I just found my new hangout spot," Dave said, giving him some dap.

"See? I told y'all this was the spot to be," Tony bragged.

The music selection was just right, with Wiz Khalifa playing in the background. They sat quietly for a while, enjoying the visual treats that walked around profiling their sexy physiques and expensive attire that enhanced their appearance. Their focus was interrupted when they heard Mark yell out.

"*Damn!*"

Tony and Dave looked up to see a female enter the club looking bad as hell.

"Yo, you see that?" Mark asked, not realizing she already had their attention. "She look just look Jessica Alba." He gazed at her with amazement.

"Yo, Mark, don't just sit there like a retard, step to the bitch before one of these vultures snatch her fine ass up. Don't worry about me, I'm huntin' ugly bitches," Dave yelled, pushing Mark toward the woman. Mark approached her as she reached in her purse to pay for her drink.

"Don't worry 'bout that, ma. Tonight, all your drinks are on me," Mark said, as he tipped the bartender. The woman looked up at him wide-eyed with a pleasant smile.

"T'anks, and what's your name?" she asked, with a strong accent.

"Mark." He grinned. Loving the way her words sounded as they entered his ears.

"Mark, dat sounds like some'ting you made up. Wha', you creeping around or some'ting? That can't be your real name," she said.

"No, Mark happens to be my gov'ment." He pulled out his wallet and handed her his driver's license. The woman looked it over and handed it back to him.

"Okay, Mark, I'm convinced." She extended her hand. "Hi, my name is Stacy. Pleased to meet you." Mark accepted her extended hand with a soft handshake.

"I noticed that you have a strong accent. What are you, Brazilian?" He took a wild guess.

The woman smiled. "Yes, I am. Born and raised in Brazil, and I can tell dat you have accent as well. So, where you from, Mark?" Her soft pink lips were so seductive. Mark was her human puppet, ready to obey her every command. The feeling he had for her was something he never felt before and had no control over.

"I'm from New York. So what's a nice lookin' woman like you doin' in this spot solo? Why ain't nobody snatched you up yet?" There was so much he wanted to know about this woman with a lovely tan and was ready to interview her for hours.

"How you know I'm not here to see someone?" She asked, looking around, as if she was waiting on a male date to show up.

Mark paused for a moment and looked around, too. "Are you here to see someone?" He asked, looking for some jealous boyfriend to walk in at any moment. Mark's weight was up and he was pretty strong. If there was any drama, he knew he was strong enough to handle it and if not, he knew Dave and Tony would have his back.

Stacy laughed. "You're easy. I'm not here to see anyone. I jus' came out to get fresh air. My girlfriends are meeting me here for a few drinks, but now dat you're paying for all my drinks, I don't need dem. So what are you trying to do, get me drunk so you can take advantage of me?"

The thought never entered his mind, but it sounded like a good idea. Mark paused with a busted look on his face. "No, I just want to get to know you," he said, but his words weren't convincing at all. She was good and must have heard every line in the book.

"Yeah right, your expression be giving you away and wha' are you, a baller are some'ting? Paying for all my drinks. I hope you can afford it, because I drink like fish." She took a sip from her glass. Mark froze again. She then broke out laughing. "You so easy."

"No, not at all. I'ma honest, hard-workin' man. You just got me all twisted."

She looked him up and down with a look that said she didn't believe him. "So, Mark Wilson. Wha' do you do?"

"Well, for your information, I worked as a manager for a security company that didn't pay well, so I moved out here for a better job and now I work doing property management. You looking for a place to stay, let me know, I got'cha," Mark bragged.

"You have any business cards?" Her eyes were hypnotic. They felt like they were the only two in the room. The crowd around him was invisible.

"Not yet. I ordered a stack to come in the mail," he lied.

Stacy held up one finger in the air to check her cell phone. "It looks like my girls can't make it tonight. I'm all by myself." She pouted with the pure expression of a little girl.

"Not while I'm here." He patted his massive chest. "I'll protect you and keep you company."

She laughed, with a look of adornment. Each time Mark made her laugh, she would pat his arms and chest. Mark wasn't slow.

He knew she was getting in a few feels of his hard muscles by the way she held her hand there for so long.

While sitting at the bar, talking and getting to know each other better, Mark was really starting to feel Stacy for more than her good looks. He completely forgot about Dave and Tony. He even forgot about Rolisha. They danced to a few songs and continued to laugh and have a good time at the far end of the club. Tony and Dave enjoyed their drinks and got a few numbers. After getting Stacy to soften up to him, Mark was able to get her into the men's bathroom located in the lower level of the club that was more private. He didn't know how he convinced her to be with him, but he did and he wasn't going to let this opportunity pass him by. Dave and Tony watched as Stacy pulled him by the hand. Mark didn't know where the private bathroom was, but Stacy did and she was down with it.

"Yo, Tone, look at this fool lettin' that bitch drag him downstairs. I bet you five dollars that bitch is gon' rob his dumb ass," Dave said, slurring his words.

"I think that fools gon' get lucky." Tony chuckled.

"I doubt that shit. I'm gon' give him two minutes. That's all he needs to bust a nut. If he don't come up, we're goin' in after him," Dave said, checking his watch.

"Fine with me, but you better hope you're wrong," Tony grumbled.

CHAPTER 56

Picture Perfect

The weather was perfect and the landscape was filled with palm trees as far as the eye could see. It was an oasis, to say the least. The clear ocean looked drinkable and the cool breeze felt good on his skin. The sun was bright and hot. It would make the best place for a good tan. Tuck could get used to this, living the rest of his life in the Dominican Republic. This was the true definition of calm. He wasn't used to seeing trees like this in the hood. Leafy oak trees that littered the ground in the fall was no longer appealing to the naked eye. There was no snow here and the winter months felt like spring. Winter coats were nonexistent here. Even though it felt like a vacation, it was far from it. This was a business trip and he had to stay focused. The beauty of the landscape made it hard to do. It was easy to get lost in the shear allurement of it. If caught slipping in any way could cost him everything, even the precious air that he breathed.

Ever since they got off the plane, Tuck saw the sudden change in Chaos' demeanor. He was very sociable upon leaving the Philadelphia airport. The one thing Tuck was able to gather from Chaos was the greed he had for money. This was the reason for him getting caught so many times by the cops, because of his recklessness and now he was short with his words. It was like Tuck was sitting next to a total stranger. Chaos had his game face on and Tuck saw the fear in his eyes. Even thought Jose Fernandez was his uncle, Chaos knew he would lay him down like a stray dog, with no hesitation, if provoked. Blood meant nothing to him. It was thinner than water. From what Chaos was telling Tuck, he could tell his uncle's greed for money was above everything else.

They finally pulled up to what looked like a military fort. It seemed as though they were on a deserted island. There was nothing else around them, just dirt and plant life, but the guards at the gate were no soldiers. They looked more like villagers with assault rifles. They wore tank tops, shorts with pockets on the side and sandals. The walls were thick enough to stop a semi-tractor trailer and at least forty to fifty feet high. A steal gate that looked as though it was designed for a state prison facility was the only way in. The high-powered assault weapons in their hands meant they were protecting something of great importance and that something was Chaos' uncle, Jose Fernandez.

CHAPTER 57

Hard Evidence

Mark got Stacy in the bathroom, which was located in the lower level of Adelphia's, ready to give it up. Mark's game must have been strong or maybe it was the drinks that got her horny. Either way, she was down with it and he didn't want to waste time thinking about it. Mark was hoping no one would bust in and ruin the mood. He knew he had to make it quick.

"I always wanted to do this. I hope you don't look at me differently for this." She dropped to her knees while unzipping his pants. She then started sucking the shit out his dick. This was a fantasy come true. Even though it wasn't Jessica Alba, a look alike was just as good. Mark's eyes rolled upward, feeling like he was ready to bust right between her beautiful pink lips that were swollen around his stiff rod. This was it and he wasn't holding back. Suddenly, she stopped just when he felt himself ready to pop like an excessively inflated balloon. She stood to her feet, turned around and lifted her skirt to reveal a perfectly round tan ass, as she bent over the sink, looking at his reflection in the mirror.

"No, not at all," Mark lied. After this, he would lose all respect for her, even though she was very attractive. After introducing him to this side of her caused him to look at her one way—an easy lay—no matter what she did in the past or future.

"Here, I want you to fuck me in the ass like a dirty little whore," she whispered, even though in Mark's mind she was already one, giving him free access to her private parts, but for some odd reason her freakiness was turning him on. He had his mind set that he would definitely call her after this and keep hitting it until he got tired of it. He would surely brag to Tony and Dave about this experience. Shit, he'd even let them hit it for general purposes. The shit ain't fun if the homies can't get none. Mark let Stacy grab his rock hard shaft and direct it into her asshole. The shit was soft and tight. Her saliva kept his dick wet enough for easy entry. The excitement caused Mark to try to ram his pole all up in that ass. Her sweet smell of roses was alluring. Mark looked down at her beautiful ass sticking out, taking all his thick, hard rod like a champ. Her sexy facial expressions in the bathroom mirror turned him on even more. Her soft moans massaged his eardrums.

"Oh...Mark...fuck me, Daddy. Yes, that big dick feels so good," she sung in a tone that only heightened his arousal.

Mark knew he couldn't turn a hoe into a housewife, but he was ready to take the risk. The way she took his dick had him falling in love and fantasizing about leaving Rolisha and getting with Stacy. *What could really go wrong?* He thought. *She's sexy as hell with a badass body and a pretty face. She is the perfect arm piece. Maybe she just needs proper guidance, a man that can treat her right.* He felt himself ready to explode all up in her ass with no protection. Her physical appearance was so attractive to him that he wanted to feel all of her. She looked safe and this was a risk he was willing to take like he did with Rolisha. No condoms were becoming habit forming. He was now in a lustful trance, feeling his inside ready to bust. Stacy's moans had now turned to screams, now heightening his fantasy and causing him to release all his hot juices inside her.

Just then, Dave and Tony bust into the bathroom with their eyes wide and mouths open. Mark didn't care who walked in, he already got his nut off and it being Tony and Dave was a bonus for him. Besides, them seeing this was a major plus. He was sure to rack up some cool points on this one. They could watch for all he cared. He was feeling himself explode all up in her as everything around him was spinning. The excitement was so intense Mark's legs weakened, causing him to drop to the floor. This was the biggest orgasm he had ever experienced in his entire life. He was now in love and ready to take it to the next level. Oh yeah, he was definitely leaving Rolisha for this sexy ass, Jessica Alba look-alike. Shit, he was even willing to share her with them at first, but after that nut, he wanted her all for himself, like a kid with a happy meal. So now, all he had to do was gather his composure after dropping to the floor. Damn, how nasty is that shit? Fuck washing his clothes; he was trashing it when he got home. Mark was so delirious he wasn't sure if the wet spots on the floor were water or piss, but it didn't matter, Stacy was well worth it.

Dave and Tony were speechless. They just stood at the door like statues. Maybe they couldn't believe Mark had hit that or maybe they couldn't get over how sexy her body was. Yeah, Mark was feeling real good about himself right about now, but little did he know, Dave's and Tony's sudden entry startled Stacy so badly, she stood up straight from natural reflexes of a frightened person. Her sudden reaction made her turn toward them and all they saw was Stacy's long….hard…*dick!* Dave and Tony were too stunned to move, let alone speak.

CHAPTER 58
Bat and Balls

"Yo, what's that, a dick?" Dave yelled, pointing, as Stacy quickly tried to push her skirt down, but it was caught on her hard pole. When she tried to turn away from their gaze, Mark looked up and saw it. He was too fucked up to believe it at first, but it was in plain sight, hard and shiny. Her dick was bigger than his. Dave and Tony cleared a path as Stacy ran out the bathroom. Mark jumped up with fire in his eyes, going after her while adjusting his pants. Dave and Tony grabbed him, trying to hold him back. They kept their backs against the wall for leverage.

"Fuck off me!" Mark yelled, as they struggled to stop him. He was too big and strong for them to hold back. He was like a running back fighting to make it toward the end zone.

"Yo Mark, the shit ain't worth it, dawg," Tony yelled. Trying to talk him down from his rage.

"Yeah, it's too late now. The damage is done. Don't attract added attention. You don't want that shit," Dave hollered through struggled breaths.

"Fuck that, that bitch played me," Mark roared.

"Yeah, we know that and second of all, that ain't no bitch," Dave cracked, still fighting to hold him back. Mark was strong and it took all of their strength to hold him back.

"Hey, Mark, chill. All those muhfuckas out there don't know that you just fucked a man in the men's bathroom, but if you go out there raising commotion, you'd bring added attention to your already crushed ego. Do you want to broadcast that shit to the whole club or keep it amongst us?" Tony said, still struggling.

His words were making sense and Mark gave up his struggle, or maybe he didn't have any strength left after that big orgasm and was too fatigued. He was now taking deep breaths.

"Let's go back upstairs and have a few drinks," Tony said, patting Mark on his back. Mark was now leaning against the wall, overly exhausted. They were all breathing hard.

"Naw, fuck all that. Take me home now," Mark ordered. The shame was overwhelming.

"Okay, if you say so. Tony take us back to my ride so I can take him home," Dave said, looking at his boy with concern. Mark was now in a daze and looking suicidal.

CHAPTER 59

Protective Shield

The ride home was long and silent. No one had anything to say until Mark decided to break that silence.

"Yo, man, I didn't even know that bitch was a dude, honest dawg," Mark tried to explain.

"Yeah...right, we believe you, fam," Dave said sarcastically, looking at Tony who was seated next to him behind the steering wheel. Mark sat in the back seat, looking at them trying to hold in their laughter. This entertaining experience was something to cherish. They kept eyeing each other with their heads still facing forward, but Mark saw Tony through the rearview mirror.

"Y'all think this shit's a joke, don't y'all?" He snapped, now getting pissed off at them.

"Naw, we don't think this shit's a joke...but for real though, dawg, that shit is funny as hell, bruh," Dave said, as Tony burst out laughing. Tony didn't say anything, he just kept laughing as Dave did all the talking. They tried, but was unable to hold back.

"Yo, dawg, I ain't gay, man. I'm straighter than Indian hair, nigga," Mark said, trying to save face.

"Mark, you just fucked a pretty boy. How you gon' say you ain't gay?" Dave inquired. Even though he was making a joke about it, there was truth in his words.

"Because, I wasn't fully aware of the shit, that's why. It ain't like I voluntarily decided to fuck a man, like I came to that club for that reason. Tony took us to that shit. I didn't know that Adelphia was a fuckin' gay club." Mark was now speaking proper.

Tony quickly glanced at him through the rearview mirror. "Yo, Mark, don't even try to point the finger at me. You know Adelphia is not a gay club. So stop with the bullshit. I wouldn't even play y'all out like that. You were caught fuckin' that bitch...I mean, dude. How come you didn't see that when his skirt was all up or felt it when you reached for the pussy? That's what I do when I fuck a bitch from behind to make sure I don't get played like you just did," Tony threw back.

"I was caught up in the moment," Mark admitted, with his head hung low.

"Yo Mark, just go home and sleep it off. By tomorrow you'll feel a little better," Dave said.

"Why, so y'all can make me the butt of y'all's jokes?" Mark argued.

"Come on, Mark, we wouldn't make you the butt of our jokes. Besides, isn't that what got you in trouble in the first place?" Dave cracked.

Tony burst out in laughter.

"Y'all makin' it harder than what it is," Mark said in his defense.

"We're makin' what harder, your dick?" Dave cracked. "Oh shit, Tony, now he wants to fuck us, too."

Now Tony couldn't control his laughter and started losing control of the wheel. With the added alcohol would surely send them to jail if the cops were to pull them over.

"Fuck you, Dave," Mark threw out.

"Naw, that's okay, I can't compete with that pretty muhfucka," Dave continued.

Mark stopped talking all together, seeing that Dave was on the roll. Tony was enjoying the shit and knew he had to put a stop to it before it got out of control.

"Okay, okay, stop it already. You killing me, Dave," Tony said, trying to catch his breath. Mark huffed trying to hold back his anger. "Mark...you know Dave just bustin' your balls," he said to break the tension in the air, but Dave kept going as they pulled up next to his car in the parking lot of the Purple Parrot. The bar was still open and it looked crowded.

"No the fuck I ain't trying to bust your balls. Boy George already beat me to the punch," Dave yelled, as Tony laughed even harder.

Mark couldn't take it anymore and jumped at Dave. Dave quickly jumped out the car and took off running with Mark giving chase. Tony cut his vehicle off and got out to save Dave. Now they were running around a parked car and Mark was on the opposite end trying to catch him.

"Yo, Mark chill, you know how he likes to make jokes about everything. That's still ya manz," Tony said.

"Fuck 'em, I'm gonna bust his ass," Mark said, with rage in his tone.

"Oh shit, he's addicted to man ass," Dave cracked some more, as Mark continued to chase him around the car. Tony had tears in his eyes. "Come on, Mark. You know I'm just fuckin' wit'cha," Dave said, trying to catch his breath.

"Yeah, save the shit," Mark hollered.

Just then, a patrol unit pulled up with the spotlight on them.

Tony walked over to the unit with his hands up. "It's okay, officer. They're just horsing around," he said, as the white, balding officer got out of his unit.

"Well, tell them to knock it off before I put them in a cell for the weekend to cool their heels," the officer threatened. He looked as though he should have retired years ago with a round belly used for storing donuts or he was just allergic to working out.

"They just had too much to drink. I got this," Tony explained, patting his own chest as if he was in charge.

"Well, I better not catch them driving," the officer said, looking at Dave and Mark now hugging and walking into the bar. The officer adjusted his belt before getting back into his unit and driving off.

Tony went into the bar to join them.

CHAPTER 60
Multiple Footsteps

It was the weekend and Chance decided he was going to take the Young Hitters out for air. He felt as though it was time for them to grow up and become men. This was when they would learn how to approach women and exercise their manhood. The night was young so he decided to head out to Philadelphia and hit South Street. He needed to unwind a little, because soon he'd be avenging Willy's death and needed to devise a plan that would cover his tracks. The Young Hitters would be utilized on this mission.

South Street looked more like a small Las Vegas strip without the people walking around with open beer bottles. The Las Vegas strip was a long street that allowed the people to walk up and down with any alcoholic beverage of their choosing. They had to stay on the main strip. Venturing off that strip and traveling to a neighboring street would cost them a hefty fine for carrying an open bottle of alcohol.

South Street was a little different and didn't allow any type of alcohol, opened or closed, to be carried on the strip. South Street, just like the Las Vegas strip, had two officers on every corner and a few walking up and down the street. Some corners would have as many as six officers on one block, but there were no casinos on South Street. The ladies were out looking for attention in their sexy outfits. Traffic was backed up and moving at a snail's pace.

"Yo, I'm feelin' this spot," Syphee said, cheesing from ear to ear.

"Yeah, but we ain't movin'. Muhfuckas walkin' right past us. Man, I rather walk," Dundy voiced with excitement.

"Y'all go 'head. I'll whip it around one more time and try to find a parkin' spot," Chance said, as the Young Hitters hopped out the ride. They were looking like kids at Great Adventure Park for the very first time. Chance knew that look all too well, the same look he saw on Willy's and Tuck's faces when they first stepped foot on South Street years ago. The cops' presence were more of an acceptance than deterrence. This was the first time they felt safe enough to keep their weapons in the vehicle. The officers never bothered anyone, but now and then, they would flex their authority, nothing major.

Chance felt his adrenaline flowing from all the stares he received by the females walking past. He was looking sharp in his all-white Nissan Marano with the convertible top down. Chance was getting very impatient and needed to find a parking spot that was close to the strip. Finding a parking spot in the overly populated city was more of an adventure. Fetty Wap was pumping softly through his speakers. He knew to keep it low. The first time Chance came to Philadelphia with Willy and Tuck, he got a hundred-dollar noise pollution ticket for pumping his speakers loud in a residential neighborhood. Right above the stores and shops on South Street were multiple apartments. There was a fire department on one corner with firemen seated outside on lawn chairs, socializing with the officers with lustful eyes. Being a young fireman on South Street was the perfect job, if you were single.

CHAPTER 61
The Questionable Hook

Chance was at the red light on Seventh and South Street when two women crossed in front of him. They were looking real good. One of the females caught his eye. She was very beautiful in her pink T-shirt, blue jeans and matching pink Nike track sneakers. It was Cancer Awareness Week and she looked good in those colors. Nothing special or too fancy. They were out there shopping for clothes and men. Everything about her sent chills through his spine. He looked upon her as if his jaw muscle froze up. It was like a struggle for him to say something before she made it to the curb.

"Excuse me, can I ask you a question?" He finally got the courage to let out. The woman looked at him while still walking. Her hazel eyes caught his gaze.

"Yes," she said in a soft-spoken voice.

"Can I flirt wit'chu?" He asked, as they stepped on the curb.

"Yes?" The girl responded with a lovely smile. That was the first time she heard a line like that.

Got her! Chance thought.

When it came to women, all he needed was a smile, which let him know it's a strong possibility she's interested in him, but Chance was a pretty boy with a thug mentality. Hooking up with females came easy, but this one was different. She did something to him that no other woman could. Maybe her alluring hazel eyes seemed to pull his heart out of his chest. No woman has ever been able to do such a thing. Or maybe it was her strong African features. The girl had a sex appeal different from anyone else he laid eyes on. She had high cheekbones and full lips that looked like they could suck the paint off a Ford Mustang. Thick nose that seemed to fit her face perfectly. She looked foreign. All the different women he slept with were all starting to look alike and that was starting to become very boring, but this woman was noticeably different. She had the look of an African Queen. Her skin was dark and looked flawless. It was looking nice and oily. Her body was breathtaking, a definite head turner. Her waist was very small and her ass was perfectly round like a half moon. She must have had a serious workout regimen to have a physique like that. He saw under her clothes that it was toned with an ironing board stomach. Her breast were somewhat small, but he was able to work with that for they stood up independently and her nipples were the size of jumble shrimp.

Chance had to get with this girl no matter what. He refused to let her get swallowed up by the tidal wave of people walking the strip. Without any hesitation, he jumped out of his vehicle while still waiting at the red light. The car's driver door was left open and the keys were still in the ignition with the motor running.

"You left your car running?" The girl said, wide-eyed and with a strong accent.

Chance waved it off. "It'd be a'ight."

"But it's cops everywhere. You're going to get a ticket." She had a shocked expression.

"Then let 'em do what they gotta do." Chance never looked back.

"Are you crazy? Somebody's going to steal it!" She uttered, still surprised by his actions.

"Listen…that car comes a dime a dozen. I got full coverage on it and can surely buy another one exactly like it, but you, ma, are a rare breed and I'd never forgive myself if I let'chu walk in and out of my life without lettin' your presence be noticed. So they can fine me and even tow it for all I care." His words flowed effortlessly as if he rehearsed that line a thousand times until it rolled off his tongue like second nature.

Suddenly, a small group of guys jumped in his vehicle, as two officers approached with pen and pad in hand.

"Someone's stealing your car and the cops aren't doing anything about it!" The chocolate princess yelled.

"I don't care 'bout that car. Like I said, they come a dime a dozen," he repeated, never looking back, as his vehicle headed down a back road.

"Then how are you going to get home?" She said, with worry in her eyes.

"I can call for my peoples or just catch a cab, but I'm not concerned wit' all that right now. You gotta give me your number now so I can holla at'cha. I think sacrificin' my whip is well worth it and I ain't leavin' until you do." He gave her his puppy-eyed look.

CHAPTER 62
Behavioral Disorder

Just from its beauty, it was hard to believe that Santa Domingo was more than just a tourist attraction. From what Chaos was telling Tuck, there was a lot of money being made in this poor county. Chaos filled Tuck in on everything he and Willy discussed prior to this arrangement that was made. When Tuck entered the fort, he couldn't help but stare at the number of wandering eyes patrolling the perimeter, heavily armed. He was not their main focus. Their eyes kept scanning the area as if they were waiting for something bad to happen. This only made Tuck very uncomfortable with making a business deal with this man. It seemed too risky. The entire view of it looked like a scene from *Scarface* when Tony Montana was in Cuba and Tuck wasn't looking forward to any helicopter rides either. A small man with gray signs of aging on his sideburns walked toward them with armed goons flanked at both sides. There was no doubt it was Chaos' uncle.

He approached Tuck and Chaos with such calm. It was like he was looking right through them. He gave Chaos a hug and then stopped right in front of Tuck to look him up and down. His eyes bloodshot red. If his posture weren't so laid-back, Tuck would have assumed they were burning with rage, but he knew that look all too well. The man was high and Tuck didn't want to blow it. He was mixing business with pleasure and getting high on your own supply was one rule you shouldn't break. This could work in Tuck's favor, if he played his cards right. The man wasn't focused and this would lead to him making irrational decisions. Tuck was only hoping he lived through this to tell Chance the whole story.

"So, you're the man they call Tuck. Chaos told me a lot about you." Jose extended his hand, while still eyeing Tuck at close range. He was well spoken as if he had a good education or he was raised in the United States. His accent was barely noticeable.

"Yes, pleased to meet you, Mr. Fernandez." Tuck shook his hand with a straight face. There was no need to show respect with an added smile. That would be a clear sign of weakness, a form of intimidation. Tuck displayed none of these traits.

"Mr. Fernandez." He chuckled, shaking his head. "We are all friends here." He raised his arms as if he was announcing it to everyone there, but his armed guards continued to parade the perimeter as if they didn't hear him. "You can call me Jose."

Tuck responded with a simple nod. Jose Fernandez physical stature posed no threat. He was a thin framed, short Dominican that lacked the muscle mass for manual labor. His malnutrition body was one of a person that skipped quite a few meals. He was so powerful that he didn't need to work out in the gym or take any self-defense classes. He appeared to be well protected.

"I hear you want to deal with me in the distribution business," Jose said.

"Yeah, the game ain't the same and my crew is starvin'," Tuck explained to him in so many words.

"Right. Chaos filled me in before y'all got here," Jose stated, as Chaos stood silently as if he had no voice. It was crazy how he had so much fear and respect for a man that was his own blood relative. Suddenly, Jose's face harden. "This right here is a family business...la familia." He jabbed his finger downwards with veins popping out his head and neck. All thirty-two teeth were fully exposed. His eyes were wide as if he were psychotic. "Not all is welcomed." Tuck saw the man was clearly unstable. This was why Chaos feared him. A result of him getting high off his own product. He was no different from Pitch. His judgement was impaired and he was unpredictable. This made him very dangerous, being a man with so much power. His psychotic look softened and returned to his calm facial expression. "But I could make an exception to the rules. You are a very powerful man in your city. This would come very productive to my business, but first I have to know if I could trust you." He leaned in closer, eyes fixed on Tuck as if he was trying to read his every thought. "Can I trust you, Tuck?"

Tuck gave him a cold stare. "You can look me in my eyes and see that I'ma real nigga and real niggas ain't afraid to die."

Jose was staring back intently, looking for Tuck to falter, but Tuck kept his poise. "I'm not familiar with that term, but it sounds convincing. I see that you had Chaos set up shop with the car business and once everything is in motion and running smoothly then I'd hook you up with my product and throw in a few keys for some extra cheese. Do we have a deal?" He extended his hand.

CHAPTER 63
Collective Shoulder Rubs

Chance was still on South Street working his magic on the chocolate princess that had him speechless. The girl looked at her friend for advice after Chance came on to her strong and they both shared a silly laugh with a few whispers. Chance just stood there smiling. She never tried to brush him away nor did she mention that she had someone. He had her and knew it. It was all a matter of time before she gave up the number. She finally pulled out her cell phone and exchanged numbers with him.

"So what is your name?" Chance inquired.

"Oni."

"I like that name. It sounds very exotic. Where you from?" Chance was so into her that he totally ignored the annoying shoulder rubs from the crowd of people passing by.

"I'm from Africa, but I attend Rowan University in New Jersey."

Chance's eyes lit up. "I'm from Jersey, too."

"Where at in Jersey?" She inquired with a wider smile.

"Camden." Chance's voice was laced with shame.

"Oh, I heard Camden is a very bad place to live."

Chance was getting very aroused by her lovely accent. It was smooth and she was very soft spoken. It was almost like a whisper.

"I never had any problems," He lied to make light of it.

"So what is your name?" She asked, after giving him the correct spelling of her name.

"Raymond, but everyone knows me as Chance."

"I like Raymond better." She added a lovely smile.

"Only you can call me that and no one else." Chance looked at her friend in a playful warning. Her friend rolled her eyes with a hand on the hip, but she couldn't hold her laughter and broke down. He could tell that her friend was feeling him, too, but his eyes were on Oni. Chance started to feel his heart slowly melting while standing there. It was something more about Oni that kept him captivated. He didn't want to leave. He wanted to learn so much about her. She was that new, exciting bedtime story, which had his full attention. Then he started thinking if the cops found the stash of guns hidden in his secret glove compartment with their fingerprints all over them, it would surely give them an extended vacation at the jailhouse. That's when he noticed his car heading in his direction. All three hitters were inside with Pemont behind the steering wheel. He was the only one out of the three who was able to get a valid driver's license. That was a good thing. At least he knew his car was safe. After Chance said his peace, he waited as Oni and her girlfriend walked off. When they were far enough away, Chance took off toward the vehicle as fast as he could without being notice. The crowd played a good part of his cover.

"Fuck you crazy lil' niggas doin?" He barked.

"We seen you puttin' yo thing down wit' that chocolate mommy. So we jumped in before those cops wrote you that ticket," Pemont explained.

"Fuck out my seat before you get my shit impounded," Tuck teased, taking his position behind the steering wheel.

Syphee was in the back seat with Dundy and Pemont was up front in the passenger's seat. Even though Pemont had his driver's license, he was still a minor at seventeen years of age. At that age, he was only allowed to travel at certain hours of the day and tonight he was past the curfew. Once Pemont was in the passenger's seat, Chance pulled off at the nearest street. He was satisfied after he got what he wanted and headed back across the bridge. The other three sat in the ride bragging on how many phone numbers they got and which girl they were going to call first. They were going through the photos of all the females they hooked up with as if they were trading cards. Chance's entire focus was on that chocolate goddess.

CHAPTER 64
So Good So Far

Tony met up with Kim at Villaggio in Cherry Hill. It came with a comfortable, old world atmosphere. She was sitting at the table looking good as usual in her orange maxi dress and six-inch stilettos. Tony was late and she thought he wouldn't show. He was looking sharp in a custom-made Armani suit. It had a dark, rich, golden color. They talked a little and Kim was curious of what Tony was out there doing with himself.

"So, Tony, what's really going on with you? You drive the fancy cars and wear the most expensive designer suits." Kim sipped her wine. The soft candlelight danced along her beautiful features. Her face was well crafted and her body perfectly sculpted. A goddess, to say the least.

"I'm just a hard working man." Tony took a long sip of wine. He was afraid Kim would come at him with more questions about his lifestyle. They have been dating for a while now and trying to keep their relationship a secret at work. They knew, eventually, they would have to let the cat out the bag, but they were willing to stretch it as far as they could.

"Look, Tony, this is me you're talking to here, not some random chick off the street. I've been watching your moves for a while now and your lifestyle doesn't fit your career. I know what you said about your father taking care of you, but something about this whole ordeal doesn't add up. If we are to continue with this relationship, that's our little dark secret from the coworkers, you need to come clean with me."

Tony knew this threat all so well. Even though Kim seemed passive in her demeanor, her actions would be all the aggression she needed to get her point across. Tony broke down and told her of his father, Frank Debartello, and how he always looked out for him. Even though he told her this lie already, he made sure to stick with the story. He could tell that Kim wasn't accepting it and knew he was lying, but she would have to prove it.

Kim, on the other hand, was different. Tony was trying hard, for a long time, to get with her and now that he had her attention, he didn't want to mess that up. After dinner, Tony walked her to her car. They said a few words and Tony handed her an envelope. Kim opened it up in front of him. It was two tickets for a seven-day cruise for her and her mother to Jamaica. Kim put in some vacation days to spend with her mother in Florida. Nothing special, but this was something they always wanted to do together. Tony was paying attention to her every word. Her mother seeing how Tony took the time for them to have a mother and daughter trip to Jamaica might cause her to accept him with open arms. Unbeknownst to her, Tony needed that time to take care of business while she was gone.

Kim thanked him with a big hug and kiss before running into the house to call her mother about the good news. Tony smiled, thinking about how much of a gentleman he was to her. The key to this game was patience. The way that everything was looking, it wouldn't take him long to get up between those thighs again.

CHAPTER 65
Slowly Tearing Apart

Pitch was on the move. His captains just got the update on the workers from the lieutenants. He was now at the warehouse with the rest of the captains for the information.

"Fuck you mean everyone's complainin'?" Pitch roared with the look of a mad dog. He was now parading around the room in circles. His eyes were blood red and his nose flared. His hair was wild and his dark grey Tom Ford suit looked as if he had slept in it. The tie was missing and the first six buttons were popped open as if he had a hard day's work.

"It ain't no work on the streets and you doublin' up on the payback when niggas borrow some ends. Only person benefittin' from this is you." It was big Balloon talking. A four-hundred-pound, six-foot-five goon. He was once a bouncer at The Whip in Lawnside. An after party spot that started filling up with partygoers after three in the morning. The place would shut down at six in the morning, as the sun rose. The pay wasn't worth the shit he got into every night. So he started hustling to take care of his heavy eating habits.

Pitch stepped in his face. "Who the fuck said this shit? You!" It was more of a challenge than a question.

Balloon was standing big like he did at the doorway of the club at night, but when Pitch approached him in an aggressive manner, his whole body deflated like a car tire, making him look a hundred pounds lighter and two inches shorter.

"Uh-ah...Pitch, I'm just the messenger," he stuttered in a timid voice. He sounded like Berry White at first and now he was sounding like Michael Jackson.

"Don't back pedal now, bitch ass nigga." Pitch gave him a long hard gaze. Balloon was silent and the fear in his eyes showed it. "Tryna talk like you runnin' shit 'round here, you gravy eatin' muthafucka. You's a easy target. You need to work on that weight, 'cause you ain't runnin' from nobody." Pitch turned and continued to parade around the room. It was obvious that Balloon's feelings were hurt by the way Pitch belittled him in front of everyone. The rest of the crew knew to keep the complaints to themselves.

"I know what the fuck goes on in these streets. I know I fell back for a minute. Somebody off'ed my lil' sistah and I still ain't got no feedback. For all I know, that muhfucka's still out there breathin'. Fuck's goin' on 'round here? What, my captains gettin' soft on me and shit? When I send y'all out to do work, I expect it to get done. I'm gon' push more product on the streets, 'cause I can see it's all 'bout the money and fuck loyalty. And all you bitch ass niggas better be out there grindin' or I'ma start taxin' the shit out y'all faggot ass muthafuckas, hard. Since I can't get what I want, then I'ma be over y'alls heads like a fuckin' drill sergeant. Now get the fuck out my face." Pitch was pissed and now taking it out on his team.

He ended the meeting and everyone quietly walked out to their vehicles. Since Pitch took over, he'd been talking to his goons recklessly. He showed them no respect and didn't care about the money. All he was concerned about was who killed his little sister, Fatima. No one knew anything and the streets were silent. Whoever did this, knew her well. Fatima had a very small circle. Pitch was refusing to let up until he found out who killed her. He was starting to get desperate and ready to point the finger at somebody…anybody.

CHAPTER 66
Aiming to Please

Chance was pissed off about the way Pitch was talking to his captains. Pitch showed no respect and talked down to everyone. Tuck was next to lead if anything were to happen to him. All Tuck had to do was give the word and any one of his goons would gladly put Pitch out of his misery. Chance was getting wound up and needed to calm his nerves. Oni then popped in his head. That sexy African goddess he met on South Street. He touched the computer screen on his dash and pushed "dial" once he found her name. The sound of a phone ringing came through the car speakers.

"Hello," said a soft-spoken female voice through the speakers.

"Hello, may I please speak with Oni?" Chance was trying to sound as polite as possible.

"This is she."

"Hey, how you doin'? This is Chance." He perked up.

"Chance…oh, *Raymond*, how are you doing?"

"Not so good. I can't stop thinkin' 'bout you. When you gon' let me see those pretty hazel eyes again?"

Oni tittered a little. "I'm not doing anything tonight. You can come see me, if you have a ride. Did you ever get your car back?"

"Nah, the cops are still on the lookout for it. Right now, I'm usin' my boy's ride, as needed to get around." Chance lied. This was all part of the hunt to get to the pussy.

"I am so sorry that you got your car stolen because of me." She was gullible and Chance was eating it up.

"It doesn't matter. You were worth it. I rather lose a thousand cars just to be with you."

Oni giggled like an innocent child. Chance had her and now he was ready to go in for the kill.

"Since you can't come to me, then I'll come to you instead." Just where he wanted her. Willing and able to make it that much easier for him.

"That would be great, because I have to drop his ride off now." Chance was now thinking of a way of hiding his vehicle.

"It's not a problem for me. Just give me your address and I'll be there by seven o'clock."

"That sounds great. We can chill at my crib. I'm goin' to let you see my cookin' skills." Chance didn't have any cooking skills, but his game was strong and whatever it took to get into that love box he was down with it. He got a kick out of playing with women's minds. This would cause them to do anything he would ask for. Even transport drugs for him.

"And what are you making?"

"You don't worry 'bout that. Just let me hook somethin' up. I'm sure you gon' love it." All Chance needed was for her to let him work his magic.

"Okay, I'll see you then."

CHAPTER 67
Taking the Blame

Afro talking to Chance about Willy's death, Melody was feeling good that she still had him to turn to. Willy was his homie, his best friend. If anyone was going to take care of the person that caused his death, Chance was that dude. Chance was a killer by nature and squeezing off a few rounds was something he did effortlessly. Giving Chance this information only puts him on a new path of his next destination. Willy wasn't into drugs and the thought of him using was none existent. Willy didn't even sell the shit, after what he had seen it do to his mother. Willy only saw it as street poison, the white powdered demon. It wouldn't make sense for someone that never used drugs to suddenly go on a crack binge and smoke himself to death. Something like that wasn't common in her world. Tony still owed Willy the money for killing that Marchantville cop, Rodeski. Is that really the reason why he killed Willy? That was the only thing that made sense to her. Tony had no other motive for doing such a thing and niggas in the hood were killed for less.

Melody began to blame herself, because if she hadn't called Tony to talk to Willy, then none of this would have ever happened. Willy never did like that redneck cop for harassing him and taking away his freedom. Willy had it in his mind that he was going to have to take that cop out one day. Hiring the hitman to help made the deed that much easier. His whole thought process was built on revenge for that cop. Willy would have been able to sleep at night knowing he was able to cover his tracks. All he needed was to get paid so Tony could hook him up with the house in Marchantville. The home would have been a steal once he used that money to purchase it. Even if Tony didn't pay Willy the money for the job, he was still in a win-win situation, because Willy already had the money to purchase the house in Merchantville when Tony made the purchased price lower than the asking price. Tony was handsome and very professional. For him to be a killer came as a surprise. Melody wasn't convinced Tony could have been the alleged killer, but there was some type of connection to Willy's murder. Tony was hiding something.

The difference between Tony and Chance: Tony knew how to cover his tracks, but Chance didn't. Chance would kill someone and walk away. If questioned, he knew nothing and refused to tell, but for how long? How long could he pull that off? If he did go after Tony, would that link everything to her? She started to get butterflies and grabbed her cell phone to call Chance. Chance never answered and it kept going to his voice mail. She then tried Tuck, but it ended up doing the same. She thought of Detective Morris, reached in her purse, and pulled out his business card. Melody remembered him giving her his business card when they found Willy in the abandoned building. She called his office to see if they had any new information. Detective Morris told her he had to drop the case, because of the lack of evidence. There was nothing for him to go on.

Melody disconnected the phone call and held the phone to her chest as she wept. She refused to believe the news story about Willy. She remembered after that night Tony never called or stopped by. That act only proved his guilt. There was something fishy about that. She wanted answers, but was too afraid to call. She had to come up with a master plan to get at him if Chance didn't come through. She then scrolled through her cell phone and came across Tony Satario, real estate agent.

CHAPTER 68
Taken By Surprise

Tony didn't know what to expect, coming to Melody's apartment. She was crying over the phone and needed to talk to him. She didn't sound suspicious at all. So there was no need to be alarmed. Willy was responsible for the death of his brother, Frankie. Larry the hitman did an excellent job making it look like a drug overdose and accidental fire, which killed Willy Mays in that abandoned building. Tony had to be calm and smart. There was no need in trying to duck her. That would only cause her to point the finger at him. What Tony didn't know was that the hitman was paid by him and Cat Daddy to take Willy out. Killing two birds with one stone was the term he said to Willy at the time of his death.

When Melody opened the door, he saw pain and anger in her red eyes. She was wrapped in a robe, wearing bedroom slippers. Tony realized she was taking Willy's death hard.

"Hey, Mel, how are you doing?" Tony asked in his polite voice. This way he saw what angle she was coming from. Tony was on guard, trying to feel her out.

"Not so good. Willy was found dead in some crack house that caught on fire. I can't believe he was getting high all this time." She cried.

Tony felt good that she didn't think he had something to do with it, but according to the detectives, she had all rights to believe so. He didn't do a good job at covering his tracks. If they discovered that Willy's death was a homicide then all evidence would lead to Tony since he was the last man seen with him. Then he thought about how Chance came at him about Willy's death while looking at houses. He shook it off. Tony was getting ahead of himself. No need to start acting paranoid. They had nothing on him.

"May I come in?" He asked. There was no need in having the neighbors hear this conversation. Melody stepped to the side and allowed him in.

"The last time I seen him was with you that night. Did he say anything to you?" She asked.

Make it sound good, ran through his head before responding to the question. "No…not really. I paid him what he asked for and left. He did seem a little overly excited." Tony lied. She was taking the bait. So far so good.

"So where did you take him? I seen him drive off with you?" She asked, as they both took a seat.

"He wanted me to drop him off at Camden High. I didn't ask any questions. I paid him and he took off on foot. It did seem strange, but I didn't know that it was that serious." Tony was putting on an award-winning performance.

Melody pulled her hair back in frustration. That caused her robe to fall open, exposing her curvy physique. If it was a distraction to throw him off his game, it worked. Now he was more focused on trying not to get a woody in front of her while giving her the right answers. Her sexy lingerie was very revealing. It looked more like a decorated two-piece bathing suit. There was no need in using his imagination, because all her flesh was exposed. Her skin was silky smooth with a buttermilk chocolate caramel complexion.

Seeing this suddenly brought his manhood to life. Tony sat forward to try to hide the lump growing in the front of his pants. If she was to ask him any question now, there was no telling what he might say. Kim no longer existed in his thoughts. Thank God, she was away with her mother on that vacation trip he hooked up.

Suddenly, Melody fell in his arms, weeping. Tony slowly leaned back, trying to comfort her, but his dick was still rising as it filled with blood. He wanted to push her off, but that would be wrong and there's no telling how she would react to that. All he could do was hope his dick went down before she saw it.

Melody placed her hand on his stomach, crying. Her soft hand rubbing his stomach felt good. Tony's dick was now hard as a rock from her soft touch. He was hoping and praying she didn't open her eyes. Without notice, her hand slid down and grasped his rock hard penis. Tony was busted and too dumbfounded to talk his way out. It was like all the blood from his brain was now between his legs. This is what millions of men go through before dealing with the consequences because of their actions.

Melody turned her head and gave him the look of shock. Tony sat there, looking stupid. What could he say? It was quite evident he was physically attracted to her. Melody motioned toward him. Tony thought she was ready to strike. He closed his eyes, preparing for the blow, but then he felt something warm and soft on his lips. He opened his eyes and Melody was kissing him. This was something totally unexpected. She reached her hand down his pants and was now stroking his dick. Tony didn't know how to react to her aggression. She was all over him like a mad woman. Tony just sat there and let her take over. Melody was now on her knees, hungrily sucking on his dick. Tony couldn't believe how horny she was. Willy was gone and maybe she needed this. Tony laid her on the floor and removed her panties. Her pussy was pink and swollen. He totally forgot about Kim and didn't even care. He climbed on top and inserted himself inside her. Tony was now fucking Melody like he was dying to do so and excited that it was finally happening. Tony badly wanted her when he first came to the house, but she had a man and he didn't want to disrespect him. Now she was single and no one had any claims over her. The pussy was available for the taking and that's what he did. He took it. It felt so good that he came hard. It wasn't about pleasing her. He fucked her for his on pleasure.

"Thank you." Melody smiled, looking up at him. She was so beautiful and her smile was infectious. Tony smiled back before getting up to adjust his clothes. Then the sounds of Carlton's cries broke the spell. He was in his bed upstairs.

"It sounds like someone needs you." Tony pointed upward.

"Yes, I'll get him. Just lock the door behind you," she said, heading upstairs.

Tony locked the door and got into his whip. He sat back and sighed after experiencing such a great orgasm. That only meant she was satisfied with the answers he gave her before giving herself to him.

CHAPTER 69
Creating An Illusion

After Chance disconnected the phone conversation with Oni, it was time to put his pimping skills to work. He called Pemont who had a driver's license.

"Yo, Chance, what up my nig?"

"Hey, Pemont, I need you to get down here and stash my whip 'til I call for you to return it later." Chance was working his magic.

"Got'cha, on my way, my dude." Pemont already knew the drill.

Before disconnecting the call, Chance gave him instructions to go to Maggiano's Little Italy restaurant in Cherry Hill and order take out. He told him what to order. This was nothing new. Pemont was aware of the routine. After he passed everything on to him, they disconnected the call.

Chance was checking the time on his watch as time passed. Pemont was running late and Oni would be there shortly. He tried calling Pemont's cell phone, but received no answer. Pemont was fucking up and Chance didn't have a Plan B. He paced around his apartment, stressing until he heard someone at the front door knocking softly. He knew that knock and ran to the door.

"Fuck took you so long, lil' nigga?" He yelled. It was Pemont with two big brown paper bags in each hand.

"The place was packed with a long waitin' list," he explained with a pitiful look.

Chance handed him his car keys and large bills rolled up. "Here, take this and bounce. I'll holla later, and don't wreck my shit."

Pemont rushed out the door while Chance prepared the food on pans and shoved it in the hot oven. He lit a few candles and had plates neatly decorated on the table. The soft sound of R. Kelly played on his stereo system. He checked his hair and clothes in the mirror to make sure everything was right. This was his way of easy passage to the pussy. He would first fuck with their minds and go out his way. When the woman would see how much time he put into making this day so special, the sex would end up being of them pleasing him.

There was an unfamiliar knock at the door. Chance cautiously approached, hoping it was Oni instead of an unwanted guest.

"Who is it?" He asked in a calm voice.

"It's Oni."

Chance opened the door with a big smile. It was contagious as she stood there smiling back. Her style of dress was different from the women he was used to being around. She was classy, which was sexy in her own way. Her choice of clothing had Macy's written all over it. She had a short hair cut on the sides and lengthy up top. Chance opened the door wider to allow her access to the place.

"Thank you very much for inviting me to your humble abode." She was now standing in the living room as her eyes wondered.

"I'm so glad you can make it and just in time. The food is ready to be served and you can take a seat at the kitchen table."

She sat at the table, impressed at how much effort he put into their dinner date. Chance saw the excitement in her eyes as they widened with curiosity at the hot pan of food he brought out the oven as if he prepared it himself.

"It smells so good. What is it?" Her excited expression displayed the hunger in her eyes.

"It's Italian," Chance said, as he prepared the plates. Chance continued to talk proper with a more business like exterior. His goal was to impress and make her want him before the night was over.

"Is this cheese ravioli?" Her tone was at a high pitch when she watched him put it on her plate. She was excited all right. Chance knew he had her now.

"Yes, it is."

"Cheese ravioli is my favorite. You made all this yourself?" She said, never taking her eyes off the spread that was laid out in front of her.

"Yes I did and now I'm ready to eat."

A smile grew across her lips, as she took a bit. "This taste just like the cheese ravioli from Maggiano's Little Italy Restaurant in Cherry Hill. How did you come to making something so delicious?" She knew their food all too well. It was time for him to make it sound good.

"I took up a few classes at a culinary art school in Philly." He lied. This was his way of making her believe he was making a difference by doing something with his life, but really, he was digging a deeper hole for himself.

"Oh yeah, what was the name of the school?"

Maybe he should have thought this through first.

"TLF Culinary Arts. It's an online course located somewheres in Philly. Majority of my cookin' was done at home while taking the course." He continued to lie.

"I never heard of them." She looked away in deep thought.

"Yeah, they're new," he uttered, hoping she wouldn't investigated it.

"What were you doing before you started taking cooking classes?"

"I used to work for this warehouse in Pennsauken, but the boss was racist and kept makin' racist remarks about my whole swag, so I ended up suing his ass. The case was settled. I'm just waiting on the money. Part of the agreement was to not discuss my case with anyone," he lied, but this would be his excuse for all the drug money he had saved up.

Then her smiley face was now one of great concern. "So, Raymond, did you ever do any illegal activities while growing up in this environment?" She must have noticed how bad the neighborhood was when she drove up.

"Yes, I used to sale drugs on the streets, but now I don't do that shit anymore. I want to do something with my life." Of course, that was a lie, of which he was becoming very good at doing.

"Good, I'm glad that you're trying to make something of yourself, but if I find out that you are still involved in any illegal activity, I don't want anything to do with you at all." Chance saw the seriousness in her eyes. Her strong beliefs and up bringing were something she took of great importance.

"So tell me more 'bout you because my life is borin." He quickly changed the topic, because it was killing the mood.

Oni stared up at the ceiling, smiling. "Well, there's not much to talk about. I was born in South Africa and my parents moved to the U.S. when I was six years of age. I haven't been back since. There's not much to tell about South Africa. I was so young and my memory of it is hazy. I'm still in school, working on becoming a doctor."

"That's good. Then you can take care of me when I'm sick." They shared a good laugh. After finishing their meal and dessert, a good two hours was spent socializing on the sofa. The conversation was so interesting that they weren't even aware of how time flew by.

CHAPTER 70
Overly Aggressive

Oni was really feeling Chance a lot and liked what he was saying. Chance was on point, selecting the right words to say. Before Oni knew it, her tight shirt was unbuttoned and Chance was on top of her, kissing her aggressively. She wasn't sure if she voluntarily allowed him to unbutton her shirt or if he physically took it there. Chance was good with his hands and was able to remove her clothing without her noticing it. Oni was now hot and willing to let him do whatever he wanted. This is what Chance wanted to do from the first time he laid eyes on her. The attention he showed and how he only had eyes for her was enough for her to give herself to him. It was as if his hands had a mind of their own, as their eyes locked on each other. You would think he had the power of hypnosis by the way she kept her gaze on him. His rock-hard penis slowly push its way inside her. He kept the head of his dick at the entrance of her walls, letting her juices lubricate his shaft for easier entry. This is how he liked it. Any other form of lubrication was unacceptable. He only wanted her natural liquids to moisturize the flesh of his manhood. They continued passionately kissing, as he felt himself going deeper inside her. The deeper it went the more he began to pump his pole in and out. He then got his entire dick down, balls deep inside her. With each stroke, there was a slight stutter in each one of her breaths. Her face tensed up from the sharp pains she received as his manhood felt as though it was ripping her delicate walls apart. Chance then arched his back and began to take longer strokes. Her juices were building and his solid love muscle was now going in and out with ease. She panted in his ear. He could feel each one of her climaxes as her walls clamped up and juices had his dick wet and slippery. The moisture excited him as he started to thrust his rock hard dick in her like a pile driver. Oni's moans where now turning to screams, which drowned out the loud clapping sound of flesh as Chance continued to thrust his pole with vengeance. That moment of pleasure was now a moment of agony. The pain was unbearable. Oni tried pushing Chance off her, but he was too strong and heavy. He then locked his arms around her waist and continued his on-slaughter. It was as if her struggling moment for freedom was arousing him even more. He had his lips on her neck and was now sucking on it like a gold fish on glass.

Oni kept screaming and couldn't take anymore. She started to beg him to stop, but he ignored her. Chance was humping on her like a madman. This was more than she had anticipated. How did she let this go this far? He no longer cared for her needs. It was all about him and he wasn't going to stop until he busted a nut. All Oni could do at this point was to wait until he finished.

Just then, all his aggressive action came to an abrupt halt. It was like someone walked up behind him and shot him in the back of his head, because his entire body went limp. Oni had dead weight on her and was unable to move him.

CHAPTER 71
Hollow Minds Tony

The heat was on and started to cause third-degree burns. Tony's attorney, Charles Hunt, was working overtime on this case. Gary Holland had a paper trail three years long. It looked to be an uphill battle for Tony and the only way out was to buy his way out or remove this problem from the face of this earth.

Then Chance popped into his head. Tony wanted to know what type of information this thug had on him. Did he know about Willy's murder or was he messing with his head? Someone had to have told him something, but whom? Maybe it was Melody or those detectives: Stewart and Morris. Now Tony was starting to see Chance as an added problem on his many lists of problems. The loud ring of the car speakers startled him. Charles Hunt name appeared on the dash screen.

"Talk to me," Tony said after pushing the "answer" button on his cell.

"Tony, you'll have to settle out of court before this Gary Holland guy pushes this thing all the way to Superior Court. I see no other option here." His voice came through the speaker.

"Fuck that and fuck him. I ain't givin' him shit." Tony pouted like a small child.

"Listen here, this ain't a game he's playing here. We have to shut him up before the state jumps in and do a little investigation of their own," Hunt Explained.

"Shit, it already made the newspaper, so it won't be long before they come knocking at my front door." Tony was filled with emotion. The Sudden visit from Detectives Morris and Stewart told him that they were already on the case. Tony explained to Hunt how they were at his workplace, threatening to put him behind bars.

"Well, it ain't happen yet, so you may have a chance to put a lid on this. I know you got the money, so let's pay this creep to keep his mouth shut so you can get back to doing whatever it is you do."

"How much is he asking for?"

"One-point-two-mill."

"He wants what? He must be smokin'." His refusal to submit was strong.

"Look, this ain't the time for pride and ego to blind your judgement. Your arrogance is causing you to refuse to take responsibility and if this goes all the way to the Superior Court, the judge can end up granting him more than what he asked for. According to his documents, you had some goons for hire beat up on him on many occasions. He even has a stack of hospital records totaling sixty-thousand dollars in bills. He even has proof that his injuries cost him his job due to his inability to work at Aluminum Shapes, which required heavy lifting. Majority of the job is manual labor. Tony, this guy is claiming to be disabled from what your goons did to him. This was the only job he was able to maintain with a criminal record. He would have to take a pay cut at a new job, if any jobs are willing to hire a known felon. From what I see here, the judge is not only going to make you pay those bills, but he'll also reward him for his pain and suffering that you caused. You took bullying to a whole new level."

CHAPTER 72

Pleasing Himself

"Raymond, are you okay?" Oni asked in a timid voice.
"Mmmm…yeah." He breathed after having such an orgasm.
"You're crushing me."

"Oh, I'm sorry." Chance quickly jumped up. He was now back to the sensitive person she met earlier. There was a big purple passion mark on her neck.

When Chance got up, Oni started to get dressed. Chance had already gotten what he wanted, but there was something about her; he didn't want her to walk out that door. If it was another female he would have kicked her out, dressed or not. Chance had no respect for women. It was somewhat of a deep down hatred he had toward his mother that even he didn't know of. His mother was mean and neglected to show the love toward him like a normal parent would. He reminded her of his father and she hated him for that. Her blood flowed through his veins, but she would fail to realize that. All his mother would see was a man who abused her mentally and physically only to leave her to raise Chance on her own. She planted a seed of hatred that grew into a man that only saw women as pieces of meat to concur and destroy. That was all he saw in them, but this one was different. She was unlike anyone he had ever met before and he couldn't let this one go.

"Oni, what are you doin'?" Chance gently held her hand. She brought out the gentle side of his character.

"I'm going home. I thought that you were different. I thought you were nice," she said snatching her hand away.

"But what did I do wrong?" He was now pulling the dumb card.

"You took advantage of me and I don't want to see you anymore. You were very aggressive and made me feel cheap." Tears rolled down her eyes.

'Oni." Chance was looking deep into her eyes with remorse. "What I did was very inexcusable. I wanted you so bad that I lost control of myself. Would you please forgive me?"

Oni wiped away her tears and stared intently into his eyes. He never flinched. There was signs of innocence. A lost boy who needed the right guidance so someone could point him into the right direction, but she held her tongue in protest.

"I meant every word I said that night I met you on South Street. If you leave me, it would surely break my heart. Just give me another opportunity to know me. I'm really not a bad guy." His words were touching, but it wasn't enough to make her stay.

"Your actions are bad and that alone is enough for me to go." She was now dressed and putting on her shoes.

"That is why I need you more now than ever. Teach me and show me how, but don't just walk out of my life this way." The words flowed naturally and it had meaning. This time it came from the heart. If Chance was going to make a change, this was the time and moment to do so. He put the charm on her, because her hard frown had now softened up.

"You don't take it from me. We both share ourselves and enjoy the pleasure together. You're a man and not a wild animal."

Chance listened as she displayed the ways of affection. She was the teacher and he was the student. She could have walked away and not have anything to do with him ever again, but there was something unexplainable that drew her to him. Something that took hold and wouldn't let go. It was how he badly wanted her. So bad that he sacrificed his nice vehicle. No man she knew of would do such a thing. This meant a lot to her. She saw more than potential in him. She saw promise.

Oni took the lead and escorted him to the shower. She didn't know his home so she listened as he told her which way to take him while still giving her full control of the moment. They both removed their clothes and got into the shower. She started by bathing him from head to toe. "The key to it is to be very gentle as if you're pampering a baby."

Chance listened, only responding with a head nod. When she was done, he continued where she left off and did the same. They stepped out of the shower and took turns drying each other off. Chance got excited like a little kid in the candy store and palmed her round, plump ass as she bent over to dry his feet. Oni looked up with a smile.

"I see you liked that, you bad boy you."

At that moment, his manhood had sprung to life from a deep slumber.

"You are a bad boy!" She teased, wide eyes focused on his hard muscle.

Chance only remained silent, soaking in everything she had to teach. No one ever took the time out to show him how to treat a woman, and that's what Oni was doing and now he was all ears, eager to learn. She then took him down the hallway looking into each room until she found the master bedroom.

She spun around, pulling him to the bed. Chance saw in her eyes that she was enjoying this as much as he was, but for Chance it was more of a treasure hunt and the pot of gold was between her thighs. Immaturely, Chance climbed on top of her ready to stick his dick in her. She held him at bay, preventing it from happening.

"No…your feeble mind is always after the first sight of crumbs. If you're patient enough and take your time you would be able to enjoy the full meal that's right beneath your nose."

Chance understood what she was telling him. Oni was very wise in her youthful age, which came from good parenting. Something Chance never had the opportunity to experience. This added knowledge she possessed, along with her beauty, was a rarity where Chance came from, which was what attracted him to her the day they met. She was more than a new toy to him.

Oni pointed to her love box. "I want to feel your lips down there," she said, with a seductive look on her face. Now he understood what she meant by saying that he'd be able to enjoy the meal that's right beneath his nose. Chance ate pussy before and didn't like it. Since then, he only fucked the chicks he got with, but at that moment, her pussy was looking very edible. It was small and swollen like big lips. The pubic hairs around it was well groomed with a perfectly trimmed outline. She treasured her pussy and put time and effort into beautifying it and that was a good thing.

Without hesitation, and like bobbing for apples, Chance dove between her thighs. Oni stopped him again and told him to take his time with it, that it's not going anywhere. Chance did as she said and gently kissed down her thigh. Oni's breath stuttered when he got down to her love box. He then kissed it gently all over, never coming up to ask questions for he already knew that she was enjoying it by her moans and body movement. He started licking on it as if it was butter pecan ice cream. His tongue came across the entrance of her sweet pussy and he slid his tongue deep inside it. Oni let out a soft, "*yes.*" His long tongue felt like a warm, wet dick. Oni loved it and she wasn't going to let him up until she hit her climax. It's been a long time since she had some. That's why her pussy was so tight.

Oni was getting so excited that she started speaking in her native tongue and then grabbed the back of his head and jolted it forward. Chance was unable to breathe as she held his head there for a few seconds. Oni had climaxed and her body went limp.

Now it was his turn to feel her nice big African lips on his hard muscle. He stood over her, shaking his dick in his hand. Oni looked up at him and shook her head.

"I don't do that to someone I just met," she said waving a finger.

"But you just let me do you."

"That's because you chose to do so and I let you. Me, I don't do that, not now. You will see me in a negative way. I must first get to know you and then maybe…and I said maybe I'll let you get a chance to see how my lips feel on it."

Chance laughed, seeing how she played him the way he played her, but really, they both got what they wanted.

"You right…you right. You got that for now and yes, I did deserve that after what I did to you earlier. I promise to be a better man from now on." As sexy as he was, she was still not giving into his demands. She was a strong willed individual.

"I'll accept your apology, but I'm still not sucking your thing." She pointed at it with a cute smile.

"I know…it's okay though. I can wait, because I will have you begging to taste this soon enough."

"In your dreams." She waved him off. Then guilt flooded her face. "I can't believe I gave myself to you on the first night. You must think I'm easy."

Chance slid his body close to her and held her in his arms. "If I thought that about you, I wouldn't be fighting to keep you here with me."

Her eyes filled with shame. "I don't want you looking down at me as some piece of meat that you can easily throw away when you're done with me."

"What? Not in this lifetime. From what just happened, I knows yous a keeper," he shouted. They both shared a good laugh as they played in the bed and before the night ended, Chance had gotten his wish. Oni gave herself to him again. Even though he couldn't get her to suck on his love muscle, it was still a well-deserved victory on his part.

CHAPTER 73

Paper Lettuce

The next day, Tony decided to start making moves early. One-point-two million was a lot of money for Tony to gather up. It would have been easier for him to have that clown waked, which means to be killed by the mafia in a hit, but it would be too risky. If those detectives weren't investigating him already, he would have taken care of Gary Holland a long time ago. Adding murder to his scheme would surely put his name on the top of the charts. He didn't want the media to make a spectacle of his name, not after his father worked so hard to keep him away from all this negativity. Getting his name blown out of proportion would be like a smack in his father's face, knowing he had the resources and the means to take care of it. Tony jumped in his whip and headed for the TD Bank on Black Horse Pike in Bellmawr, New Jersey. The bank had a few customers waiting to check their accounts. A young, attractive looking Hispanic girl approached him.

"Hi, my name is Linda and your name is?" she said, with an extended hand.

"Tony," he responded in his professional work tone before greeting her with a gentle handshake.

"Thank you for coming to TD Bank. How may I help you?" They both took a seat at her desk.

"I need to make a withdrawal from my account." He handed her his driver's license for proof.

"And how much do you wish to withdraw from your account?" she asked, typing his name into the computer.

"I need a cashier's check for one-point-two million dollars."

The bank officer's eyes darted toward his and locked on. Tony saw the excitement that replaced her professionalism. She was ready to drop drawers hearing those numbers. Tony's head was too worked up for him to notice the woman's beauty. Her professional style made her look like a mannequin, but seeing the amount of money in his account made her want him to the point that she forgot where she was. Tony paid her no mind. She must have caught on and readjusted her sudden laid-back posture.

"Hold on a minute. I have to get my manager. One-point-two million is a lot of money, Mr. Satario." She giggled.

"Do what you gotta do," he replied, now annoyed by her flirtatious jesters. He was pissed that Charles Hunt wasn't trying to work some lower figures, but Gary Holland was refusing to bend. He was stuck on one-point-two million.

The manager hurried over and greeted Tony with a firm handshake. "Hi, I'm George Freeman, the bank manager here." He explained everything to Tony about withdrawing a certain amount of money from the bank and that's why he has to be called on. After what seemed like an hour process, Tony finally got the cashier's check and left.

Suddenly, his cell phone rang. Kim's name appeared on the screen.

"Hey Kim, what's up?"

"Don't 'Hey, Kim' me. What is this with your name on the front page of the newspaper?" Her voice was stern. She must have been checking her news app on her cell phone, but that article happened days ago and she's just getting it.

"It's nothing, all lies. Don't worry about it. I'll take care of it." Tony tried calming her down. She was supposed to be enjoying her vacation trip with her mother.

"Well you better. You know how I feel about getting involved in illegal activities that would cost me my freedom." Anger laced her tone.

"I know. That's why I'm all over it now. Don't worry about it. I'll straighten out this whole mess before you get back to work on Monday," Tony said before the line disconnected.

CHAPTER 74

Polishing a Bargain

Tony drove across the Ben Franklin Bridge and was now entering the city of Philadelphia. He attempted several times to reach Kim by phone. She refused to answer any of his calls after reading the rental property scam that reached the front page of the newspaper article. He was meeting up with Polo the Don to discuss business. The plan was to sell all his properties and make his problem disappear. He owned over one hundred properties and if the price was right, he could walk away with close to six million dollars. Taking out the one-point-two-million put a hurting on his account, but he made sure to drop off the cashier's check to Charles Hunt. When it came to good lawyers, Charles Hunt was the best there was in getting the job done right. Whatever it took, legal or illegal; it didn't matter as long as his clients came out victorious. It was all about winning one case at a time. Suddenly, his cell phone rung through the car speakers. Tony pushed the green "answer" button on the touch screen.

"Talk to me Charles," he said, seeing Charles Hunt name pop up on the screen.

"Hey, Tony, good news. Gary Holland took the money."

"Did he say anything or give you a hard way to go?"

"No, not at all. He signed the agreement and nearly broke his neck leaving. I told him cases like this takes years before reaching a settlement and it may not fall in your favor. After the lawyer gets his fees and IRS gets their tax cut, you may not have enough to buy a decent home. I guess after that speech he didn't feel like waiting."

"Good. Now with that out the way, I can focus on more important matters."

"No problem. If there's anything else you need, feel free to give me a call."

"Will do," Tony said, disconnecting the call. Everything was starting smoothly. All he had to do now was get Polo the Don to pay him six million for his properties so he could start his new business. Tony accepted set back, but never tolerated failure.

Tony got to the meeting spot with a black leather briefcase in hand. It was a big office building on Twelfth and Walnut Streets. Richardson LLC was a front for his operation. Nothing more than smoke and mirrors. The business wasn't real. This is where he held his meetings and a few more other spots in different parts of Philadelphia and New Jersey. Tucan was at the door, mean mugging Tony.

"What up, Tone? What you doin' here?" He spoke with revelation.

"I'm here to see Polo. Where he at?" Tony said, with earnestness.

"Hold on." Tucan spoke to someone using a radio. Then he walked Tony to an elevator. The elevator opened with two thugs inside. Their cocky attitudes let Tony know that they were packing heat. One of the thugs stepped out and pat-searched him before taking him up. They never checked the briefcase for any concealed weapons. Maybe they felt as though Tony wasn't a threat or Polo the Don didn't want his crew to know what was inside. Tucan rode up the elevator with both thugs on each side of Tony. Nothing was said as they took the elevator to the top floor. The building was twelve stories high with all empty offices on each floor. Once the elevator reached the top floor, Tucan escorted Tony to Polo the Don's office. The other two thugs stood by the elevator.

"Tony!" Polo the Don yelled with excitement. "What a pleasure to see you here. It's been a long time. So what brings you here?"

"I'm looking to sell my property business and I know that you're the right man to come to." Tony skipped the formalities and went straight to the chase.

"And what are you asking for?" Polo the Don inquired with anticipation.

"Ten million." Tony started high to work his way down.

"And why would I be interested in buying your business in Jersey when majority of my business is in Philly?"

"Well, last year I grossed close to three million and once you decide to grow the business you could make a killing." Tony inflating the price was his way of making a quick sale.

"And all you ask for is ten million? Is it because of that guy pressing charges on your illegal scam?" It seemed as though Polo the Don was keeping up with the current news.

"That's been taken care of." Tony tried brushing it off.

CHAPTER 75

Lost Wages

"So tell me how this business work." Polo the Don was taking the bait. Now it was time for the pitch. Tony explained how he would buy the homes and sell it to others who couldn't be approved for a mortgage, mainly those that used blood money and couldn't account for it. He would rent it out until its paid for. Once they came up with enough money to pay the remaining balance, they would own the property outright. High interest rates and added inflated fees were the main key to his lucrative cash flow.

"So why would I be interested in buying your business when I can buy my own business and do the same thing?" Polo the Don stated.

Tony was hoping he wouldn't go that route.

"You have a valid point there, Polo, but check this out. I can get you all my properties at a discounted price and they're all occupied. So the cash flow is there already."

Polo the Don thought about it for a moment. He was a smart businessman who wanted nothing to do with any illegal business that was drawing so much attention, but the cash flow was too tempting to turn down.

"You know what? I can get those properties off your hands, because I see that you need my help and I like you, Tony." His sinister smile revealed the characteristics of a king cobra.

Tony saw the lies before it departed from his lips. Polo the Don is about money and his greed would one day cost him.

"If you say so." Tony replied with sarcasm. He knew that Polo the Don was going somewheres with it and it wouldn't be in Tony's best interest.

"Okay, I'd give you two million for everything." He was starting low, a little too low.

Tony's face dropped. "Two million. I can get more than that at whole sale."

"But it would take you to long and I know you need someone to get it off your hands fast. That's why you came to me." Polo the Don was right and a hard person to get over on.

"You're right. I'm at least honest about that." Tony was now feeling himself back pedaling.

"So what's wrong with the two million?"

"I'm not a fiend so two mill is out of the picture. I'm willing to sell it to you for eight million." Tony was trying to stay within the six million dollar range.

"Okay, I can see the desperation in your eyes." Polo the Don chuckled.

Tony sighed, trying to keep his composure. Eight million was a major plus and more than he bargained for, until Polo the Don threw out…

"Four mill."

Tony bit down hard as his jaw muscles pushed out the side of his face.

"Seven million." It was more of an auction than a business deal.

"Four mill," Polo the Don repeated.

"Come on, Polo. You're killing me here. I'd give it to you for six million." Now Tony was at his ideal price range. All he needed was for Polo the Don to break.

"Four million and that's my final offer."

Tony saw that Polo the Don wasn't willing to bend.

"I can't afford to go that low. What about five million." Now Tony was in the negative and Polo the Don could hear the desperation in his voice. Just like a snake, Polo the Don had his fangs in Tony's flesh the minute he walked in the door and now he was pumping his venom into his blood stream.

"Then it's a pleasure doing business with you. I hope you can find someone else that's interested in your business." Polo the Don stood from his chair with an extended hand. He was hard to break and Tony didn't see this one coming. He was losing Polo the Don and knew he couldn't find anyone else that would buy an illegal business from him.

Tony dropped his head in shame. Polo the Don's venom was taking affect and not accepting his offer would kill him. His offer was more of an anti-venom and his means of getting his life and Kim back.

"All right, you win, four million then." He pouted. If it wasn't for Kim ignoring his calls, there was no way he would have accepted that deal.

Polo the Don's face lit up. "Tony, my man. You just made my day." They shook hands in agreement.

"You're a hard man to do deal with," Tony complained. The loss was a minor setback. Tony knew it wouldn't take long for him to get back on his feet again.

"You draw a hard bargain, but any time you want to do business again, feel free to look me up. I'll have my peoples get with your peoples. Until then." Polo the Don snapped his fingers and Tucan approached Tony with a duffle bag. He dropped the bag at his feet. "This is my down payment for now. Five hundred thousand."

Tony unzipped the bag and started looking through the money.

"Don't worry, Tony, it's all there." It was like he already knew Tony was selling his business. Who else, besides Floyd Mayweather, walked around with that much money at his leisure?

Tony looked up at Polo the Don with a smirk before popping open his briefcase. He showed him a copy of all the titles to his properties that was in a brown envelope. "Don't worry, Polo, they're all there." He slid it over to him. Polo the Don was to receive the original copies once all the paperwork was completed.

"I'll have my men escort you to your vehicle, so you can make it home safe. It's not healthy to walk around these streets with that amount of cash." Polo the Don smiled as Tucan, along with two more thugs, escorted him out the building.

CHAPTER 76
The Letter

The bright light of the sun burned his eyeballs as he turned his head. Chance stretched out his arm, smearing his hand across the bed, but it was cold and empty. His head popped up and Oni was gone. There was a note on the nightstand. That only meant she left and it was probably a while ago. How did she sneak out without him even knowing? He read the note.

Sorry I had to leave and I didn't want to wake you. You were sleeping so peacefully. Last night was very enjoyable. I can't stop smiling. I hope that your feelings haven't changed toward me. Call me whenever and if not, I'll understand.

Yours truly,
Oni

Chance bald up the letter and tossed it in the wastebasket by the bed. He was going to let her sweat a little. Chasing women was something he didn't do. He headed to the bathroom to freshen up. The hot shower felt good. It gave him a moment to analyze last night. Even the following day he couldn't stop thinking about her. After a good shower, he checked his cell phone and Pitch had left a text message that read TIME FOR PRACTICE in capital letters, which meant for him and the other captains to meet up at the warehouse. Chance grabbed his wallet and car keys and headed for the front door. That's when he noticed he didn't have his ride out front. He quickly called Pemont to come get him. Pemont got there with Syphee and Dundy in less than five minutes.

Chance headed for the door again, but stopped in his tracks. He turned around and ran back upstairs to his bedroom. He grabbed the balled up letter that Oni wrote out the wastebasket and did his best to straighten it. He took one of his shoeboxes out the closet, dumped his white Jordan's on the floor, and placed the wrinkled letter inside and put the lid on top. For some odd unexplainable reason, that wrinkled piece of paper was more valuable than his three-hundred-dollar, custom-made sneakers. He stuffed the box in the top corner of his closet. He didn't know why he did what he did with that letter, but deep down he knew that letter would come in handy in time of need.

CHAPTER 77
The Verbal Beat Down

Majority of the meeting consisted of Pitch complaining about no one finding Fatima's killer. Little was said about the diminishing financial problems. Even though he put product on the streets, it still wasn't enough to go around. Pitch did this on purpose to keep the hunt on. This was Pitch's way of starving everyone out. When a nigga was hungry enough he'd eat anything. Well the same rules applied to this shit, but it was getting worse than he expected. His goons were getting so desperate for money they started framing jokers to admit to killing Fatima. Pitch had to hit them hard for their actions. This desperate act only brought more heat to his front doorstep. He would get captains to send his goons to stump the shit out them for trying to play him out by framing someone to take the wrap. Then he would charge them a hefty fine for their stupidity. This would deter them from making the same mistake twice.

As for Chance, he became numb to the screams that came with each beat down. Maybe it was because he knew they would survive the beating or maybe it was because of the numerous killings on the streets that came from his own hand.

Chance pulled out his cell phone and scrolled down the list of names. He stopped at Oni. A smile grew on his face before dialing the number.

"Hello." A sot female voice answered.

"Hey, Oni, how you doin', ma?" Chance stepped outside to get away from the blood-curdling screams.

"Hey, Raymond." Her tone perked up. "I thought you weren't going to call me."

"And why would you think that?"

"Because I gave myself to you without a challenge and I left without saying goodbye. I'm sorry for that, but I had morning classes and you looked so peaceful resting."

"Well, if you're lookin' for my forgiveness you gone have to let me take you on another date."

"I'm with that, but I want to pick the place."

"No prob. We can make that happen."

CHAPTER 78

Expensive Suit

A man in a very expensive suit entered the city jail and approached the officer seated at the front counter. "How may I help you?" The officer asked rather flatly. He was busy writing notes in his log, never looking up to acknowledge the man.

"Yes, I'm here to see Quadeer Ingram," the man said in a pleasant voice.

The officer looked up at him. He had the officer's attention now. "And, you are?"

"Joseph Borowicz, attorney-at-law." It was Larry 'the hitman' Payne posing as a lawyer. He handed the officer his ID card and information before entering the facility.

Once in the waiting room, Cat Daddy entered with chains and a hard look to go with it. He sat at the opposite end of the table and waited for the officer to leave before he spoke.

"Just the man I've been looking for," Cat Daddy said, adjusting his jumpsuit. He looked so uncomfortable wearing it.

"I haven't heard from you lately, but I do see how they're gathering up all this evidence that seems to be falling from the sky. From the looks of it, I can tell when you need my services. So why are you still here and what can I do for you?" Larry offered. His eagerness was quite evident.

"Someone out there is giving these pigs all this shit. I'm not sure how, but I know that there's a snitch amongst us." Cat Daddy bit down hard as his jaw muscles tensed up.

"Oh, how I hate snitches," Larry expressed, pumping his fist.

"I need you to find out who it is and take care of the cop, Detective Steward. He's in charge of this whole investigation and whoever the snitch is, is giving him more shit to plant on me. This fuckin' cop has a hard-on for me. Take care of him before he fucks me."

"We don't want that to happen." Larry chuckled. He was excited and couldn't wait to murder somebody.

"How much to make all this disappear?" inquired Cat Daddy.

"This right here would be the most expensive favor that I have ever done for you. You're asking me to take care of a cop. Cops are more expensive than regular people. Taking out those ghetto thugs was easy. They ended up being gang-related. That's why it came so cheap. No one gives a fuck about them, but this right here will take time. I have to find out who's turning tapes and how to clear your name to get you out of here."

"But can you do it?" Cat Daddy's voice reeked with desperation.

"Can I do it? Cat, Cat, Cat, they don't call me the hitman for nothing." His grin was tainted with evil.

Cat Daddy dropped his head and laughed in silence. "You's a funny guy." He looked around and leaned forward. "I heard about that mob boss who went out with a bang. Word on the streets say that his crib was secure like Fort Knox. Only one person was capable of pulling that off and that's you. I don't know if it's true or not, but didn't you work for him?"

"Cat, Cat, Cat, I am not the type to kiss and tell. You'll have to ask him that yourself and from what I hear, he took that little secret with him to his grave."

Cat Daddy dropped his head again in laughter.

"So I assume that you'll be doing the same thing as well?" Cat Daddy quizzed about him keeping their secret to the grave as well as he was doing with Frank Debartello.

"I see that you're a very smart man." He waved a finger. "I would like to assume that you'll bless me as well as you did from the last job." A sinister grin formed on his evil face.

"You already know."

CHAPTER 79
Reflected Image

Chance drove Oni to his mother's house when she sent him an urgent text message. He tried calling and she wouldn't answer. His mom was diabetic and had high blood pressure. She wasn't taking her meds like she was supposed to and there were times she would end up spending days in the hospital recouping from it. This was supposed to be Oni and Chance's date night, but he couldn't ignore his mother's call.

"Mom, where you at?" Chance called out upon entering the house with Oni.

"I'm in the bathroom, shittin," she yelled from upstairs.

"Just have a seat. She'll be down shortly. As you can see, she's off the hook. So don't pay her no mind. You care for anythin' to eat or drink?" Chance offered, as she gracefully sat down and crossed her thick legs. Even her sex appeal was unique, very sexy and smooth.

"No thank you. I'm okay," she said, so properly. She was different from any of the girls he'd dated in the past. Her mannerisms displayed her strong upbringing. The sound of the toilet flushing drew their attention toward the stairway. Then there was a loud squeaking sound, followed by running water. That was a good thing to know that she had good hygiene. Chance approached his mother as she came down the steps, giving her a big hug.

"Hey, Mom, is everything okay?" Chance asked, before releasing his embrace. He was a good son and that put a smile on Oni's face.

"Yeah, I'm fine. Give me some money," she blurted out with her hand extended, palm up.

"Damn, Mom. Couldn't you work it out much smoother than that? You didn't even give me a chance to walk in the door."

"I ain't stupid, you know. I'm just sick. I heard you come in while I was shittin'. So you been here long enough to eat a big bowl of Fruity Pebbles like you always do." Chance dropped his head in embarrassment. "I need me some money to pay this damn cable bill. They want so much money and you need to do something wit' all them girls calling—"

"Mom."

"Don't 'Mom' me. You's just like yo father, thinking he's God's gift to the world to do as he pleases." She continued to argue.

"Mom…I'm not like him. I would never do you dirty like that. He was a cheater."

"And a dog," she threw out there. "You may not hurt me, but those women are no different from your mother. If you…" Her words trailed off when she noticed Oni sitting in the living room. Oni stood when their eyes made contact. "You didn't tell me you had company," she mumbled, smacking him across the back of his head.

"You wouldn't give me a chance to."

She bumped him out the way to eye Oni up and down. Her whole demeanor had changed. The room was silent. She was now staring at Oni as if she was covered in green mold.

CHAPTER 80
Filling the Gap

Tony had his eye on owning a funeral home. The four million wasn't enough to start his new business. This would be the perfect front for all the illegal shit he had going on. To get the business started, he needed to make some extra moves to get the funds he needed. He found an old building in Voorhees. This would be the perfect spot to get started. The majority of the people living in Voorhees were loaded with cash. The building was an old farmhouse he had to remodel. It needed a lot of renovation and that meant he needed a lot of cash to do so.

This is good…this is real good, he thought.

He was finally ready to get the wheels turning. This new business venture would be racking in more money than the rental property. All he needed was an extra few million to get started. So instead, he used some of the money he had to purchase him a new home.

As for Kim, she needed some work. She still didn't trust Tony and needed some time to get her head straight. This didn't happen until after the big article of him running an illegal rental business. Tony worked too hard to get to this stage of their relationship. Selling it now and clearing his name was for the best to get her back. That only pushed him back and now he had to start all over to rebuild her trust. His uncle Bill never took him back as a realtor. Tony was more of a liability and Bill couldn't deal with all of his side businesses. It was bringing too much attention to The Home Reality Association. This was messing up his money. Home Reality was good for his rental business, but now that it's sold, he no longer needed to work for that company. He could now focus all his attention on his new business. Now it was time for him to venture out and do things his way.

As for Melody, Tony found himself spending more time with her at her place. This was more sexual than mental. Melody wasn't in Kim's league at all. Kim was a go-getter, a business woman that stayed focus on having bigger and better things in life. Melody just wanted a happy home to settle down in to raise a family. The main difference between the two was that Kim was willing-to-work-hard-for-it type of person and Melody was we-can-work-it-out type of person.

CHAPTER 81

The Tumbled Lie

"Mom, this in Oni, and Oni this is my mom," Chance introduced, trying to break the silence.

"Oni..." she repeated in deep thought as if she heard the name before.

"Pleased to meet you, ma'am." Oni extended her hand.

Chance's mother looked at her hand as if it was dirty and gave her a weak handshake.

"You're different. Where you from?" she asked Oni as if she was an alien from a different planet.

"I'm from Africa."

"Africa, yeah. I knew you were different. Where at in Africa?"

"Sudan. My parents moved to the United States when I was very young. If I were to visit my country, I would feel like a complete stranger."

"So let me guess. You plan to marry my boy so you can become a citizen?"

Chance shook his head in disbelief, leaving Oni on her own as she continued to press her with more questions.

"No, ma'am. My parents and I became US citizens when we arrived here long ago."

"Oh...okay." She lit up her cigarette. "You seem like a well-mannered young lady. What do yah do?" One eye was cracked as she released clouds of smoke.

"I attend Rowan University in Glassboro."

"So what's your major?" She frowned as if Oni knew what she was getting at.

"I'm studying to become a doctor."

204

"A doctor?" She looked at Chance. "I see you have a smart one here." She then turned her gaze back at Oni. "You seem like such a good girl. How did you end up with my boy?"

"Mom," Chance uttered, but Oni continued to answer her question as if she didn't hear him.

"We met on South Street. He ended up getting his car stolen that night." She blushed as if she was dying to tell more about how they met.

His mother quickly looked at him, cigarette dangling between her lips. "Car stolen? Raymond, you never told me that someone stole your car."

"I didn't want to worry you. It's nothing. My insurance took care of it," he lied. Insurance companies take weeks, even months to settle cases like these. Oni was aware of this, but she thought he was only saying this so she wouldn't worry about it.

"That was a very nice car. I hope they find the bastard who took it." She waved a fist in a fuss, forgetting to take a puff from the cigarette that was building ash.

"Don't worry about that, Mom. It's nothing. I could get another one," he said with such calmness.

"It's nothing." She looked him over before laying the cigarette in an ashtray. "What'cha high or something? You never act this way before. That car was your baby. I had to beg you to take me out in it. And, when did all this happen?"

"Two weekends ago on that Friday," Chance stated.

"Two weekends ago! But you took me to the doctor that Monday in it. That was fast, what they…"

"Mom…that was Tuck's truck, remember? We got the same ride." Chance was throwing hints at her, but she wasn't catching on.

"No…I thought he didn't like—"

"Mom…fall back. It's bad enough that someone got my shit. I don't need you rubbin' it in, okay?" Chance argued, trying to make his mother think he was still upset about it, but it was a weak attempt.

"Whatever, it's only a car. You'll get something that would put a smile on your face. I know how you are about your reputation on the street. What you call it, street credibility or whatever street slang y'all use now-a-days, but she looks like a good girl, Raymond." She jumped back on Oni, now realizing the stolen car story was a lie, but from the look on Oni's face, she caught on as well. "I don't want to hear you broke her heart like them other floozies that won't stop calling here."

"Come on, Mom, really?" Chance huffed.

"Boy, stop cryin'. It ain't like I'm lying." She frowned.

"No, you just sayin' a little too much."

"Well, give me some money then and I'll shut up. I need to pay this damn cable bill," she said, with her hand out again. Chance reached in his jean pocket, pulled out a drug knot, and slipped it in her hand without counting it. Her eyes widened as she quickly stuffed it in her bra.

"Damn, is that what it takes? Oni, you're more than welcome to stop by anytime you want. If you call in advance I'll make sure to bake you some of my delicious oatmeal cookies," she said, with excitement. That amount of cash gave her an instant adrenaline rush.

"I love oatmeal cookies. Then that's a deal." Oni chuckled as they embraced before leaving.

CHAPTER 82
Show of Force

Cat Daddy was escorted into a room where Detectives Stewart and Morris waited. He stood in the doorway, refusing to enter.

"Don't just stand there, come on in," Morris said, seated at the table beside Stewart.

Cat Daddy did as he was told with a hard attitude. His massive size was intimidating to anyone he stood near.

"Quadeer Ingram, aka Cat Daddy, can I ask you a simple question?" Stewart said after the guard left the room.

Cat Daddy responded with a cold stare. He already knew Stewart was going to come at him with stupid questions to piss him off. Morris was more observant.

"Where on God's green earth did you come up with the name Cat Daddy?" Stewart questioned.

Cat Daddy kept a cold stare on Stewart as a slight smirk rose on the right side of his cheek. Stewart was trying to piss him off, because he wasn't on his payroll. If Cat Daddy hired him like Pitch told him to do, he wouldn't be in this mess in the first place.

"'Cause I'm good at gettin' so much pussy. That's why your bitch's pussy taste like my dick." His words were cold and harsh.

Stewart motioned forward; ready to attack Cat Daddy, but some unseen force held him back. Maybe he didn't want Cat Daddy to know that he was getting to him. No matter how hard he tried to piss Cat Daddy off, it always seemed to backfire or maybe he didn't want to do anything with the camera pointed at them. This would be a hefty lawsuit if he were to attack him, which might cause him to lose his career. He knew the temptation wasn't worth the risk.

"Let's see how long the jokes last while you're rotting behind bars," Stewart threw out.

"Whateva, cop. Fuck you bring me out here for? 'Cause, I ain't givin' you no confession," he boomed.

"Well, you should, 'cause Eddie had a lot to say before he OD'ed off your shit," Stewart lied. He was trying to bait Cat Daddy into saying it was his product and confessing that he distributed the drugs.

Cat Daddy knew Eddie knew nothing of his operation and the crack that killed him belonged to Polo the Don. Cat Daddy paid Larry to give him that beat bag for his disrespect for his organization. Eddie was sloppy and he was stealing money to support his addiction. These acts were a clear sign of laziness and Cat Daddy wasn't having that. It only showed him that Eddie couldn't be trusted and for the right price, he'd sell his own soul.

"I find that hard to believe, plus I barely knew the muhfucka. So come a little stronger than that, cop, 'cause his dumb ass ain't here anymore to fill your ears with more lies and I don't hang with crackheads either," Cat Daddy voiced, with hatred in his tone.

"You think you real smart. Let's see how far all that knowledge gets you in an eight-by-eight cell." Stewart threw a folder on the table with photos of dead victims. "Do you recognize any of these photos?"

Detective Morris just stood in the corner silently. Cat Daddy looked through the pictures and pushed them away.

"Nah, never seen them before." Cat Daddy leaned back in his chair, arms crossed.

"Well you should, these are the victims whose life was taken away by your own hand. I'm the lead investigator on this case with enough proof to put you away for good." Stewart said that with so much confidence that Cat Daddy started to believe it, but he was not willing to let him know that.

Morris finally stepped in. "Listen, Mr. Ingram, I was just added to the case to help Stewart with his investigation and from what was gathered, you don't have a leg to stand on."

Cat Daddy saw that they were playing the good cop, bad cop role. This old school tactic was played and getting old.

"Since you put it that way. I refuse to say another word without my attorney present. I'm sure you heard of him…Charles Hunt. He's a good lawyer who'll have no problem with eating this case alive. A weak case fabricated by a dead crackhead. His confession holds no weight when he's not here to verify that statement." Cat Daddy said that with so much ease both Morris and Stewart were impressed. Cat Daddy wasn't easily intimidated.

Stewart was hot with a very short temper. His face turned beet red. "If that's how you want to play this game, then fine. Just remember this. Eddie isn't the only snitch in your camp. My newfound birdie is going to help me put you away for good."

With that being said, Cat Daddy was worried. Who was this snitch? He had to get rid of him quick.

"You know what, detective? You do a good job at acting like yo shit don't stink. Does your partner here know 'bout your second job?" Cat Daddy said, with a motive behind it.

"What the fuck you talking about? What second job?" Stewart was clueless of where this conversation was going.

"Yeah, you bein' a cop and crooked at the same damn time." Cat Daddy chuckled.

"What is he talking about?" Morris asked with a puzzling expression.

"Fuck would I know? And why you asking me this shit?" Stewart barked at him. His response only revealed he was hiding something. Stewart was very defensive toward Morris, which made him look guilty. Cat Daddy had him just where he wanted.

The distrust between the two was evident and now it was time for him to put the nail in the coffin.

"Oh yeah, not only are you on Polo the Don's payroll, you also work for that mob boss, Frank Debartello." Cat Daddy paused for his response.

Morris and Stewart looked at each other, then at Cat Daddy and then to each other. They held it in silence and then it went back to Cat Daddy.

"Don't believe this lying ass scumbag. He's just making all this shit up to piss me off." Stewart giggled, never taking his hard gaze off Cat Daddy. He tried to play it off, but it was hard for Morris to believe him with perspiration forming on his forehead and his complexion looking rosy.

"Morris, if you're looking to take down a scumbag, make sure you check his phone records and bank statements. I'm sure there's enough shit on it to make headlines." The room grew silent. That was Cat Daddy's cue to leave while he was on a roll. "Now fellas, this completes my day's entertainment. It was enjoyable while it lasted. And like I said, I have nothing further to discuss without my attorney present. So if you would excuse me…guard." An officer entered the room. Cat Daddy raised his arms, as the officer pat searched him. He then gave Stewart a sinister grin with an added wink before leaving the room. Stewart rubbed his head in a frustrated pout. He looked up and noticed Morris's questionable gaze.

CHAPTER 83
Deeply Felt

"Your mom is funny," Oni said while driving Chance back to his place. This was a date and she chose to spend it at his place.

"Yeah and don't pay her any mind. She's gettin' old and don't know what she's talkin' 'bout," he murmured.

"Oh, she knows what she's taking about. She's just a parent trying to protect her son. I can respect her for that."

"Yeah, you could," Chance said, with excitement in his tone.

"Yes, I can, but that doesn't mean that you can go around emulating your father. I know how female are and if they know that you're in a good relationship, they would try everything in their power to destroy it. I don't know what I'd do if I find out that you were cheating on me." Her wavering tone showed how emotional she was about it.

"Oni, you don't have to worry 'bout that. I'm really feelin' you, ma." Chance stated with honesty.

"I know you do, that's why you worked so hard with that '*truck means nothing*' line to get with me. You should have given your mother the heads up before I got there." Oni teased. Chance was busted. There was no need in prolonging the lie.

"I know, but it was smooth while it lasted though." Chance admitted. He was surprised to see that she wasn't offended by his deceitfulness. In other words, she was a good sport after all.

"It was. I know you went through a lot of trouble to keep it away. So where is it?" She asked. Her eager expression glowed with excitement.

"I got my peoples holdin' it for me." Chance finally opened up truthfully.

"You think that you can trust him with it," she said, with a worried look.

"I thought I could until you brought it to my attention. I'll make sure to get it from him today." Chance took it lightly until he thought about how young his hitters were and how he did dumb shit when he was their age. Holding the keys to Chance's car didn't sound so good now.

"I'm not mad at you. I'm kind of turned on by it. I never had anyone go out their way like this for me," she said as her face lit up. Even though he was caught in a lie, the mere thought of it was still strong.

"Like I said, I'm really feelin' you ma." Chance gazed into her eyes with such meaning.

"So what did your mom mean about street credibility." Oni asked.

"Ah, that's nothing. She knows how I feel 'bout my pride and ego. The ones I grew up with know how I get down." Chance said, with such calm that it bothered her. It wasn't what he said that did it; it was how he said it.

"So how do you get down?" She was digging now and Chance could feel the interrogation coming on. Her playful tone was now serious.

"You know. It's a male thing, lettin' everyone know that I ain't no punk." He tried to convince her.

"That type of behavior shows the characteristic of a small minded individual. One with little room to grow. I hope that your world doesn't evolve around this." She made him feel shallow.

"Damn, now that you said it like that. You sure know how to downplay a person's belief," Chance said in a discouraging tone.

"If you ask me. I wouldn't call it a belief. It's more of a lifestyle...a choice. A man chooses his own path that suits his own needs and desires."

"Girl, you deep; I'm scared of you." Chance realized she was on a totally different level than him. There was no playing mind games with her type of intellect.

"You shouldn't be. My father told me that knowledge is the number one key to survival. Never stray away from it. It makes a big difference between leaders and followers."

Chance nodded, letting it all soak in. Oni was very deep and that's what he admired most about her. She never let her beauty keep her from learning. Intelligence was more important than a person's appearance.

CHAPTER 84
Twisted Turns

"So is this why you've been ignoring all my phone calls?" a female said, breaking Chance's train of thought. She was a pretty girl, with nice curves and a few tattoos that looked sexy on her. She had no problem exposing them. She was very attractive, but her demeanor revealed her wretchedness. Two other girls stood next to her, ready to start some trouble.

"Erika, it's over. Don't be comin' 'round here startin' yo shit," Chance yelled at her while Oni stayed in the car.

"After all the shit I did for you? This is how you treat me? I did time for your dumb ass," She barked with anger, but her hurtful eyes displayed her desperation.

"And that's why I stopped fuckin' wit'cha. You talk too damn much."

Erika quickly redirected her anger toward Oni.

"Bitch, you's mine, just wait 'til I catch yo black ass." She pointed at Oni, who just sat there behind the steering wheel with a puzzled look.

Suddenly, Chance's exterior changed. His eyes formed slits and his voice steady. He had a calm demeanor of a cold-blooded killer when he said, "You are so out of pocket right now. Don't make me force my hand, Walonda…Zakia, get yo girl before she ends up in the red zone."

At that moment, both girls had a look of fear in their eyes and the aggressive stance deflated. They knew the red zone meant murder. The girls quickly escorted the crying Erika to their car and drove off. Oni was still sitting there in shock of the power Chance had over them.

"Raymond, what was all that about?" Oni asked, as they got out the car, but she remained there looking for answers.

"Some crazy girl that's been stalkin' me for a while now." He was back to good old Chance now.

"That looked like it was more than just some girl. What are you, a pimp?" Her eyes held a look of concern and they were prepared to soak in everything he was telling her.

"A pimp! Oh no, pimpin' ain't in my blood. If I were a pimp you would have known that already. One way or another that would have come to the light by now."

"I just saw a totally different man. And the way you talked to those girls was unlike anything I've ever seen. What are you then, some type of king pin drug dealer?"

Chance paused before answering. "No, I'm not a king pin drug dealer." That was the truth. Chance never told her that he was a drug dealer that worked under a kingpin by the name of Cat Daddy.

"What did that girl mean when she said she did time for you?"

Chance looked her in the eyes as he tried to select the right words. "I wasn't always innocent. I did some dirt and shit happened and that's all I'm gonna say."

The delayed response was a clear sign she caught on to what he was saying. She knew that whatever he did in the past would surely cost him his freedom, but something deep down inside her had to know. Before she decided to move forward with this relationship, she had to know what type of man she was dealing with and if he was the kind of guy she wanted to spend her life with. For some strange reason, she knew if she continued to dig deeper into Chance's past, there's a strong possibility her safety or her life would be at risk.

"The more I get to know you, the more you start to scare me. I think I'll go home now. I need time to think."

Chance could see her shaking in fear. "Think about what. I would never hurt you. Don't do this to me." He was becoming emotional, as his voice got deeper.

"I'm not slow, Raymond. I know a player when I see one. I'm not sure of what angle you're coming from, but I'm sure it's bad and you know how I feel about this. Especially about drug dealers. I can't support a black man that kills his own people for a profit." Her words were stern with meaning behind it.

"I don't do that shit anymore. You made me a better person. That's why I've been takin' those classes." He was spending so much time with Oni that he neglected the business, but he was really taking a break.

"Seeing you interact with your mother was a strong indication that you care a lot about her and that tells me that you would do the same for me, but what I just witnessed gives me pause."

She was starting to have second thought about him and he knew it. It was only a matter of time before she found out he lied about his cooking classes.

"I think that it's best that I go home to gather my thoughts."

CHAPTER 85

Bob and Weave

"So, Dee, what the fuck was all that about?" Morris said, talking to Stewart like a true friend.

"That piece of shit was just fucking with your head. He ain't got shit on me. He knows I'm on to him so he's looking for an outlet." Stewart was trying to make light of the situation, but Morris knew him all too well. The puzzled look that Stewart gave him was a pure sign of quilt.

"Dee, we've been partners for a very long time, right?"

"Come on, Andy, don't go there. That fuckin' cunt made that bullshit up!"

"Just tell me the truth. Are you working for those scumbags we work so hard to put away?" Morris was looking for answers, but Stewart wasn't giving him what he wanted to hear.

"Listen, I want to get rid of those scumbags as much as you do." He was dancing around the question, refusing to respond.

"Just answer me. Are you or are you not working for them?" Morris's tone was laced with frustration.

Stewart saw the hurt in Morris's eyes. They were more than partners, they were buddies. If there was anyone that truly had his back it was Morris.

"Hey, Andy, I'm your friend here. You know me better than that. This is me, baby. Your right-hand man. Don't let that lowlife come between us. He was trying to get all in your head with that nonsense. I wouldn't jeopardize my career. The shit ain't worth it."

Morris could tell this conversation was going nowhere. He wanted to believe his friend, but deep down he knew Stewart was lying. If Stewart was to tell the truth about the situation then maybe they could work together to save his career and maybe his freedom. Stewart holding back only forced his hand and made him do what he's known for and that's working a case. There was no need in questioning him any further because he was only wasting his breath. Morris knew he would have to do some investigation of his own.

CHAPTER 86
Wine and Dine

Tony took Kim to The Chop House in Voorhees. They ate out on the deck at the fire-pit. The view of the lake, outlined with oak trees, was breathtaking. For the last few months, Tony was doing a very good job at wowing her on every date. She was now convinced Tony wasn't a bad guy after all. His shiny, curly hair and *GQ* persona was looking better with each date. She found his smooth baby face and bedroom eyes very attractive. His swagger was turning her on. He did his homework and she was impressed.

Kim started the conversation. "I see you took care of that little rental situation."

"If they bothered to look, they would have seen that I sold all those properties to some slimy company months ago. I didn't know that they would still try to use my name in the process." Tony lied to avoid Kim from interrogating him.

"So is Bill taking you back?"

"I never looked back to find out. I'm starting my own business," he said prideful.

Kim ignored all his calls and kept her distance. Tony knew what it was and gave her the space she needed. Once he cleared his name and covered his tracks, it was back to rebuilding their relationship.

"Doing what?" She frowned as if she was prepared to cut their date short.

"I'm starting my own funeral home business."

"Isn't that scary, let alone depressing?" Kim's reaction showed Tony she wanted nothing to do with it.

"I own the business, which means I leave the rest to the employed to handle. I'm not ready to deal with the horrors of running a funeral home yet." Tony was no stranger to death, but deep down he knew that telling Kim wouldn't be a wise decision. The sounds of glass and silverware filled the air.

"I have to admit, you have been doing a great job of keeping a smile on my face. So, Tony, let me ask you this, if you don't mind." He played it off like it was nothing, but every time she asked a question, he had to be on point, because Kim was good at that detective shit.

"Nah, go right ahead, I'm all ears." The butterflies were playing football in his belly.

"Since you've been putting in so much time into me, I have to admit that it's been quite the experience. So now that you got me away from home again, what are you planning to do with me?" Now this was the question he had no problem answering.

"I plan on taking every opportunity of my free time to get to know you better and hopefully build something out of this," he said, with honesty.

"That's very interesting." She replied as if she was starting to get bored.

"So what do you think of me so far?" He asked, still maintaining a pleasant smile.

"You're a'ight," she teased.

"Really, Kim, that's how you feel about me?" They both shared a good laugh. She was slowly coming back to life.

"I should be asking you that question, seeing you work so hard to impress me."

"You're a'ight," Tony teased back.

They both continued to laugh. Their giggly moment was interrupted by the waitress who was ready to take their order. Tony ordered the porter house steak and Kim ordered the lobster tail. They shared the macaroni and cheese with lobster meat. The white wine was enjoyed with their meal. Money was no issue for Tony. His main concern, over everything else, was getting with Kim.

CHAPTER 87

In the Wake of…

Detective's Stewart and Morris had been partners for over five years. The two started as good drinking buddies that ended up growing into a very close friendship. It was hard for Morris to accept that his partner was crooked, but his demeanor proved otherwise. They started gathering up all their paperwork in silence. Morris had more questions to ask Stewart, but knew it would be a waste of time and effort. Stewart was hiding something and Morris was willing to find out. No words were spoken between them. How could he do such a thing when their whole career was bringing down those that disrespected the law?

Morris wasn't sure of what Cat Daddy's master plan was. With all the evidence Stewart had on him, it didn't seem to bother him at all. The angle Cat Daddy was coming from became the main focus of his investigation, but what Cat Daddy said about Stewart was puzzling. Each time he mentioned Stewart, there was a look of discomfort in his eyes and the automatic defensive screen that Stewart put up that bothered Morris the most.

Lately, Stewart's actions and attitude had changed for the worse. He suddenly had extra spending money and his style of clothing had become more expensive. These were the main reasons Morris questioned Stewart's loyalty to the force. There was no ignoring the shit anymore. Morris now had a yearning to know the truth. Even if it would cost him his friendship.

Retrieving a copy of Stewart's bank and phone records seemed like the hardest thing Detective Andy Morris had ever done in his entire career. Stewart was a good friend to Morris and doing this made him feel as though he was betraying him to the point that he was stabbing Stewart in his back. Morris had to pull strings to get it. Thank goodness he still had friends in high places. He stayed up all night going through all Stewart's paperwork. Morris couldn't believe the things he found. There were sums of money added to his account from unusual accounts that were untraceable. His phone records were filled with untraceable numbers. The majority of the numbers were from disposable cell phones. This would take some deep investigation and video surveillance footage from various locations that Stewart was known to frequent. The deeper Morris got, the dirtier Stewart was looking.

CHAPTER 88

Eyes Wide Shut

After Oni had time to cool down, Chance was able to take her out on a date that didn't include his place or the streets of Camden. Oni was firm in her beliefs and Chance didn't want to risk losing her.

Chance took Oni to the movies and out to dinner. They later went to her dorm on the college campus. Oni stayed in Willow, a female dorm. Chance was excited. This was his first time in a female dorm. A few doors were opened, giving him a bird's eye view of all the lovely ladies walking around in their T-shirts and panties. Chance felt like he was at a strip joint. All he needed was some extra one dollar bills so he could make it rain money up in the place.

He fought hard not to let his excitement show. Seeing him walk through their hallway caused them to rush to the doors, greeting him with seductive smiles. They all looked like T-bone steaks.

Oni got him into her dorm room, which was at the end of the hallway and locked the door. Chance scanned the room. It was decorated with photos of her friends and family on the walls. She also had stuffed animals on the bed. Her sheets and blankets were printed with Sponge Bob Square Pants. Her room was clean and everything stacked neatly. She had a Macbook Pro laptop on the desk with a stack of books next to it and on the floor.

"This is cute," Chance said, with a hint of sarcasm.

"Cute! This is better than cute. This is my mini palace." She giggled.

"So, from what you're telling me, this is your first time away from home." He pointed at the cartoon blanket set.

"Yes, I needed a break from my father's watchful eye and iron clad fist." She balled her hand up as she flopped on the bed.

"So your parents are strict," Chance said, still visually inspecting the room. It was amazing how a person with so little, cherish it so much.

"Yes, to a certain extent. Now that I'm grown and on my own, they untied the leash of torture and let me run free. My father said that experience is the best teacher. I'm now old enough to make my own decisions." She seemed excited at the thought of it.

"Is that why you felt the way you did when you came to visit me the first time?" Chance sat beside her, giving her his full attention.

"Yes. I allowed my emotions to get the best of me." She looked so innocent.

"So that explains your action."

"My father warned me about bad boys and then I met you. You seem so nice and no one ever came off at me like that."

"I know...my charm is somethin', ain't it?" He laughed.

"Shut up." Oni pushed him.

"Hey, I thought you were gonna feed me. You ain't got no kitchen up in here. All I see is a microwave and that ain't gon' fly." He quickly changed the subject while lying across the colorfully cartoonish bed.

"Don't worry about that. I promise to satisfy your hunger. I ordered something that I know you will enjoy and I'm the dessert."

"You go, girl. I see you's a naughty little girl and for that I'ma spank yah." He motioned toward her with a raised hand.

"Oh, I've never been spanked before." She pulled her jeans down and stuck her ass in his face.

"Now that's what I'm talkin' 'bout." Chance grinned as he lightly smacked her round ass repeatedly.

Her phone rung, destroying the moment. "Hello," she answered. "Okay, I'll be right there." She hung up the phone.

"Is everything okay?" Chance asked with weary eyes.

"Yes, that was the front desk. Our food has arrived. I'll be right back." She pulled her jeans up and headed out the door. The door was left open, giving Chance a bird's eye view down the long hallway. Girls were walking up and down the hall, going from one room to the next like headless chickens. Chance was enjoying the scene, sitting on the bed as if he was watching a blockbuster hit.

CHAPTER 89

Walking on Eggshells

"So, Kim, where do we go from here? I know it's getting late so if you want to call it a night, I'll gladly take you home," Tony said, looking at his Rolex watch after the waitress handed him the check.

"Well, tonight I really don't have a curfew. So it's all about how long you can hang."

Tony surely didn't prepare for this. Their dates always ended after dinner. This was a test. Nothing more than a mind game that she loved to play. He fucked up once and was taking this relationship very slow. Kim never said anything, but her actions showed it. She was distant and wasn't interested in going out. Tony knew it was the newspaper article that revealed his illegal activity. Plus he knew how Kim distanced herself from anything unlawful. Something in her past must have spooked her.

"Well, it's after ten and nothing's open unless you want to go to a club." He was free-styling a few suggestions, but it wasn't what he really wanted to do.

"Nah, been there, done that. This has been a long day and all I want to do is relax."

Tony was doing good so far, but he had to choose his words wisely. So far, she liked what she was hearing.

"You're more than welcome to come chill at my place, if you don't mind, of course." He struggled to keep his composure, but inside he was ready to explode with excitement. Kim had been distant from him since he was fired from the job. She slowly worked herself back once he cleared his name of all charges. Tony was so determined to get her back, he was willing to do anything.

"Oh yeah, and what can we do at your place?" She was still quizzing him, making sure he didn't slip up.

"We can watch a movie or just sit and talk. I'm really feeling you, Kim, and there's so much I want to know about you. I can talk to you all night and even make breakfast for you in the morning, if you end up staying that long." He threw it out there, hoping she took the bait.

She stroked her chin in deep thought. It's been a long time since they made love and Tony's sudden erections were a pure sign of withdrawal. He wanted that pussy so bad. Melody wasn't good enough. He needed something more than just physical and Kim was the total package for him.

"I like that. You're willing to talk to me all night to get to know me better. That was smooth, but your game ain't that strong." Her smile faded and now she was giving him a hard gaze.

"Well, you can't knock me for trying." Tony gave her his pitiful puppy face. It was good while it lasted. He was all out of ammo and shooting blanks.

"Cute, but another weak attempt. I do admire your determination. So I'll let you take me to your spot to relax and maybe watch a movie or two. Who knows, you may end up making me breakfast in the morning. It all depends on how strong your game is."

That drew a smile on Tony's lips. So far he was passing the test. Now he had to select his words more carefully. They talked during the ride to his house. Kim was telling Tony that she grew up in the worst part of North Philadelphia, and how hard she worked to get out of that drug-infested area. She stayed in school and joined every activity they had to stay out of trouble. She became a full-time student of Temple University, which was close to home. She graduated with a bachelor's degree in health and fitness, which explained her sexy physique. She was now willing to come see how he was living, which meant he passed the test. The time they spent dating, Kim had never been to his home. He always took her out. Now let the games began and that's seeing how far he could go to get to the ultimate prize.

CHAPTER 90
Forgotten Past

A female entered the room. She was pretty and looked as though she was Spanish and Black. She was built like a thick hourglass, with pink glossy lips and short curly hair dyed blonde. Chance watched the girl walk around the room as if she had lost something, but he knew she was giving him a free advertisement of her killer curves. Blood quickly rushed down to the little man between his legs, seeing her ass shake in her extra tight nighty shorts that were high enough to show her butt cheeks.

Then the girl turned her focus toward Chance as if she didn't notice his presence.

Yeah…right.

"Uh, you're cute. Where's Oni?" The look in her eyes was craving dick. Words were not needed to say so.

"She just stepped out to grab some food and your name is?" He asked, still keeping a stone expression.

"Kiesha," she said, licking her lips like he was an edible treat. Chance wasn't slow. He knew how devious females could get. He saw that she was a slimy bitch and he was hoping she and Oni weren't friends, because he would have to worry about his conscience bothering him for putting some dick up in her.

"I'll make sure to tell her you stopped by." Chance never lost his cool as he thought of all the different ways he could fuck the shit out that bitch before Oni returned. Friend or no friend, it didn't matter, because she was an easy lay from the look in her eyes.

"Okay, see you later, handsome," she emphasized as she departed the room.

"No prob, ma." He stared at her hypnotic ass. This girl had a mean walk and enough confidence to make the President stutter, but Chance still remained cold as ice.

When she exited the room, Chance dropped his face in his hand. She almost broke him.

"Damn, nigga, how you gon' act like you don't know me?" Keisha's voice startled him as she re-entered the room. He looked up with squinted eyes.

"Who's you?" He frowned.

"I just told you earlier…Keisha," she voiced, now with an attitude.

"Never heard of ya. Now spin off." He huffed. She was doing too much and the shit was turning him off. For all he knew, this could have been a set up.

"Wow, Chance, you forget all the bitches you done fucked?"

She said his name without him even telling her. That only meant she did know him. Chance had fucked so many women, he lost track of their names and faces.

"Only the one's that can't fuck," he said still keeping his composure.

"Does Oni know how you get down?" She quizzed, but it came off more as a threat than a question.

"Fuck you just say?" Chance rose to his feet, nose flared and chest heaving like he just had an adrenaline rush of fury.

"You heard me. You and Tuck came over to my cousin's, Wanda's, crib on Eighth and Lime two months ago for some ass and then bounced. You could have hollered at a bitch or somethin'."

Chance was more upset with himself than her. He couldn't believe he fucked a picture-perfect bitch and didn't remember it. A good fuck or not, she was too fine of a woman for him to forget. A female looking as good as she did, he would have taken his time to teach her the right tricks for his own pleasure and then gave her the boot after dogging her out.

"Real talk, I don't remember. That haze and lean got me all fucked up in the head." Chance was now blaming it on the weed and liquor. He was now thinking of a way for a rematch. She looked good and he didn't know how he could forget a dime piece like that.

"Nigga, I got that good, good and never had a complaint. You just need me to jar that memory," she offered. The bitch was literally throwing the pussy at him, but he was fumbling the ball. Yeah, I don't think the President could have done any better with this chick.

CHAPTER 91

The Wow Effect

Tony pulled up to his estate. The home was well lit with beams of light showcasing it. There were also lights aligning the brick walkway. The estate looked more like an elementary school with the amount of windows it displayed from the front. One could tell it was easy to get lost in the multi-bedroom home. All the lights came on by the use of motion detectors.

"Okay, Tony, I knew you were doing it big, but not quite like this." Her excited eyes scanned the landscape. Tony smirked, seeing how impressed she was. He knew her pussy had to be moist. All he had to do now was work his way inside her love box.

"So you like it?"

"Me liking it is more of an understatement." She visually scanned the place as a feeling of exhilaration swept through her.

They entered the front double door entrance into the foyer. The crystal chandelier dangling three stories in the air was massive. Its design was unique in its own way. It was the most impressive chandelier she had ever seen. Tony then gave her a nice little tour of his mansion. It took over ten minutes.

"I've been in many homes, but none quite like this one. I am very impressed. What are you doing on the side to afford such a thing…wait a minute; don't respond. I have a strong feeling I would not like the answer. So I'll stick to the story you said about your father, the mob boss, helping you out." Tony could tell she wasn't buying that story.

There was a long pause as guilt was written on his face. Tony had to think fast and change the subject before she started to pry into his business like an investigator.

"So what do you think about the back yard?" He asked, hoping she'd drop the topic.

Kim beamed at him as if she was ready to dig all in his shit for trying to be slick with it, but instead she twisted her mouth up into a smile.

"I loved the…what you called it again? The back yard, right? It looks more like a waterpark. So how much is your water bill?"

"It really isn't that bad. It's recycled water," he lied. The pump alone added an extra zero to his electric bill.

"Oh, I like that and it's private. I know it has a lot of history with it."

Tony responded with a sly grin and an added wink.

"Maybe one day you'll go for a swim," Tony flirted. He was gaining his confidence back, seeing how she was still interested in the home.

"That sounds good. I love to go swimming." Kim started removing her clothes. Tony watched in silence. He couldn't believe his eyes. Kim saw the shocked expression and she loved it. She was now in control. Tony wasn't sure if this was one of her mind games. If so, she was winning because he was too dumbfounded to make any attempts of a comeback. She started with her blouse, slowly unbuttoning it to expose her nipples pointing from the firmest breast he'd ever seen. They were both pointing at him like heat seeking missiles. She wore no bra for they needed no support. Her arms, shoulders and stomach were well toned like an athlete.

"Hello…Tony…are you still there?" She teased, breaking his lustful thoughts.

Tony then realized he was standing there like a dumb caveman. No matter how many times he saw her body, he was still at a loss for words by her physique.

"Words cannot express how amazing you look. Please don't let me stop you."

Kim gave him a seductive look as she pushed her tight skirt down to her ankles. She stepped out of them and was now wearing string bikini underwear and high heels. The combination was fascinating. Tony couldn't control the tent like bulge that formed in his pants.

"So, are you going to join me or am I going to swim alone?" She said, walking out of her heels and into the backyard. She looked back at Tony, who was still in his dumbfounded state as she walked into the pool, removing her panties.

Tony shook it off and quickly removed his clothing. He was too impatient to remove each button from his Brooks Brothers silk shirt, so he pulled it apart, causing all the buttons to pop off. He entered the cold water. Outside he remained cool, but inside he felt like a kid at the playground.

CHAPTER 92
Private Party

Chance's aggressive stance had softened. Now he was contemplating how to get another sample of Keisha's pussy. When it came to pussy it was like kryptonite. He was too weak to turn it down, but tonight his focus was on Oni. He wanted to get Keisha's number, just in case he didn't already have it. So he could smash that ass when he was done with Oni, but Oni had returned with the food in hand before he could get a word in.

"Keisha, why you flirting with my man?" Oni said playfully. She didn't catch on to the tense atmosphere.

"Oh, there you are. I was goin' to ask you if you wanted to go with me to the frat party tonight at Edgewood apartments, but I see you already got company and you got food, too." Keisha realized they weren't going anywhere no time soon.

"Yeah, girl. This is for us only." Oni entered the room gripping the bag like a running back with a football breaking through the middle for the end zone.

"Oh, I see you got your own party going down. Then I'll leave you two lovebirds alone. It's been nice meeting you. What did you say your name was again?" She was doing an award winning performance at playing clueless. That only meant she was good at keeping secrets. This would come in handy if they were to take it there.

"His name is Raymond and he's my man. Thank you very much." Oni answered for him.

"Raymond!" She responded in a high pitch tone. He was only known as Chance in the hood. So she wasn't sure if that really was his government name or he was playing her out.

"That's what I said and don't dog it out. Bye Keisha." Oni pushed Keisha out of her room. Oni came back and made sure her door was shut and locked.

"Glad to get rid of her nosey behind." Oni sighed with her back pressed against the door like a doorstopper. "I can't trust her as far as I can throw her. There's something real shady about her. I just can't put my finger on it." Oni was now in deep thought.

"Then why are you friends with her?" He inquired, but he couldn't stop thinking about how bad he wanted to fuck her.

"They say keep your friends close and your enemies closer. At first, I thought she was a friend. Until she fucked every guy that tried to get with me. That only made her out to be a campus hoe. I hated her for that, but then I realized that she only does this out of pure hatred and jealousy toward me. I have done nothing wrong to her. She wasted so much time and energy trying to take away my happiness that it ended up backfiring on her. Her status as a woman is way below average. The guys show her no respect and call her out of her name. As of right now, she has no friends…only me. I kind of feel sorry for her. She lost herself and I'm hoping that maybe deep down she'll find out that I'm really a true friend."

"Wow, Oni, that's deep. Even after all she did to you." Chance was impressed. Her whole thought process was different from anyone he knew. This uniqueness only made him want her more.

"And I forgave her for that."

CHAPTER 93

Holding His Title

Tony was now standing in the center of the swimming pool, while Kim remained in the corner, leaning against the wall, waiting for him. It was four feet deep were they stood. It only got deeper if they were to venture out. The pool was three times the size of an Olympic-sized one. It came with different sections with unique features. In the lower level, where they stood, was a bar that could easily seat eighteen people. In the deeper end was a seven-foot-wide waterfall that was two stories high. A curved sliding board ran down the side of the waterfall. It also came with slow moving water rapid that flowed on the outskirt of the entire yard, designed for those with floatation devices for a soothing ride for a better view of the entire yard. The light display in and out of the pool was amazing. There were a few fire-pits around the perimeter. The most impressive was the fire shooting from the waterfall. There were lots of fake palm trees that gave it that Caribbean look. The yard alone looked like he spent over five million dollars to build a backyard oasis that was the perfect getaway. It was enough to make Kim drop her drawers and now it was time for him to reap the reward.

He pressed his chest against hers as they silently gazed into each other's eyes. He wanted her bad and from the expression on her face she wanted him, too. He leaned forward and kissed her lips. They were soft to the touch. She leaned in, kissing him back. They kissed, as his lips pressed hers open, allowing his tongue to enter her mouth and their tongues danced to the non-rhythmic tone of their heavy breathing. Kim ran her hands south and grabbed hold of his manhood. Tony's breathing stuttered. She began to stroke his hard pole. Tony wanted her bad, but knew to take it slow. He wanted this to last. It wasn't about him tonight. It was all about Kim. He wanted to make this the best sexual experience of her life. He wanted her to keep coming back for more like a fiend. This was why he selected this home in the first place. The goal was for her to fall in love with it and make it her home. Hopefully, he could get her accustomed to this new lifestyle that she would ignore his wrongdoings. He didn't need any Viagra. This was real. A fantasy come true. He wanted Kim for years, ever since he first laid eyes on her. This was a fantasy that he cared less about the consequences. This was all about the here and now.

CHAPTER 94
Tangled Sheets

Chance paused for a moment. Oni was a very sweet-spirited person. There was no woman that he knew who talked or acted as she did. He had discovered a newfound feeling for her. Something deeper than the lust that overpowered the way he perceived her. She had a good heart and that's what he admired most about her.

"You know what, Oni? You're not that bad at all. I like you."

"Thank you. I suppose." She shrugged. "I'm just being me. This is how my parents raised me."

"Then you have some great parents. I hope to see them someday." This time he meant every word of it.

"Well, that won't be any time soon." She looked in the brown paper bag, pulling their meal out. "So all this talk of Keisha got our food cold. I'll have to heat it up in the microwave."

"What is it?" Chance looked at the big brown bag.

"My favorite, baked pizza turnover." She pulled it out. Each one was wrapped in white paper.

"I never had this before." He watched with inquisitive eyes.

"Then you'll love it." She bit down on her bottom lip.

Oni heated it up in the microwave and watched as Chance bit into it.

"Mmmm. This shit is bangin," he thundered.

"Sssshhhh, not so loud, potty mouth." The walls were thin and everyone outside the door could hear him.

"Oh, my bad. I think it's delicious," he said sarcastically. They both laughed.

After the meal, Oni cleaned up everything and went into her playful mode. She started reaching her hand under his arm and tickling him. Chance unaware that he was ticklish burst into laughter as they playfully wrestled on the bed. They paused to catch their breath. Oni climbed on top of him and gazed into his big brown eyes. She admired his strong features and sexy lips.

"Can I ask you something?" She said, as if she was afraid of his answer.

"Yeah, go head, ma." His warm smile was welcoming.

"Do you have any kids?" These were the questions she should have asked when they first met.

"No. I'm not ready to start a family yet."

Her question only meant she was ready to take it to the next level.

"Do you have any goals and if so, what are they?" This was her way of feeling him out and he knew it. Chance realized that his answers determined how far this relationship would go from here. He did what he was doing from the first time he laid eyes on her and that's lie.

"My plan is to become a chef and then hopefully own my own restaurant." His words sounded so convincing.

"What's the name of this so call restaurant?"

"I don't know yet, but I do have a few names to run with."

"What are they?" Her eyes were of an innocent child eager to learn, but the questions were starting to sound like they came from a prosecutor.

"Yeah right. So you can steal my idea. I don't think so." He started tickling her. He wasn't planning on her to come at his neck with so many questions. He needed a distraction and playing in the bed until he gets her clothes off was the perfect solution. Chance was smooth. Smoother than she thought. Before she could think of the next question to ask him, he had his lips pressed against hers and was now removing her clothing. By that time, Oni was already in the mood and just went along with the flow.

CHAPTER 95
Reflected Enjoyment

Kim lifted each leg and wrapped it around Tony's waist, as his rock hard penis slowly entered her love box. This time and place was perfect and this moment would be unforgettable. He palmed her thick ass cheeks, holding her steady as he slowly stroked his dick in and out of her soft pussy. They gazed into each other's eyes, reading one's expression. It was enough to keep going, as Tony began to stroke harder. Kim's head fell back as her eyes rolled upward. She was in pure bliss. Tony was feeling like a champion, trying to maintain his title. Everything he said over the years about his sex game was now up to the challenge and he had to prove it, once again. The water began to splash as Tony increased his thrusts. Kim moaned, grabbing the back of his neck to keep her balance. Tony was getting so excited that he started to lose himself with each stroke. Kim took her right hand and grabbed his waist.

"Take it slow. We got all night," she whispered, looking at him with her seductive eyes.

"Oh…Okay." Tony breathed. That immature action made him seem like he lacked the experience needed to please her. This was a learning lesson and he was soaking it all in like a human sponge. Coming now would ruin the moment and set him back to step one of rebuilding this relationship.

Kim stared into his eyes, as he took his time pushing and pulling himself in and out of her. Kim's eyes rolled again as her head fell back. Her nice hairstyle was going to have to be redone. She was now getting it wet each time her head went back.

Suddenly, Kim pushed Tony off her. Tony just watched, waiting for her next move. Kim got out of the pool and entered the house with water dripping off her smooth skin. Tony stared at her, as her ass swayed left to right. It was very hypnotic. Her legs had the thickness of a track star and her body was well toned. All she needed was a tennis skirt and you would think that Serena Williams was letting him wax that fat ass. Tony didn't lay down any towels for them to dry off. All she left was a wet trail to follow. She looked back at Tony.

"Now take me to your bedroom," she said with an extended hand.

Tony got out the pool, allowing his dick to lead the way like a compass. He grabbed her hand and took her to his master suite. The double doors to the bedroom was huge as if it was designed for Mighty Joe Young. The doorknobs looked like dumbbells. He pushed the door open and the bedroom looked like a small cathedral, with a large seating area with a fireplace and a big one-hundred-inch 4K Smart television. There were two walk-in closets, each one the size of a living room, a seating area with a huge mirror. The bathroom was big enough to throw a party, with a huge custom-made Jacuzzi for eight and a massive shower that looked like a studio. Two vanities with a huge mirror and two toilets with private doors. Tony walked Kim over to the round bed. Kim was still inspecting the room in amazement.

"This room is a woman's paradise," she said, lost in astonishment. Though she toured the home earlier, she couldn't control the wow effect it still had on her.

Tony wrapped his arms around her, kissing the back of her neck with his long pole pressing against her backside. "This could be your paradise if you just let me in."

Kim giggled. "You must say that to all the girls."

"I don't deal with girls, only women and you're the only woman I've ever brought to this house."

"Why…because you just brought it?" She said, causing Tony to stop kissing her on the neck. She must have hit it on the bullseye.

Tony spun her around. "Damn, you're good. And to be honest, yes, I did just get the house. It took a while to get it where it is and the interior decorator cost me a fortune. I—"

Kim pressed her finger against his lips. "Ssshhh. I didn't remove my underwear to talk." She pulled him down on to the white sheets. She looked up and saw the mirror on the ceiling. It put a bigger smile on her face. She enjoyed watching his ass move as he waxed that pussy. She loved how his ass tightened with each stroke. The way his back muscles moved just turned her on. Kim hadn't had Tony touch her in a long time, since she distanced herself from him after the newspaper article and tonight she needed this, all of it, as Tony took her away.

CHAPTER 96

Wet and Wild

Chance started kissing and licking the salty flavor of Oni's neck and chest. He worked his way down to her thy, but she stopped him before he got to her love box.

"First, I must freshen up," she said, jumping to her feet and running to the bathroom. Chance could hear her turning on the shower, as he stood on the opposite side of the door. He wanted to join her for some wet and wild sex, but he waited a few and decided to play on the laptop instead. It was powered on so he pushed a few buttons to take the screen out of safe mode, but he needed the passcode to access the computer. Chance started to snoop around, looking in the drawers and closet to see if he had any heavy competition. So far she was clean and there were no signs of anyone pushing up. Maybe she had something on her computer, probably her social media page. As for now, he needn't be concerned. Oni seemed to be on the straight and narrow. Neither her cell phone nor her dorm phone rang the entire time he was there. That alone was a good sign. Unless she had the ringer off. He checked to make sure. The ringer was still on. Everything was looking good so far.

Just then, the running shower water stopped. He quickly sat on the bed. Oni came out the bathroom wearing just a towel.

"Don't just sit there, get your stinking ass in that shower," she teased.

Chance couldn't help but laugh at her silly ass. She could always keep a smile on his face and that's a plus. He entered the bathroom to see another door on the opposite end. That only meant that she shared the bathroom with someone else, but who? He knew it was another female and he wanted to see for himself.

He reached to turn the doorknob, but it was locked. Chance shrugged it off and got into the shower. Afterwards, he came back into her room to find Oni under the blankets.

"Let me guess. You want to play hide and go seek," Chance said, crawling under the blankets. Oni laughed as she allowed him to continue where he left off.

She watched as the lump in the blanket slowly moved toward her pussy. Leaving a wet trail of kisses along the way. It was as if she lost control of her muscles as her body jerked from his lips touching her sensitive spot. His lips were soft and his tongue was warm and wet. It felt so good. He was doing it right and enjoying it. She liked how he was licking her in all the right places. She moaned with pleasure, spreading her legs wider. She wanted to feel his whole mouth. What Chance was doing was too much for her to handle. It was like an atomic bomb went off in her pussy, as the wave of energy shocked her entire body. It took her a minute to gather herself. She pushed him off the bed and on to the floor and climbed on top. She inserted his solid wood inside her and she gyrate her hips. Chance just watched as she moved like an amateur dancer. Her rhythm was a little off, but she still looked sexy doing it. Chance was in a lustful gaze when it hit him. It happened so fast he didn't have an opportunity to prepare for it. He reached his climax with so much force he growled like a bear and then let out a loud yell. It was enough for the entire dorm to hear. Oni covered his mouth.

"Raymond!" She yelled at him to hush. It would be such an embarrassment if the entire dorm knew what was taking place behind her door. He tried standing to his feet to shake it off.

"I'm sorry. I don't know what hit me." He was enjoying this newfound sexual experience. Taking it slow and being none aggressive felt better than he thought. Chance could get used to this new type of lovemaking she had introduced to him. He climbed back in the small single bed and held her in his arms. There was nothing else to be said. The panting and heavy breathing was enough to answer the questions of pleasure. Satisfaction was what put them into deep slumber.

CHAPTER 97

The Perfect Man

The next morning, Kim woke up in an empty bed. Tony was in the bathroom brushing his teeth. The sound of the water running must have awakened her. She had a smile on her face from such a wonderful night that Tony had given her. He treated her special and made her feel like a woman. Her body felt so relaxed in his comfortable bed. She stared at her reflection in the mirror above her. Her hair was a mess and needed to be done, ASAP. She looked at a remote control on the nightstand and picked it up. The remote was the size of an iPad mini. She touched the screen and pushed a button. Just then, the mirror on the ceiling turned into a television screen. How incredible was that. The volume was loud and she quickly turned it down. The controls were very simple to use. Tony stuck his head out the bathroom with his toothbrush still in his mouth.

"Good morning, sleeping beauty," he teased, with her hair looking like a train wreck.

"Whatever." She laughed.

He went back into the bathroom to finish freshening up.

Kim pushed a few more buttons, causing the curtains to open up. The view of the landscape was breathtaking under the sunlight. She sat up with the sheets still wrapped around her, enjoying the view.

I could get used to this, she thought as she stared out the window.

Tony startled her with a kiss on the shoulder. She was in such a trance that she didn't hear him approach her. Maybe the Persian rugs made his footsteps so silent. She shook her head with hands covering her face in embarrassment.

"I have everything you need to freshen up. You take your time doing so while I make us some breakfast." Tony laid a clean robe on the bed and headed for the kitchen.

Kim took advantage of the moment and looked all through his things. She wanted to know what he was really about and to make sure he wasn't gay. She should have taken care of these things before she gave herself to him, but before they ended up taken this relationship further she had to know. *Can't no man be this good without no flaws.*

CHAPTER 98

Scared Killer

Chance didn't know why he couldn't stop thinking about Oni. The women he got within the past were considered bitches for dropping the panties on the first night, but Oni was different. There was an innocence about her. She wasn't fast or loose, even though he got the ass on the first night. She was just naive and clueless to the game. She got played by a hustler with street knowledge and he felt guilty for taking advantage of her innocence. He even felt bad about wanting the fuck Kiesha.

Naw...not really.

That would be some bonus pussy, an easy nut. Oni liked him a lot and was willing to do anything for him. That's the type of girl he needed by his side. A woman that would hold him down in time of need. A woman that would have his back when times got rough. A woman that would love him for who he was and accepted his flaws. Not the same old hood rats that would leave him at the drop of a dime for another hustler that made more money. Oni wasn't that type at all. Even though he couldn't see it, he could feel it deep down in his heart. When they would go out, she always volunteered to treat, believing he had no job or money. She was unique in every way. Oni was a keeper.

His cell phone started ringing as it came through his car speakers. The screen read: Oni. That put a big smile on his face like a playful kid. She was the only woman capable of doing such. Chance never smiled so hard in his life. Some days his face would end up being sore from it. Those unworked muscles weren't used to it. He hit the touch screen.

"Hey, ma, how you doin'?" He cheesed.

"Hey, Raymond, baby. You miss me?"

She was the only person allowed to call him by his government name and it didn't bother him at all. It just sounded good coming from her lips.

"Oni, you already know."

"Good, I'm coming to get you."

"Oh yeah? Where you taking me?"

"To meet my parents."

There was a long pause as he struggled to find the words. He wasn't prepared for this. Even a killer has a moment of fear. No matter how minuscule it seems.

"Don't you think it's a little too soon for me to meet them?" He was worried he wouldn't make a good impression.

"Don't act scared now, Chance," she teased, using his street name.

Chance chuckled, trying to hold back his laughter. No matter what type of mood he's in, she would always draw a smile from him.

"My heart don't pump no fear, ma." But it did. This was their relationship on the line and he would have to muster the best performance of his life to keep her.

"Oh, listen to the tough guy. What, you had a tough batch of milk and cookies?"

They both shared a jovial laugh.

"You's real funny, ma." Chance caught his breath.

"Naw, seriously. You have to come. They invited us to dinner. That would be considered rude if you didn't attend, plus you get to taste my mother's cooking."

"You make it sound like a good thing."

"Well, for them it is. My father believes that if he gets the opportunity to get to know this man sleeping with his daughter, then he can determine if you're right for me before my feelings get involved."

"Don't you think it's a little too late at this point?"

"No...not really, 'cause if my father doesn't approve of this relationship then I'll have to dump you, bruh."

"Ah...it's like that, ma?" His pitch high from laughing so hard.

"Listen, it was fun while it lasted and now it's time to give you the boot." She giggled.

"You make it sound like you're gettin' rid of me now." He couldn't stop laughing.

"That depends. Are you coming or not?"

"Since you put it that way, then yes. I'll be there. What time you gonna be here?"

"I'll be there by four o'clock." They continued to play on the phone. This was what he admired about her the most. Her playful side. Chance adored her for that, because making him smile came easy for her. Oni became the perfect distraction without him even knowing. Chance was so into her that he had completely forgot about Tony...for now. She was able to bring out his softer side. A side that no one in his inner circle had a chance to witness, let alone his crew, which only got his colder side. Only time Chance loosened up was when Tuck was around. Since they only experienced his dark side, it would be hard for them to believe that he was capable of smiling, let alone falling in love. The cold-blooded executioner now soft and cuddly like a teddy bear.

Unacceptable.

CHAPTER 99

Keeping Secrets

Tony entered the room with a tray of bacon and eggs with toast, orange juice and a banana with green grapes. They sat by the fireplace with the big screen television, watching an episode of *Power*. Kim sat across the couch with her feet on Tony. He massaged her feet while she enjoyed her meal. Finally, a man that was doing everything right.

"Tony, can I ask you something?" Kim was in her curious mode and Tony didn't know what angle she was coming from.

"What is it?"

"Do you think about Nick?"

"All the time, he was my peoples. It's messed up how his life took a turn for the worse." Tony couldn't believe he killed three people and took his own life. He seemed more like a family man and wanted the best for them.

"Remember his last day at work?"

"Yeah, he stormed out the building like a bat out of hell." Tony tried stopping him and blamed himself for it. If Nicolas never left work none of this would never have happened.

"Did he ever say anything to you when you came into his office?"

"No...why?"

"Because he was fine when I left and when you came in he suddenly stormed out the building." Her conscience was starting to get the best of her. The day that Nicolas Coles left work and ended up getting locked up for two more murders was the day that she allowed him to fuck her on top of his office desk. Was it her that caused him to lose his mind? Nicolas did try to stop her when she aggressively took the dick.

"He never had a chance to say anything. His phone rang and then he stormed out. It was an emergency phone call. Bill excused him from work. I had never seen him like that before. Then the next thing I know he was locked up for murder. I wish he had talked to me. Maybe I could have done something to prevent it." Tony lied to save her dignity. He knew she gave up the pussy to him that day at work. The scent was in the air when he entered the room. According to the news article, Nicolas Coles thought his wife was cheating on him when he discovered her in their bed with another man. Nicolas ended up murdering the both of them, not knowing she was being raped by the Merchantville rapist. He did save her life only to take it away by his own hand.

Kim sat in deep thought. It was like she was ready to confess her dirty deeds. She shook it off and gazed into his eyes. "You think everything that happened to him was intentional?" She threw out.

"I strongly doubt it. He wasn't like that, but who knows? We only knew him for a short period of time."

CHAPTER 100
Display of Dominance

Oni took Chance to her parents' home in Franklinville, New Jersey. Only twenty minutes from her college campus and forty minutes from Camden. The home was surrounded by a wooded area with wild turkeys and deer parading across the landscapes. Her parents' home was the size of a mini mansion on two acres of land. The exterior was red brick stucco. The roof, double doors and windows were trimmed in black. It had a three-car garage. The interior had five bedrooms and four full bathrooms. The basement was finished with a wet bar and game room. The five-thousand-square-foot home was new from the additional homes that were still being built in that development. Having Oni do all the driving was a major plus. Hopefully, no one would recognize him. With all the females he laid pipe to, he didn't want any of that drama to come to Oni.

Chance felt awkward meeting the parents of the girl he played house with every night for the past three weeks. She was a good girl and he was a thug living a lie. A lie he had no interest in at all. Only interest he had was being with her, but deep down he was changing for the better. For the first time, he decided to leave his crib without bringing his weapon along.

"Raymond, glad to finally meet you. Oni told us so much about you. It's like I practically know you," Oni's father said with a firm handshake. This was the alpha male in him displaying his dominance.

"Thank you, sir, and I appreciate you inviting me to your beautiful home," Chance said, not paying attention to the testosterone levels slowly building by her overly protective and aggressive father.

"Don't pay Jimmy any attention. He's just being extra. Hi, I'm Salina," her mother said, giving him a big hug. "Now come on in and have a seat at the kitchen table. The food is all ready."

Oni's mother was very pleasant and attractive. Beautiful, dark skinned and curvy. This was what Chance was looking for, something he needed to see for himself. The look of Oni's future. If her mother looked this good now meant that Oni would look just as good. Maybe even better. It was all in the genes.

CHAPTER 101
A Feeling Came Over Me

Tony and Kim were really pulling it off. Kim felt like she could tell him anything. They had so much in common and they enjoyed the same foods. Out of everything, pizza was their favorite and they both agreed on that. Going out on dates wasn't a struggle because they both loved to hang out. Dinner and a movie was cool, but going to different movie theaters and restaurants was adventurous.

Tony was putting so much time and effort into the relationship that he started neglecting his business. He bought an old farm, but kept rescheduling with the designer. The building was just sitting there collecting dust. Kim was feeling him now and he didn't want to lose her. This was the perfect time for him to take advantage of the situation. He was determined to keep her as his own, no matter what. Everything else was secondary. Tony would always fantasize about her, hoping and wishing for the day to make her his own. He would even send her roses and chocolates to her office with no name on it. He didn't want Kim to know he was her secret admirer, but then he broke down and admitted he was the one sending her those roses. She was surprised and impressed with the way he went out to put a smile on her face. She never had a clue that it was him. Tony was real smooth about it. He would act just as excited as she was whenever the gifts kept pouring in.

Kim made Tony see things in a different light. He never felt this way about a woman. She kept a smile on his face whenever she was round. He couldn't go a day without hearing her beautiful voice. He even lost interest in other women, including Melody. Their relationship was just physical. There was no need to call and

254

explain anything to her. Kim was his main focus. Yeah, he could do this. This was something that happened once the feeling came over you. A feeling that can't be described. The feeling was strong, like an addiction for something his body constantly craved. Something he couldn't live without. That feeling was called love. A very powerful thing. Something he craved more than the air he breathed. Something he would give his own life for without hesitation. He saw in her eyes that she had the same feeling. This was the perfect time for him to break the big question, but he'd have to do it right.

CHAPTER 102
Overly Protective

"I want to thank you for a well prepared meal," Chance said in his best well-mannered tone.

"Thank you very much. It was nothing." Her mother blushed. She seemed like a very nice person and that was another plus on Chance's mental checklist.

"So, Raymond, what are your goals and ambition?" her father asked, wiping the crumbs from his mouth with a napkin. This was the test of approval. No one was good enough for his daughter and the look in his eyes showed it.

"I'm taking up a class in culinary arts. I plan to be a chef one day and even start a business of my own." It sounded good at first when he introduced it to Oni, but this time it didn't feel so right. Even the words didn't come as natural. He was hoping they didn't catch on to his bullshit. There was an extended pause as everyone's eyes danced around the room. Maybe they did catch on or his standards were too low to be with Oni. Either way, the look in their eyes made him feel uncomfortable.

"So you think cooking would be good enough to support a family?" her father continued, and Chance knew the direction this conversation was heading. Buttering up to him wouldn't be good enough. It was time to make his story sound more believable.

"Cooking would only lay the foundation as I slowly build. Until I get my restaurant," Chance said with meaning. He was impressed at how it sounded so good coming straight from the head. He was now free styling all his answers.

"I'm pretty sure to start a business is costly, even the so-called foundation," her father said. The thick tension was felt in the air.

"Well, I'm not fortunate to have the luxury of buying a business. So with hard work and determination I know I could make it happen." Chance's speech was so convincing that even he believed it, but Oni's father was becoming more defensive as his nose flared up like saucers. He took Chance's words as an attack on him.

"So you think that this family is fortunate enough to do so?"

This caught Chance off guard and made him feel out of place.

"No…I ain't mean it like that," he responded in his defense. He was struggling to maintain his fake character. His respect for her father was dangerously at *fuck it* levels. The thug in him was dying to reveal itself. He knew her father was no match for him one-on-one. Resolving matters was always done through violence and he saw her father starting to power up with rage.

"Then what did you mean by that sarcastic remark?" Her father boomed with fire in his eyes. He leaned forward as if he was ready to pounce on Chance, but Chance held his composure.

"Daddy…what are you doing? He's a guest…Mom?" Oni cried out in protest.

"Jimmy, knock it off this instance," her mother voiced.

Jimmy sat back, still keeping a hard gaze on Chance.

Chance was unaware that he was giving him the same hard stare until he felt the stiff elbow from Oni in his ribs. He quickly softened up his hard stare in silence. The way her mother shut him down displayed a strong woman in his presence. After a performance like that, it was time for them to leave. Oni's mother walked them to the door, while her father marched upstairs. Hopefully, she put him on timeout for his childish behavior.

"He could be a little difficult at times, but what do you expect when it comes to his little angel?" Her mother explained.

"Mom, I'm not a little girl," Oni uttered.

"I know, dear. It's going to take a while before your father realizes that."

CHAPTER 103
Lost Words

Tony took Kim to Las Vegas and stayed at the MGM Grand. The hotel had the valet to park the car and carry their luggage. Tony got the Skyline Terrace Suite with a balcony overlooking the city. He took Kim to the Stratosphere for dinner. The restaurant was over one hundred stories high. From this height, the ground looked like a map. They were too high to see the details of what was on the surface plain. The food was great and the atmosphere was perfect. The waiter's presentation of what the place had to offer made it hard for them to choose their meal. They still ended up enjoying what they ordered and the waiter was so helpful that Tony gave him a big tip. Afterwards, they left the restaurant to see Kevin Hart, who was her favorite comedian, live on stage at the Las Vegas Strip. Kim couldn't stop laughing at all his jokes. She enjoyed Kevin Hart because he always had her in stitches from laughing so hard. Suddenly the spotlight beamed on them, catching Kim by surprise. Kevin Hart made jokes about them being all lovey-dovey then his mood changed to serious.

"You two look very happy. What is your name, sir?" Kevin asked Tony.

"Tony."

"Tony…and ma'am, what is your name?"

"Kim."

"Kim, I just want to say that you look very lovely tonight. Tony must be the luckiest guy on the planet. You know he loves you, right?" Kim responded with a head nod.

Kevin Hart was talking as if they were close friends. He never questioned their relationship. It was as if he knew already. "Speak up. You look stupid. Rocking your head like that." Kevin started mocking her by rocking his head back and forth. It was funny how he overly exaggerated it. "What, you rode the yellow bus with a helmet, licking the glass?" He continued with more jokes as the crowd busted out laughing.

"All right…all right. Everybody calm the fuck down. You're destroying the moment here." Kevin paused, taking one big deep breath as if he was preparing an important speech. He exhaled, blowing hard into the mic. "I never did no shit like this before, so here it go. Now, Kim…Tony wanted me to ask you will you marry him," he threw out, catching her off guard.

Kim's mouth dropped open. She looked over at Tony with her face stuck. Tony was on one knee holding a small black box in his hand. When he opened it, there was a fourteen-karat engagement ring. Her eyes nearly popped out her head. Kim was in shock, now put on the spot. She never had a man purpose to her and with such a big audience made it even harder to speak. She couldn't move her jawbone to respond or to close her mouth.

"Now you looking stupid again. I told y'all she rode the yellow bus." The crowd laughed, still in anticipation for her answer. Kevin was now standing over her with his mic in her face. "Now this is getting ridiculous. Kim say something. Breathe, at least," he joked.

"Yes…yes," she said in a low whisper.

"What was that? He didn't hear you," Kevin Hart continued to press.

"Yes, I will," she yelled with excitement, as the crowd cheered. Kim was overjoyed. To get someone like Kevin Hart had to be very expensive.

CHAPTER 104

A Chilling Event

"Now you see what I was talking about," Oni said as she drove with Chance reclined in the passenger's seat. "Well, that explains how I was able to get in those panties so easily," Chance teased with a sly grin.

Oni shoved him with an elbow. "Whateva." They shared a hearty laugh together while crossing Camden's border. The gloomy conditions was enough to deflate the happy moment, as the peaceful ride seemed more like a memory. Camden gave off an eerie silence as they sat there like spectators at an opera. Chance reached over and turned the volume up a little on the radio to kill the silence. The streets were a reminder of who he was and where he came from. Deep down, he no longer wanted to live this way. He was starting to see himself spending the rest of his life with Oni. He even thought about having children and a house with a white picket fence. As geeky as it may sound, this was something he strongly looked forward to having. His moment in the dream state was interrupted when a black SUV with tinted glass cut in front of them illegally with bass pumping through its speakers. Oni quickly blew her horn while slamming on the brakes. A middle finger stuck out the window of the SUV.

"Can you believe these idiots?" Oni yelled out as Chance beamed in silence. Oni was so frustrated, she continued to blow the horn at the SUV that refused to move while staying idol at the green light.

Then the music stopped as the SUV was thrown in park. They could tell by the way the SUV jerked and the white reverse light flashed. Suddenly, all the doors swung open. Four goons with their guns drawn surrounded the car. Chance reached for his banger and realized he wasn't packing. They were sitting ducks, waiting to be plucked. The goon on the driver side tapped on the glass. Oni was too afraid to look at him, but she saw the goon motioning for her to wind her window down. Oni looked at Chance, who could do nothing but sit there. This was his girl with fear in her eyes, pleading for help. Chance was overcome with anger seeing this and hopped out the passenger seat in a rage. He knew these goons were only trying to scare them or they would have sprayed the car up before he exited it.

All guns were now aimed at him. He gave all the gunmen a cold stare. It was cold enough to send chills through Oni. She never seen that look before. He was now playing with death and she wasn't sure if it was the look that gave her the chill or the fact that he was willing to die with no fear. It was the look of a cold-blooded killer. Without saying a word, all four gunmen tucked their weapons away and got back into the SUV. Oni thought she had gone deaf for a moment until she heard the slamming of doors and the tires of the SUV peel off with a loud squeal and white smoke. It was like they communicated by means of mental telepathy, because there was an understanding. The look that Chance gave them seemed to put fear in the four goons that were holding guns. Four of the toughest looking men that she had ever laid eyes on, but one weaponless man was able to put a stop to what looked like either a robbery or an execution with just a look.

"What was that all about?" Oni asked, as Chance got into the car.

"Nothing…just some wannabe thugs tryna make a name for themselves, that's all." Chance watched the SUV disappear into the distance.

"No, I'm not talking about them. I'm talking about you, Raymond. Those guys looked at you with fear and respect. What are you, some kind of boss or killer? I know when I asked if you were a king pin you said no, but you're something close to that nature. I don't know what it is, but I do know that you're hiding something from me and I don't like it."

Chance reached over and grabbed her hand. "Ma...relax. You're making this bigger than what it is."

"Raymond, you're a nice guy and all, but I'm really not feeling this picture."

CHAPTER 105
The Cold Flush

Mark and Dave were at Cooper Hospital, patiently waiting for Tony. The days were very stressful for him. His sensitivity levels were on tilt. They both had to select their words and be very cautious with his emotions. Tony's father was in a coma on life support with second and third degree burns on sixty percent of his body. If he were to pull through he would have to go through extensive surgery, dealing with skin grafts that may take several years before completion and even with that he wouldn't be at one hundred percent. His major concern was for his father to pull through. He had lost his one and only brother and wasn't prepared to lose two loved ones in a single year. Hopefully, he would be able to give a name and description of the person who did this to him, so he could personally deal with it himself.

"Damn, Dave, you were in there blowin' that shit up, Iraqi style. I was 'bout to send the medical staff in there to make sure you was a'ight," Mark teased, after Dave sat beside him.

"Bathroom got that automatic flush. Shit was annoyin'. I musta fell asleep," Dave explained, with along sigh.

"You musta did somethin', as long as it took," Mark continued to crack.

"But the fucked up part is that I had this crazy ass dream I was fucking the shit out this snow bunny. She was big and so was her pussy, but her pussy felt tight as shit. That shit was feeling so good that I bust a nut. This bitch got so wet that somehow my ass got wet."

"Man…I don't think I need to be hearing the rest of this story." Mark shook his head.

"But wait a minute. It gets better. Let me finish."

"A'ight, go head," Mark huffed as if he was going to regret letting Dave continued.

"Well, the shit was cold as hell. It was so cold that it woke me the fuck up. When I looked down, the toilet was overflowin' because the automatic flush wouldn't stop flushin'. I tried to jump up, but I couldn't. Come to find out, my dick was stuck in the hole. With it constantly flusin' made it feel like a wet pussy. Can you believe that shit? I might have to take me another bathroom break to get another feel of that white porcelain.

"Man…fuck outta here with that bullshit. You always talkin' stupid," Mark barked as Dave continued to tell more funny stories with a serious expression on his face.

CHAPTER 106

The Boom Dot Com

The next morning, Chance was awakened by loud movement. He looked up to see Oni gathering her things. She was now fully dressed and looking beautiful as ever with her deep hazel eyes. It took Chance a moment to soak in his new surroundings. It was weird to wake up in an unfamiliar place, but he was willing to get adjusted to it.

"Hey, ma. What'cha doin'?" His voice cracked.

"I have an early morning class and I'm free after that. I should be back within an hour or so. Make sure you're up and ready when I get back."

"No prob," he said as she gave him a kiss before heading out.

It took Chance a few minutes to gather himself. Oni left a brand new toothbrush and the password to her computer. *She is all right after all,* he thought. He got on the computer to play Mr. Detective, but there was nothing on there to cause him worry. Ever since that incident with Erika, her two girlfriends, and those four goons waving a gun, looking for trouble, Oni seemed intimidated by Chance's actions. If he raised his voice or seemed upset, fear would cause Oni to be silent and stiffen up. Seeing this reaction was starting to bother Chance. His feeling for Oni was deep. She was definitely worth keeping.

Chance was really feeling good about himself. After a few minutes of horsing around, he freshened up. Once in the shower, he took a long hot one to let the water massage his muscles. He ran the water on his face to wash away the suds as someone entered the shower. He felt warm breasts pressed up against his back and soft gentle hands on his dick.

"Oni, is that you ma?" He said, as his dick suddenly got hard. He tried to open his eyes, but the burning sensation from the soapsuds prevented that.

"Um hum." She put a blindfold over his eyes before he could dry them off. *There's no need to worry. The door is locked and Oni is the only one with a key to the room,* he thought as he played along. Oni was full of surprises.

"Oh, you want to play a new game? Okay, I'm wit' it."

She spun him around with his back pressed against the wall. She dropped to her knees and started giving him the best head of his life. She was going deep with no gag reflexes. Chance was trying to hold on to something. Her lips were driving him crazy. She was sucking his balls through his dick, forcing out the cum. She placed his hands on the back of her head, forcing him to go rough. He didn't want to do it, but it was feeling so good he lost himself. She was sucking like a pro. He was ramming his dick all down her throat and she moaned in pleasure. She was taking that dick like a champion. He was pumping his dick as she took two hands and clutched it like an Italian hoagie. Chance couldn't fight it and just let himself go as his dick exploded down her throat. She never let up and slurped it up like it was a strawberry milk shake and kept sucking. Chance never knew Oni had it in her like this. She sucked his shit like she was in a dick sucking competition, fighting for the crown. For a girl with this much skill she put on a good front, but for now he was willing to enjoy the moment. No need in fucking up a good nut. He felt the excitement rising in his loans as she sucked and kissed on his head. It was too much for him to handle. Her soft lips was causing him to bust another nut between those soft lips. This girl had mad skills and a mean suck game. *Is this why she was holding back on me?* This much skill came from sucking a whole lot of dicks. Oni wasn't as innocent as she led Chance to believe.

He removed the blindfold only to see Keisha on her knees, looking up at him with his dick still in her mouth. Her eyes were smiling up at him. Chance wanted to push her off. He was angered that she played him, but excited she was sucking him off with the best blowjob he ever had. He lift her from bended knee and raised her legs in the air as he stuck is dick in her and fucked her hard for the hoe she was. Even though he was pissed off that she played him, beating the pussy up felt like the logical choice of punishment. Keisha smiled and encouraged him to nut inside her.

"This pussy is the bomb dot com," she whispered, as Chance was lost in the pleasure zone. This bitch was bad and her body was tight. Hoe or not, he was going to fuck this bitch until he got tired of the pussy and today wouldn't be that day. They took it in her bedroom and she let him beat that pussy up until his heart was content. Chance was stroking it like a wild man. The pussy made him feel like he had just got out of prison from doing a ten-year bid. Chance pulled out his dick and came all over her face. She smiled as his hard dick kept spitting in her face with aggression. She smeared it off with her fingers and ate it.

"Damn, you's a nasty bitch," he breathed with pleasure.

"Yeah, if you weren't so drunk that night you would have remembered this pussy."

That's when Chance realized why he couldn't remember her. He was right when he blamed it on the alcohol and weed; he was fucked up that night. He knew he wanted to come back for more. Her sex game was all that. So they exchanged phone numbers and he went back into the room to wait for Oni after taking another hot shower.

CHAPTER 107
Competitive Egos

Tony was in the mood for pretzels and water ice, so he headed over to South Jersey Water Ice in Somerdale. He was sitting in his ride, enjoying his mango-flavored water ice when his cell phone rang. Dave's name appeared on the screen.

"Hello." He answered with food still in his mouth.

"Yo, what up, Tone? Let me tell you 'bout this big black Herman the Monster lookin' muhfucka right here. I didn't catch you at the wrong time, did I?"

"Naw, go ahead. I'm listenin'." Tony knew this would be very entertaining by the tone of Dave's voice. With his father's condition stressing him out, this would make for the perfect distraction.

"Yo, we were on our way back from the Purple Parrot in Cherry Hill when this nice lookin' dime piece was broke down on the side of the road. She had the hood open with smoke comin' out. We pulled over to help, but was really tryna check her out. Not only was her body tight, but she was pretty as hell and we both were fightin' to hook up wit' the bitch. Come to find out, she had her grandma in the car chillin'. I got her out in case the car caught fire. I was workin' my magic on the grandma for her approval. Then super-save-a-hoe here ended up givin' the bitch his whip and told the bitch that he was gonna take care of the car. This fool is gon' pay to get her shit fixed while she still cruisin' in his whip. I told the nigga that she gon' take his shit, after dropping the grandma off, to a chop shop and have her cousins strip it down to the framework. He put a lot of bread on tryna customize his shit like yours. This fool is stupid. I can't believe him."

"Hold up, Dave. I thought you were into ugly bitches."

"I am, but Tone, you gots to see this bitch. She was bad enough to make me change my mind."

"Where y'all at now?"

"At the shop. He's talkin' to the mechanic now. A cab's supposed to take us to my ride as soon as it gets here."

"But, Dave, that was a strong power move on his part," Tony tried to explain.

"Yeah, I'll give him that, but if the nigga don't smash that, I'm gon' clown the shit outta his ass, fo' real."

"Damn, Dave, I sense a little animosity there."

"Nah, it's all-good 'til Rolisha finds out. I want to be there when it all goes down. Hopefully, a fight breaks out and I get to see some ass and tits."

"You sound like a pervert."

"I never said I wasn't." They both shared a laugh.

"I hope you still got his back when Rolisha tries to do some dumb shit."

"Don't worry 'bout that. I always got my dawg's back, but he be talkin' that, he ain't worried 'bout that shit. She ain't gon' do shit anyway, 'cause she's in unfamiliar territory. I told that fool that this ain't Vietnam, but when Rolisha finds out 'bout this sexy ass bitch, he's gon' think its Vietnam."

Dave continued to give Tony an earful as he laughed and tried to calm him down. Dave was hot and Tony never saw him this worked up over a female. He must have really been feeling this woman. Tony was only hoping that it didn't cost them their friendship, with both of them fighting over one girl.

CHAPTER 108

Lies and Deceit

After the scaring of Erika and those four thugs, their relationship became questionable. Oni had love for Chance, but was afraid that he would hurt her. Not just physically, but emotionally as well. Chance could tell by the way she reacted toward him. Her fear of him was quite evident. One thing about Oni that Chance admired about her was that after she questioned him about anything and he gave her an answer she wouldn't nag or hulk him about it. Chance never felt any pressure behind being with her. This only made him fall even deeper for her. Something that he never felt before.

While Oni left for her morning classes, Chance would sneak into the next room and fuck Keisha until Oni returned from her classes. The sex with Keisha was good, but the betrayal to Oni was eating at his conscience. This went on for weeks and Chance wasn't tired of the pussy yet. Keisha was right, she had that good pussy and Chance was enjoying every opportunity he had to get some. The fact of easy access to get it whenever he wanted it was starting to get boring. Unlike Keisha, he was starting to get tired of their little sex escapades and wanted to come clean with Oni. Their whole relationship was built on lies and deceit. Him being dishonest with her made him feel worse than a disloyal soldier. It started to hurt him more and more each day to look into her innocent eyes and fill them with more lies.

Oni was the one he wanted. He wanted to spend the rest of his life with her. This feeling now made him want no other. There's no telling how long this feeling would last. For all he knew, it could have been a phase in his life and down the line he may go back to his old ways. Who knows, this feeling he had could be real. Only time would tell. All Chance knew was that this was how he felt right now at this moment and didn't want to lose or hurt Oni behind his selfish deeds.

Today would be the day that he would lay all his cards on the table and come clean with Oni. Chance was ready to open up and reveal all his dirty laundry and hope that Oni would find it in her heart to forgive him and make this relationship work. If this doesn't work and she decided to leave him, he'd be crushed and there's no telling how long it would take for him to get back on his feet. It was time for him to man up and do the right thing. If anyone could help him be a better person and walk a straight path to a more productive lifestyle, that person would be Oni. He had to make a stand in order to move forward, but there was one more thing he had to get rid of in order to make this relationship work and it was on the other side of her bathroom door.

CHAPTER 109

The Very First Time

Tony was at the Purple Parrot with Dave and Mark. They were having conversations about them losing their virginity.

"Yeah, I was fourteen years old when my best friend's sister gave it up to me. She was sixteen years old. I thought I was in heaven," Mark said.

"I was fifteen when I lost mine to my math teacher. I was in love, but couldn't tell anyone because she would have gotten in trouble. I eventually got over her when I got to high school. That's when I started getting pussy by the pound," Tony bragged, as they shared a laugh.

Then Dave jumped in, ready to tell his story like an elementary school kid during show and tell. "I remember Ms. Jackie. She was the baddest chick in the hood. Everybody wanted that ass. Then one day a guy that was hustling on my block told me that she got hooked on crack and was trickin'. I didn't believe him until he called her on the phone to come over so I can get some. Guess what this bitch said?" He asked them.

"What did she say?" Tony and Mark said simultaneously.

"This bitch said that her pussy was sore and she couldn't do anythin' right now."

"Damn, she was gettin' a lot of dick," Mark uttered.

"Hell yeah, she was. I'm telling you the whole neighborhood was hittin' that, but I didn't give up. I was determined to lose my virginity one way or another. Then my birthday came and I was now seventeen years old and still didn't get any pussy yet. The boys from around the way decided to hook me up. It was killin' 'em, seeing me walk around full of cum. So they rented a motel room up in Brooklyn and told me to go inside 'cause there was some pussy waitin' for me. I didn't care who it was as long as I finally got a chance to see what the shit felt like. When I entered the room, guess who was butt-ass naked on the bed?"

"Don't tell me, your sister, right?" Tony teased, as Mark sat there like he was in the movie theater watching a motion picture.

"My sister! Naw, man. Stop talkin' crazy. You're ruinin' the story."

"Then stop bullshittin' and finish tellin' us already. You're startin' to put me to sleep here," Tony said in his New York accent.

"All right…all right. It was Ms. Jackie, still lookin' sexy as hell, too. She was all like, 'Hey there, big daddy, I heard you wanted me to be your first.' I nodded my head. I ain't gon' lie, man, I was shook. Then she told me to come over and get in bed with her. I took my clothes off quick and jumped in, dick hard as a rock. She got me on top of her and put my shit in that pussy. I was so excited I thought I was gonna bust right then and there. I wanted that pussy so bad for so long that I didn't care about protection. I just ran up in that shit raw-dog. I started humpin', but the shit was rough as hell like sand paper. She asked me what was wrong and I told her that it hurt. If pussy felt like that I would have kept my virginity and never fucked again. She then told me to hold on and ran into the bathroom. I was waitin' for a while, hopin' that my shit stayed hard. There was this big ass cockroach crawling across the ceiling. The shit was disgusting, but I managed to keep my shit up. She finally got out the bathroom and jumped back in bed. I let her put my dick in her pussy and that shit was wet as hell. I was so excited that it started to make that clappin' sound. I knew right then I was gon' bust, but she stopped me and told me to eat her pussy. I never ate pussy and didn't know what I was doin', but she was lovin' it. I know she came because the shit kept squirtin'. It was nasty and the pussy was smellin' like a dead cat, but I didn't give a fuck. I thought that was why they called it pussy. This was my dream come true and I was gonna make the best of it. I was beatin' the pussy up and every time I was about to cum, she would stop me and make me eat that stinkin' pussy. Then all of a sudden I bust all up in that pussy. I didn't know what was goin' on until it hit me. I got real dizzy and my body got weak. I fell out and the room kept spinnin'. That's when reality hit me. I knew that this was the way to make babies and then I started to get scared. She must have seen it written all over my face. She tells me not to worry. She can't get pregnant. I was so relieved to hear that. Then I asked her how she got her pussy so wet when it was rough at first and if all pussy felt like that. She said no. Pussy don't feel like that. Then she ask me if I remember the time I had that guy call her to come down and break me off. I told her yeah I remember. 'You said that your shit was too sore.' She was like 'Yeah, from everyone comin' at her at once.' Then she was like, 'Well when you tried to hit it and it was dry, makin' your dick sore, I went into the bathroom and pilled the scab that was formed to let the puss leak.' I jumped up and looked in the mirror and there was green shit and tiny maggots crawling around my lips and stuck up in my teeth."

Tony's face was locked with a discussed look. Mark dry heaved, trying to keep his food down.

"Man…that was the nastiest shit I ever heard," Tony said, with a stunned look.

"That shit ain't true, he's lyin'. He never told me that story and we grew up together," Mark said, still dry heaving.

"Well, that ruined my appetite for the rest of the day," Tony replied.

Dave tried to hold on as long as he could until he burst into laughter.

CHAPTER 110

There's a Scam Going On

O ni entered her morning class filled with students of all colors and different races. The professor was up front at the large, green chalkboard giving one of his boring speeches. He was an older, foreign looking man. He could have been Chinese or Japanese; it was hard to tell. He spoke very well as if he was born and raised in the United States. He was thin build with salt and pepper hair. It was hard to make out his age because he had no wrinkles. He was somewhat attractive, but nothing like her boo, Raymond. The stuff the professor was talking about could have been done back at her dorm, online. With Chance being there she knew that she wouldn't get anything done. This felt more like a waste of time, but Oni decided to stay in case she missed something. Oni was eager and willing to do well in school. Not just for her parents, but for herself as well. If she didn't do well, she would get an earful from her parents. This wasn't for them, it was for her and she knew it.

Oni wanted to have a good future and starting young would be the best thing for her. She never thought of settling down and having a family like a normal girl would. She wanted to be something and do something that would make a difference in everyday life. Being a superhero was more for dreamers; it was unreal. She chose to be a doctor and in modern times that was considered a hero. A doctor does save lives. Oni was so lost in her daydreaming that she completely lost track of what the boring professor was talking about. At this point, she would have to go online to catchup.

Suddenly, she was overwhelmed with curiosity. The temptation was too hard to resist. She then reached for her iPhone and started searching for TLF Culinary Arts online, but nothing came up. Chance said that it was a cooking course online and she was interested in seeing what it was all about. Oni tried other search engines and went down a list of all culinary art schools in Philadelphia, but nothing came up. She also tried searching for all culinary art schools in the United States and there were none with the name TLF. Oni continued to search other countries that may have it and still no results. Either Chance was lying or they took the class off the web. Oni took it as far as believing it could have been a scam website that took Chance's money. There are companies out there that do that. Oni loved to watch *American Greed*. It was her favorite television series. It talked about all the different companies that scammed people of their life savings. Oni had to make sure that they were not trying to get over on her man as she tried to find a way to sneak out of class undetected to warn Chance.

CHAPTER 111
Making a Choice

The next morning, Chance was awakened by a knocking sound. He opened his eyes and got out of bed. He opened the door and no one was there. He was in Oni's room looking down the hallway of her dorm. It was silent with no movement. He was thinking that he was hearing things and climbed back in bed. Then he heard the knock again and noticed that it was coming from the bathroom door. He went over to open the door and there was Keisha standing there in her robe.

"Yo, what up?" Chance quickly perked up.

"Oni just left. You can come to my spot." She opened her robe to reveal her nudeness.

Chance shook his head in frustration. "Look, Keisha, it's over. I'm done."

Keisha closed her robe and gave him a hard stare. "What, you in love now? Nigga, you can't just cut it off after I let you hit this. You think you gon' just treat me like a hoe and then play house with my girl, Oni? Naw, fuck that."

Chance gripped her by the neck. "Bitch, you better watch yo fuckin' mouth, unless you ready to be added to my body count." He shoved her backwards and slammed the bathroom door in her face. Keisha started kicking and banging on the door with verbal threats. Chance knew that cutting it off with her feeling some type of way about him wouldn't be a good move on his part. This was why he hated dealing with ratchet bitches from the projects. He had to shut her ass up and find another way to end it. Her loud mouth was starting to draw unwanted attention and this was not needed. Chance swung the door open and dragged her into her bedroom.

"Is this what you want, bitch?" he roared, slamming Keisha on her own bed.

"Yeah, give it to me," she said, letting him have his way with her.

Chance was giving her hard dick and she was taking everything he gave her. She was a nymphomaniac and he was the only drug for her addiction. After he bust his nut, he knew it wouldn't be easy to get rid of her. Killing her would be simple, but that would only bring heat to his doorstep and right now he was trying to stay under the radar until Tuck got back.

"I'm sorry, Chance, for yelling at you. I don't know what I'll do if you leave me," she confessed, covering her nudeness with her bed sheets.

"You make it sound like it's a relationship. You just a fuck and that's it. Nothing more," he said, slipping on his underwear.

"Don't say it like that. It can be more than that. You know my fuck game is better than Oni's."

So this was her plan all along. Not only was she crazy for the dick, she was catching feelings.

"But she's wifey material. You's a campus hoe and I can't make you no housewife."

Keisha was nothing more than a love-struck fan of a killer. Chance was hood famous and Keisha thought that her sex game would make him leave Oni, so she could be his main bitch.

"That so-called relationship you got is a lie. She doesn't even know that you're a captain in the drug game. She heard of Cat Daddy and how big he is from us having girl talk at night, but she really doesn't know what goes down. If she did, you know she'll run for the hills and never look back."

"You just stay in your lane. I'll tell her when the time is right," he ordered, but deep down there was no right time. Kiesha was right, telling Oni would only chase her away.

"And then what? Y'all live happily ever after? The shit don't work like that. Oni ain't built for that lifestyle."

"Look, I'm done talkin' 'bout this. You just stay out of our business unless you want me to add your stinkin' ass to my hit list," he threatened her again. Keisha's eyes widened. She knew too well of his murder game and didn't want any part of it. The first time he threatened her with it, she was too upset to pay it any mind. She just wanted him to see her as being more than just a fuck, but her reputation on campus stained her credibility of being someone's girl.

Chance left the room to wash her scent off his skin. When he entered the bathroom, he noticed Oni sitting on the bed with her head down. Her face was covered in tears.

CHAPTER 112
A Deaf Ear

Chance entered the room as Oni's protector. A natural reaction of a man. "Baby, what's the matter," he said, leaning into her.

Oni looked up at him with a cold stare. Her red piercing eyes were strong enough to be felt. It was quite obvious that she was angry at him and he knew he was busted. He was hoping she only knew little. That would make it easier for him to work his way back into her heart.

"How long have you been fucking her?"

Chance was hoping she didn't smell her scent on his body. Not being able to wash it off, he was now sporting it like cologne.

"What are you takin' 'bout?" He frowned to add more affect to his lies.

"Don't play with me, Raymond, I've seen and heard everything. You've been lying to me all this time." Her words were unwavering.

Chance opened his mouth to speak. He had to say something, because he was losing her fast. Someone must have pushed the mute button on his vocal cords. He just couldn't get anything to come out.

"How could you, Raymond? How could you fuck Keisha, of all people? After what I told you about her?" Her tone was laced with pain and grief. She used the word fuck twice. This was his first time hearing her use curse words. Oh yeah, she was definitely pissed off at him.

Chance sat there silently. He didn't know what to say.

"So all this time I've been dating a big drug dealer who's ranked as a captain, slash killer, and who knows what else you do out there on those streets. Having a high rank as a captain means that you have been doing this for quite a while now. That's not the characteristics I've been looking for in a man. I can't follow you in that path of destruction. There's no future in that. Plus, you're a dirty, low-down dog. Fucking Keisha only shows that you're nasty and unfaithful. I don't have time for feeble, one-track-minded, little boys."

"But, Oni, give me a chance to explain."

"Explain what? How you lied to me about making that cheese ravioli and had me believing that you wanted to be a chef. Or how it wasn't you fucking the shit out my friend for God knows how long. It doesn't matter, because your mind state is programed to lie to get ahead in life. Fast money, fast women is all you know in the game you play. The game you call life and I don't want to be involved. Now I have to get tested and hope to God I didn't contract any STDs behind this stupid act."

"But, Oni, baby—"

"No…don't 'Oni, baby' me. Just get your shit and get out. I'm going to ask you this one time or it's going to get really ugly up in here. I knew I should have listened to my father, he was right. Experience is the best teacher and you taught me a well…so get the fuck out of my room." She swung the door open as Chance walked out without saying another word. He saw the seriousness in her eyes and knew she was at her breaking point. "And don't think about calling me either. I'm changing my number. I can't afford to let you ruin my future." She slammed the door in his face.

CHAPTER 113
Newfound Interest

When Chance got to the meeting it was the same old same old. Pitch crying about Fatima's death and how no one found out who did it. And for the very first time, Crystal was no longer a distraction. All he kept thinking about was Oni. The meeting was nothing more than just hot air. He just couldn't stop thinking about her. Chance was no longer interested in the hustle game. He didn't want to dog out women either. The thrill of the hunt was played out. Now he wanted a relationship and all he dreamed about was Oni. She took away his hard exterior and kept a smile on his face. She was the one. The one to take him away from all this and show him what the real world looked like. The problem was how he was going to explain to her the truth about him being a captain of a drug cartel and lying about being a chef. That shouldn't be too hard since she heard the conversation with him and Keisha in the other room. The biggest problem was getting her to forgive him for cheating on her with Keisha. He was hoping she would understand it was all physical and not emotional. She was an easy fuck. What did she expect from a campus hoe? Chance was trying to create a good story that was persuading enough for her to take him back. She pushed up on him in those sleazy ass shorts the first time he came to visit, so was it really his fault? What he did was something any man would do. Men were hunters and women were the prey. This was his way of flexing his dominants.

After the meeting, Chance forgot what Pitch was wolfing about. He spent the entire time at the meeting day dreaming about Oni. This lifestyle of criminal activity was played out. There was more to life than spending it living underground like a Teenage Mutant Ninja Turtle, breaking the law and hiding from cops. Oni had possessed his mind and polluted his thoughts. Chance was now looking at his life outside the box. From what he saw, this was not what he wanted in life. This life only brought sorrow and misery. Only retirement plan that came with this lifestyle was six feet under in a pine box or prolonged prison time and that's guaranteed. There was no future in this illegal drug business. An illegal business like this is only short lived.

He had now seen the light, thanks to Oni. Deep down, he knew he would have to answer for the trail of bodies that was laid to rest by his own hand. If he were to die today he would surely burn rotisserie style. An army of his victims would be waiting to greet him with closed fists to unleash an eternity of ass whippings. They lived that same grimy lifestyle as he did. They just got caught slipping and Chance beat them to the punch.

If he changed his life around and asked God for his forgiveness, then maybe he could spend eternity in heaven with the righteous. Chance was so serious about changing his life around. He wanted his girl back and thought that if he laid his cards on the table, she would find it in her heart to forgive him and take him back. He was ready to ask Oni for her hand in marriage, but not right now. There was one more thing he had to take care of first and that was getting her back.

Pitch, on the other hand, took his actions the wrong way. There were no prolonged gazing at Crystal during the meetings and Chance stopped making comments of how bad he wanted to hit that ass. Pitch's whole thinking of this new mood swing that Chance was going through only meant one thing...he fucked her.

CHAPTER 114
Addicted Love

Seeing the hurt in Oni's eyes after finding out that he was cheating on her with Keisha really bothered Chance. He enjoyed the moments they spent together. Her being out of the picture caused him to go through a state of depression. He became distant to everyone around him. His demeanor was cold and he kept his sentences short and to the point. Everyone around him noticed the change in his attitude and couldn't put it together, so they gave him space. This sudden change was unexpected. Chance was a cold hard killer and there was no need in provoking him. That's when Chance realized he was going through something. Something that he had never felt before and that something was separation anxiety. He was withdrawing, but without the shakes. Women were always chancing after him. To have Oni cut him off was different. He was now doing the chasing.

There was no need in bullshitting around. He needed to make moves and get shit done in order to get her back into his life.

Chance tried hard to get her back. With flowers and gifts. He kept sliding letters under her door. It was starting to look like he was borderline stalker material. He wrote her letters, telling her that he had no interest in the drug game, but he lied again. Quitting the game isn't that easy, unless he didn't like living. Chance had the Young Hitters making all the moves while he took up classes to become a real chef. This time he was for real and ready to change his life around. Tuck was still in the Dominican Republic with Chaos. There was no way of reaching out to him. Tuck sent short text messages to let Chance know that he was okay, but there was no verbal communication. Tuck didn't want to take any risks. It was all up to Chance to handle the business until he got back. This was a prolonged business trip, a test of his loyalty to Jose Fernandez. Tuck would be back once he passes the test and that no one knows. This was all Jose Fernandez's rules of becoming part of the family. Tuck would work for him while building his trust. There was no crossing Jose Fernandez once Tuck returned, because he would have full control of his life. Tuck failed to realize that he had just sold his soul to the devil himself. This deal could never be broken. Tuck would come back to the United States more powerful than Polo the Don and Pitch combined, but the longer Tuck stayed away, trying to build a new family, the more Chance was losing his interest in the drug game and wanted to be with Oni, living the American dream.

Pimping females was no longer in Chance's blood. He wanted Oni and was willing to do anything to get her back. That's when he went into his closet and grabbed his Michael Jordan shoebox. He opened it up and pulled out the wrinkled letter that Oni wrote to him.

CHAPTER 115

Liquid Pain

Chance entered his mother's home to check up on her. She hadn't called nor answered any of his text messages. That alone was a clear sign that she wasn't taking her medication. She was avoiding his long scowling speeches of why she should take her medication. Chance was always available for his mother and there was a reason for this. She never showed him any love growing up and this was done to make him hard. This was the only way she knew how to make him a man. He showed her all the love he could give and his heart wouldn't rest without her showing him the love that he lacked. The love he desired before she departed this world without doing so. Upon entering the home, he noticed Oni sitting on the couch. His mother's baked cookies and a glass of milk was on the center table in front of her. There were only two cookies left. One was bitten into and the glass of milk was empty. That meant that she was there for a while, but he knew she didn't come over to enjoy her baking skills.

"Hey, whatchu doin' here?" His voice cracked. Chance struggled with his words. He was nervous and excited at the same time. It felt good to see her after many attempts at trying to do so. She was looking so beautiful. He saw the excitement in her eyes as well. Even though she still maintained a blank expression.

"I missed you. I tried so hard to stay away from you and ignored all your advancements, but I'm not built like that and needed someone to talk to. So I came here instead. My parents wouldn't have been a good choice," she confessed with honesty as she kept her gaze away from him in shame. That only seemed to soften his hard heart.

A slight grin grew to one side of his face. "You're not built like that. What, now you talkin' street lingo?" He teased, but was still a little nervous. Oni being at his mother's house was not a good thing. There's no telling what his mother was telling her. She wasn't loving or affectionate like a normal mother would be, but there was that strong sense of obligation he had to make sure she was okay. Maybe it was guilt from all the women he dogged out and mistreated, but no, it was bigger than that. He was simply doing his best to receive the love and affection she held back from him.

"I've been with you so long I must have picked it up from you." She still refused to give him eye contact.

Chance motioned toward her. He missed her so much and all he could think about was scooping her in his arms and holding her tight. He never felt this way about anyone. Killing was what he knew best and this feeling was more alien to him, but it felt so good and so right. This was something he yearned for. Something he strived for and always needed to make him whole. Something he never received from his mother, which made it so easy to grow into a cold-blooded killer. His advancement toward her was halted by his mother's voice.

"Raymond, what you do to this poor little girl here?" She argued, upon entering the room.

Oni was now gazing into his eyes like a curious kid waiting for his response.

"Mom, why you ain't answer my calls? I've been—"

"Don't fuckin' slick talk me," she yelled, slapping him across the face.

Chance never flinched and kept his regular expression as if it didn't happen or he was used to this type of treatment.

Oni's opened mouth and wide eyes let him know that she witnessed it. His mother seemed to smack the taste out of his mouth as he stood there silently, letting his anger simmer.

"I told you about dogging these females out and look at what you do. You go find an innocent girl that's trying to do something with her life and you try to destroy that, too. You are jus' like your father," she scowled, standing in his face as if she was ready to take him on toe-to-toe. Chance was a killer; he would take a joker out for just looking at him the wrong way. His mother putting her hands on him was something unheard of, but hey, it was his mother and she automatically got a free pass.

"Mom, I've been making it a daily ritual to let her know how sorry I am. Let me try to work this one out. I love her and don't want to lose her," Chance said, with hot tears forming in his eyes. Chance never cried and he opening up was something new.

"Then work it out." She walked away into the next room. Seeing her son opening up like this was starting to affect her emotionally. She tried to stay hard as long as she could. Being affectionate was something she wouldn't do. She believed that would make him soft. So instead of holding him and letting him know that everything was going to be all right, she walked away to let him deal with his sensitive side by himself.

Being hard for so long he didn't know how to stop his emotions from running down his face in liquid form. Chance fell into the nearest chair, too ashamed to look at Oni who was pitifully watching. He was broken and didn't have a leg to stand on. He never thought he would fall for a woman and yet he did. He couldn't believe that this would have happened to him. He was now weak and his feelings were crushed as he sat there slumped over.

Suddenly, he felt warm soft hands slide between his arms and around his waist. He looked up to see Oni staring up at him with watery eyes. She was on her knees, between his legs. Nothing was said. They could read each other's thoughts through wet gazes. Oni was his heart and soul and he knew then he couldn't be without her. They stayed there in a tight embrace, sealing their love for one another.

Suddenly, his mother walked in ready to throw a hell storm of angry words at him, once she got herself together. Seeing the tears coming down from both Oni's and Chance's faces caused her to turn back around into the kitchen so they could have their private moment. Chance was finally opening up and she didn't want to destroy the moment. Chance looked up, wiping the tears from her eyes. Oni did the same to him. At that moment, they both shared a warm smile. This moment only strengthened the bond between them. Chance kissed her forehead and walked her to her car. They went to his house for deep passionate lovemaking.

CHAPTER 116

Sealing the Bond

Chance walked into his home, which was decorated with fresh roses. It looked like a flower shop as the sweet aroma filled the air. With so many roses Oni didn't recognize the place and thought that they were trespassing on someone's property.

"What's up with all the roses? I hope these didn't come from another chick. Like that Erika or something," Oni said with fiery in her eyes.

Chance stopped and turned with sincerity. "These roses are for you. Not only was I sendin' them to you every day, I also kept some here just in case you were to come. Those other females are in the past. I truly love you with all my heart and meant every word of it."

"I want to forgive you, Raymond, but I can't get those images of you sexing Keisha out of my head." She squeezed her head.

"Sssshhh," Chance said, as he pulled her close to him.

Oni melted in his arms like putty, allowing him to have full control of her body. Chance wanted to get her upstairs in his bed, but his lustful needs was too powerful. They fell on the couch with their mouths glued together. They were practically tearing the clothes off their backs. Oni grabbed Chance's hard penis and tried to insert it into her wetness. He stopped her and pulled her hand away. He wanted to be in control and today she was going to let him do so.

Chance kissed and licked her all over like she was chocolate candy. He paid attention to her teaching and took it slow. This wasn't the sex she was expecting. Oni loved the way his tongue slid in and out her wet walls. Every muscle in her body started to tense up before it exploded from inside out like the Fourth of July. Her body went limp as she looked down at Chance still enjoying her pussy like he was eating a banana sundae. He was keeping her aroused. She began to grind her hips to his tongue, grabbing the back of his head. This time he was bringing the freak out of her. She just let herself go and let the beast out. This was the wild side of her. A side even she didn't know about. She was now all over Chance, riding his hard shaft like she was in the rodeo, refusing to get off the wild bull. Chance couldn't take anymore and let out a loud scream as all his strength was released inside her like warm milk. He collapsed on the couch.

CHAPTER 117
What Lovers Do

The strange noise of movement woke Chance from his deep slumber. It was Oni putting on her clothes. He fell asleep on the couch and didn't remember anything after his big orgasm. It was daybreak and he wondered where she slept, if she got any sleep at all.

"Hey, ma, what are you doin'?" Chance mumbled in his weakened voice.

"I have an early class and I can't go in looking like this." She giggled, displaying her torn shirt and panties. They both shared a good laugh. Chance grabbed Oni by the hand and pulled her on the couch with him.

"All this time I've been sending flowers and writing you letters, why haven't you responded?"

Oni shrugged. "I wasn't planning on coming back. So I moved out and stayed at my girlfriend's apartment. That dorm was too distracting for me. I couldn't stand another day sharing the bathroom with that whore. After being gone for so long, I came back to find stacks of letters and flowers. One day when I had nothing better to do, I opened the letters and started reading. The words melted my heart. Then you sent me the first letter that I wrote to you. That was special and meant a lot to me. So I came to your mother's house all confused. I couldn't stop thinking about you. I thought you moved on until you came over. I saw in your eyes that you missed me as well."

Chance sat upright, still in his nudeness. Oni couldn't keep her hands off his chiseled chest.

"Look, Oni, why don't we go to Vegas and tie the knot?"

292

Oni playfully pushed him. "Not if you gon' ask like that."

Chance sigh deeply. "Oni," he said, now on bended knee, looking up at her. "It would be an honor to have you as my wife. So, Oni, will you marry me?" He pulled out a small black box from under the sofa cushion and opened it up to display a huge diamond engagement ring. Oni's mouth fell open as if she had no jaw muscle. She was not expecting this at all. Chance was smooth with it. A little too smooth and there was something about a naked man on one knee that turned her on.

"I don't know. I have to call my parents and get their approval... No, you have to call... No, go over there and ask for their approval... Aw, what the hell? Yes!"

They hugged and kissed and for the first time made love. This time it was different. They held each other like true lovers do and gazed into each other's eyes. The lovemaking was the best sex that either of them had ever experience. One that even words couldn't explain.

CHAPTER 118

Blending In

Syphee was in the computer store looking like a shopper, but he was really there keeping an eye on the Geek Squad. This is the name they gave them and wasn't quite sure if they really had a name for themselves. Syphee was the youngest of the three-man crew and to unfamiliar eyes; he looked just like a regular little kid out shopping. His baby face posed no threat. This made it easy for him to get around undetected. They kept a tail on the Geek Squad for quite some time. They knew that they were getting money, but there was no form of traffic coming or going to their place of residence. So the money had to come from somewhere else. If it were through the computer, sooner or later the feds would catch on and run down on them. The Young Hitters were working on suspicion only. They suspected that the Geek Squad used their home as the stash spot. They were just out trying to find out where the cash was coming from. Syphee had his cell phone on FaceTime so Pemont and Dundy saw what was happening.

"They headin' out," Syphee whispered as he quickly rushed out the store and jumped in the back seat of the car with Pemont behind the wheel and Dundy in the passenger seat. The Geek Squad was at the counter waiting to pay for whatever they purchased. The Young Hitters were dressed like Catholic schoolboys to throw off the geeks. No one would expect these three innocent faces to be young killers. Dressing up in thug gear would attract weary eyes, so they would change up their style of look to fit the everyday normal look of the regular kids in that particular area. This was something that Pemont picked up from playing different video games that dealt with stealth and different camouflages to sneak up on his enemies. Plus, they didn't stand out when patrolmen were out looking to put young black hoodlums behind bars.

"Here comes them geeky ass muhfuckas," Syphee said as they watched them hop into their own whip and head toward Camden. If they were to get a quick glance at the Young Hitters, they would have probably said the same thing about them. That's when it hit them. These geeks were probably doing the same thing as the Young Hitters were doing. Using this geeky style of dress and attitude to throw off unfamiliar eyes.

The Geek Squad pulled up into the Parkside section of Camden. They had hit three different mac machines, withdrawing a big sum of cash from various bankcards. One drew the cash while the other two were lookouts with their back to the machine to seal him from any onlookers, but the Young Hitters knew what they were doing. They saw from a distance that the cash they were withdrawing was being stuffed in backpacks. When they got to their secret hideout, Pemont pulled out his cell phone and called Chance. It was about to go down tonight.

CHAPTER 119
Getting Out the Game

Chance was startled from his deep sleep by his cell phone ringing. He opened his eyes. The room was dark. It was night. The screen of his cell phone lit up the room. It read Pemont.

"Yo, what up?" Chance answered the phone. Oni was still sleeping with her head on his chest. The entire day consisted of lovemaking. Chance didn't know he had it in him. He didn't know Oni had it in her either. This act caused her to miss all her morning classes, but it was worth it.

"It's 'bout time, my nig. We's all here. Where you at?" Pemont said with an attitude. The job was done and they were waiting for Chance at the meeting spot to count the cash.

Chance looked at the time on the screen. It read 12:34. "Give me a minute to get myself together first. I had to handle some business." They knew that line all too well. Chance was doing what he was well known for besides killing—getting pussy.

"No prob. We'll keep everything on ice 'til you get here…one." They disconnected the call.

Oni got up off Chance and started putting her clothes back on.

"So you still gon' leave me?" He pouted like a little kid.

She looked at her watch. "Well, I did have morning classes. I'll have to make them up tomorrow."

Chance reached out to pull her back onto the couch.

Oni pulled away. "Oh no mister. We are not going to do this again. I can't take anymore."

This was all new to Chance and he was enjoying it so much that he couldn't get enough of it.

"After what I seen earlier? Girl, you know you still got it in ya," Chance teased.

"You might be right. So come to my spot and let's see," she said now ready for some more.

"No prob. Just give me a little to take care of somethin' first."

Oni's face hardened. "Take care of what, Chance? I hope it ain't illegal," she snapped.

"No, not at all." He lied. "I got enough saved up to buy a new house and have a big wedding at the same time. So what do you think about that?" He did have enough for both and with the job he had lined up with the Young Hitters would be icing on the cake.

"That sounds good, but how did all this happen?"

"I finally got my lawsuit money I was telling you about." He lied some more, having her believe that he sued his last job for racial profiling and discrimination.

Oni wasn't accepting his story and answered with a "Yeah, okay," as she continued to get dress. She didn't forget about him being a captain of a drug cartel. This was eating Chance up. He lying to her like this was weighing on his conscience.

"Oni, I can't do this to you anymore. I lied 'bout the lawsuit money. It's from me sellin' drugs and I don't want to do this anymore. I want to be honest wit'chu and come clean. I can't keep hurtin' you like this."

Oni's eyes began to water. "I can't be with you if you're killing your own people for a profit." The thought of leaving him began to tear her apart.

"That's why I want out of the game. I love you, Oni and I want to start a new life with you. We can go somewhere far and start a new life. I have enough money to do so. I would even pay for all your college courses and take up some classes myself to become a hardworking man. Just say yes you'll go with me." Chance eyes began to fill with hot tears.

"I love you, Chance and I'm willing to give it a try so the answer to that is yes, but I want to know, where are you really going?"

"I can't just walk away. That would be straight suicide. I'm a captain, so I gotta hand over my position so I can walk away with a clean slate." Chance was ready to make that move and let the Young Hitters know after counting the money from the last job, but first he wanted to take care of Tony Satario, the realtor who killed Willy. He'd wait for Tuck to return from the Dominican Republic before breaking the news to him.

"Good, I'm so proud of you, Raymond." She smiled, giving him a big hug.

"Setting up for a wedding takes so long. I just want you to be mine and let the whole world know this," Chance said with excitement. Even after all he did to her she had a love for him that was strong enough to overlook his sinful ways.

"Chance, I love you and I do want to spend the rest of my life with you," she confessed with watery eyes.

"Then it's settled. I'll meet you at your dorm later on tonight and from there we head to Vegas for the weekend, after your classes and come back as Mr. and Mrs. Cobbs."

CHAPTER 120

The Price is Costly

D ave drove Mark to the mechanic to pick up Yolanda's car. It was a BMW 730 with black leather interior and woodgrain panels. She had custom rims that looked good on the car. Not too big and not too small, it was just right. Everything about this car had money written all over it.

"You better hope that pussy's well worth the price of getting her whip fixed," Dave argued at Mark for getting her car fixed. It would have been a strong move if the car was a cheaper brand, but anything with the letters BMW meant that it's going to cost him a lot to get fixed. Dave would make fun saying that BMW stood for *Big Money Whip*.

"Don't hate 'cause my game was stronger," Mark teased like a little kid bragging about his trick or treat bag.

"Whatever Captain Supa-save-a-hoe. Let's see how much this pussy cost you," Dave demanded as they approached the mechanic at the counter.

"Hello, gentlemen, how may I help you?" The mechanic greeted with a friendly smile.

"Yes, I called in about the white BMW that was towed in," said Mark. Suddenly he started feeling cramps in his pockets like it was a female's monthly cycle. *Dave was right*, he thought. *This is a very expensive car*. All Mark wanted to do was impress the woman that owned it and hopefully build something out of this, but now he was too afraid to find out how much all this was going to cost him.

"Oh yes, she's ready to go. It appears that she ran into something. We're not sure what it was, but it did some extensive damage underneath the hood."

"So how much did everything come up to?" Mark's tone showed signs of nervousness after he manage to ask the question.

"That would be thirty-seven hundred dollars and eighty-six cents." The mechanic's attitude was very pleasant, but with the cost of getting the car fixed was expected. Mark started to feel lightheaded as he reached for his wallet.

"You better hope she swallows and take it balls deep in the ass 'cause that is one of the most expensive pussies I have ever seen in my life," Dave whispered to Mark. He was enjoying this.

Mark tried to remain cool as beads of sweat started to form on his forehead. He pulled out his Visa card, ignoring Dave as he continued to make jokes about it.

"You could have gone to three strip joints, made it rain and paid to get two nuts off and still wouldn't come close to what you just spent on one bitch." Dave was on a roll, as Mark got into the car and headed for Yolanda's house.

CHAPTER 121

Hard Evidence

"That's all I got. So is you gon' kill me or what, 'cause this shit ain't funny," Chance complained after explaining the whole story to Pitch. The rope began to burn as it cut into his flesh with each turn of the wrist. Syphee, Pemont and Dundy could do nothing. They were still hand cuffed from behind. Tuck and Chance raised them to become cold-blooded killers. So Pitch wasn't taking no risks. Removing the cuffs from either one of those young thugs would surely lead to a blood bath. All three young thugs stood there with hard looks, but they couldn't control the pain that ran down their faces in liquid form. Chance was their mentor. He and Tuck practically raised them to become the young men that they were. Whenever in need they could always count on Tuck and Chance to have their backs. Now in the time of need, they couldn't return the favor. All they could do was watch the man they looked up to as their shepherd. The man they never, in their lives, had to witness being tortured in front of them.

"Oh, you think that I'm fuckin' jokin' wit'cha, huh?" Pitch yelled, putting away his cell phone and pulling out an iPad. He then handed it to Bones, who past it around so everyone saw the poorly recorded video of two people making out in the back of Cat Daddy's body shop. Pitch had both videos on two devices. The iPad had a bigger screen for everyone in the room to get a better view of it. They saw the two making out in the backseat of a car, but it was hard to make out who the guy was. It was quite clear that it was Crystal, because the close-up recording of her entering and exiting the shop came into focus. Even her license plates came in clear. After everyone got a good look at the video, including the Young Hitters, Pitch snatched the iPad from Bones who was still viewing the video. Even though he was having a secret affair with her, he still couldn't believe that she cheated on Cat Daddy with another man.

"So what the fuck is this then, huh?" Pitch roared with venom. While sticking the iPad in Chance's face so he could get a good view of the video, Bones stood silently trying to figure out what type of woman Crystal was. Was she a hoe or was this deeper than that?

"Fuck is that shit 'posed to be?" Chance hissed.

"Pussy, don't act stupid now. That's you stickin' yo dirty ass dick in Cat's bitch."

CHAPTER 122

It Was on Video

"Fuck outta here. Yous trippin'. That shit ain't me and you know it," Chance uttered.

Pitch was on a mission and Chance was his prime target.

"Muhfucka, that's you," Pitch thundered, still breathing hard. He was fueled on hate and anger. Hurting something was his way of alleviating it.

"Prove it," Chance challenged.

"I jus' did wit' this video." Pitch waved the iPad in the air for everyone to see.

"That weak ass video don't mean shit," Chance disputed.

Pitch reached in his pocket and pulled out a small note pad. He then started reading off the times and dates of all the comments Chance made about how bad he wanted Crystal and was willing to do anything to get it. Chance was now on trial and Pitch had all the evidence he needed to prove his case. Explaining that he no longer had an interest in Crystal and moved on wouldn't work. No one in the room knew of or even heard of Oni. Their entire relationship was nothing more than a secret. Chance never brought her around any of his crew members and the only friend he had was Tuck and Tuck never seen nor heard of her either. Worst of all, Tuck wasn't even around to defend him. Chance was on his own with this one.

"You's lying, I ain't say that shit." It was a bad move on Pitch's part, because they didn't know what he may have on them. If the feds run down on him and him keeping records written down like this would surely jam them up. This was another form of dry snitching.

"Oh yeah, out of all the shit I read, did anyone here not hear at least one of the comments I just read off?" Pitch addressed everyone in the room, but there was no response. It was looking real bad for Chance. Even the puzzled looks on the Young Hitters' faces weren't looking good at all. They were starting to believe the story as well.

"I rest my case," Pitch said, as if he was an attorney.

"Oh now you's a cop," Chance barked.

Pitch smacked him hard across the face. "Nigga, watch yo mouth."

Chance shook it off, spitting a mouth full of blood on the floor.

"That don't mean shit. You just want an excuse to body a nigga." Chance knew Pitch couldn't wait for this moment by the way he looked at him every time Crystal's name came out his mouth.

"No I didn't. I like you. You and Tuck was my right-hand man." His tone reeked of sarcasm. Everyone knew that Pitch always had them by his side when he made moves, which made it hard for the crew to believe that he didn't like them, but the weird thing was the way he said, *you and Tuck was my right-hand man*. That was used in the past tense, which only meant that he was trying to get rid of Tuck as well. The Young Hitters knew that they would have to warn Tuck and the way they all looked at one another meant that they were all thinking the same thing.

"Yeah, you expect me to believe that shit. I'm tellin' you that shit ain't me," Chance tried to explain, but the blood lust in Pitch's eyes made it hard for his words to get through to him.

"Then who the fuck is it?" Pitch growled in anger.

"I don't fuckin' know, but it ain't me," Chance lied. He knew it was Willy on that video, because Willy confessed to him and Tuck the night they caught him at the Inn of the Dove in Cherry Hill. He thought about telling Pitch the truth so he could get off that hard pool table, but that would jeopardize Willy's whole family. Cat Daddy would take it out on Melody and her son if he found out it was Willy, but little did Chance know that Melody's son wasn't Willy's child. Pitch already knew, but Chance believed with Willy being dead and gone his family would still catch Pitch's wrath. A rule that Cat Daddy created and Pitch was willing and eager to stand by it.

"I knew you would plead the fifth," Pitch said, now walking over to his tools of torture. Seeing this made Chance swallow hard. The knot in his throat felt like it was the size of a baseball.

"Does Cat know you doin' this shit?" Chance asked, knowing the answer himself.

"No, not yet. I'm runnin' the show here and after I'm done I'll pass it on to him," he stated as if it was something minor like overcooking his dinner or borrowing his car to make a quick run.

All three of Chance's hitters wanted to say something, but they knew that Pitch would take it as a challenge and end up giving them the same treatment. Pitch started with a sharp drill and drilled holes in Chance's shin bone. Everyone cringed as his bloody flesh and bone splattered all over the place. Some got on them. Chance's screams were unbearable. A few of the guys covered their eyes, but was forced to watch. A few others lost their meal in the process.

The pain and torture was too harsh to bear. Physically, there were no means of escape, but mentally, even for a few split seconds, Chance had a way out. He closed his eyes and thought happy thoughts…about Oni.

CHAPTER 123

Rubbing It In

Later on that night, Dave got home with bags of groceries. After eating up all the food in the house, there was nothing left in the refrigerator. Even if there was food in the refrigerator Dave was not willing to take the risk of eating it after the last incident that sent him to the hospital. Mark was still circulating the video on the internet of his swollen face, after the allergic reaction from the peanuts that Mark put in the food. It received a lot of hits and the number of viewers kept growing.

When he entered the house, Mark and Yolanda were on the couch adjusting their clothes.

"Dave, what the fuck you doin' here?" Mark said in a hint like tone.

"I live here. What the fuck y'all doin'?" Dave said, ignoring the hint.

"Nothing, just talkin'." Mark's stuttering tone revealed his nervousness.

"Then get a hotel room or something. I like to chill on that couch and y'alls about to put some DNA all over it, eww." Then Dave stopped with a look of recognition. "Yolanda, is that you?"

"Yes, hi Dave," she said, looking uncomfortable.

"My bad. I understand. My boy pumped out a lot of bread to get that whip fixed and if he couldn't afford a hotel room please don't be hard on him."

Yolanda sat there, not knowing what to say. How was she to respond to a comment like that? If Dave was trying to mess up the mood, he was doing a very good job at it.

"Don't mind him, he's a clown. Come on, let's go to my room," Mark said, escorting her upstairs.

"You should have done that in the first place, instead of trying to rub it in my face, you know?" Dave yelled out with jealousy. He knew Mark wanted him to walk in on that. Mark was good for that. This was his way of getting extra cool points from the fellas, but to Dave it was a childish act that shouldn't get any recognition. He was hoping Yolanda had a dick bigger than Stacy's. Then he wouldn't be so upset in Mark fucking her, but then he thought, if Yolanda was a dude and Mark fucked her, then there would be no denying the fact that he's attracted to men. This would be a sign that he was meant to be gay, if he chose to accept it or not. Suddenly, there was a hard knock at the door, but not just any old knock. This knock was loud and rapid. Dave ran over, swinging the door open. Whoever was on the other side of that door had a serious beat down coming to them for disrespecting his crib. Dave's hands were now in fists, but he froze at the sight before him. This was real and the timing was way off. Now standing in front of him was Rolisha and she had fire in her eyes.

"Where's that nasty ass nigga at?" She yelled loud enough for the whole neighborhood to hear.

Dave held her back from entering the house.

"Rolisha, what are you doing here?" Dave yelled, still trying to hold her back. He was hoping Mark could hear the commotion from upstairs.

"Why the fuck you blocking the door and why you talking like that? You got something to hide in there?" She tried to push by.

"Yo, don't be comin' up in here tryna start yo mess, girl." Dave tried to sound off with an authoritative voice, but she wasn't buying it.

Just then Mark came running down the steps. "Hey, what's goin' on here? Rolisha, why are you here?" Mark acted like he was surprised by her visit.

"Why haven't you answered your phone? I've been callin' you for the last two hours."

Mark pulled out his phone.

"Look, babe, I haven't been ignoring you. My battery is dead, see?" Mark said as she snatched his cell phone and tried to power it on. He had a spare dead battery that he switched up when he heard the commotion. "See? Had I known it was dead, I would have recharged it. So what's goin' on?"

Rolisha's hard stare softened. "Someone broke into the crib and took everything. I got the kids in the cab now. I'm scared to go home by myself." She cried. Her catching a cab from New York was very expensive. Paying that cab fare on top of the money he spent getting Yolanda's car fixed was killing his pockets, but he saw the urgency in her eyes. She was looking for an excuse to stay there so she could spy on him. Mark knew better and wasn't having that. He was dying to know if everyone was all right and if she called the cops, but this would only prolong her stay and he couldn't take that risk with Yolanda still upstairs.

"Okay, I'll get my wallet and keys right now." Mark ran up the stairs.

"I'll go with you." Rolisha ran up behind him. Dave tried to stop her, but she got past him before he knew it. Dave's mouth dropped, knowing the outcome of this scene. He ran up behind them to see her reaction when she saw Yolanda in his room. Little did Yolanda know that Rolisha was the type that would mess up her flawless face and leave permanent scars if she found out that she was messing with her man. They got into the room and Yolanda wasn't there. Where did she go? Maybe she jumped out the window, but the window was jammed and couldn't open. Then she was under the bed. Mark grabbed all his things and ran off with Rolisha. When they left, Dave checked under the bed for Yolanda and she wasn't there. He checked the closet and she wasn't there either. Where could she have gone?

He looked in his bedroom and to his surprise, Yolanda was laying in his bed looking like a frightened cat. She removed her clothes and was only sporting her bra and panties.

"They're gone now. Everything is fine now."

"He didn't tell me he had a crazy baby momma that just got out the psych ward." Her gullible ass believed that story. This only put a smile on Dave's face as he closed the bedroom door behind him. If she was gullible enough to believe that story, wait until she hears what Dave had to say.

"Yeah, she's a piece a work. Let me tell you what she did that got her in the crazy farm."

CHAPTER 124
The Confession

The loud drilling sound and the pain that followed radiated through Chance's entire body like a bolt of lightning. It quickly snapped him out of his happy dream state of mind and back to reality. The room was a bloody mess. The horror would surely haunt everyone's dreams forever. The torture of Chance went on for fifteen minutes before he finally broke.

"Okay…okay! No more!" He yelled, coughing up a mouthful of blood.

Pitch smiled with Chance's blood dripping down his chin as he leaned into him. Either he wasn't aware of it or it just didn't bother him at all.

"Okay, I'm listening." Pitch laid the drill beside him.

Chance's good eye danced around the room at all the wide eyes staring in anticipation.

"You win. It was Willy. Willy did it," Chance cried out. He knew that he sent a death wish to Willy's family, but he knew that once Pitch sets him free he would take him out before he had the opportunity to deliver the message. He wasn't sure of what excuse he would have told Cat Daddy or what would happen afterwards with so many witnesses. It didn't matter at this point; he needed relief. This was his way out of this game of pain and he was willing to deal with whatever followed.

"So you tellin' me that she was fuckin' that corny ass nigga, Willy? Fuck outta here." He was refusing to accept that. Queen Pin was bigger than that and Willy was too minuscule to even matter.

"Yes, she was. I caught them together at the Inn of the Dove in Cherry Hill and he told me everything. I wouldn't lie to you 'bout that." But he did when he left Tuck out the picture. Tuck was there that day and he got an earful. Chance didn't want any harm to come to his best friend.

"I don't fuckin' believe you. Why him?" Pitch questioned, but from the look in his eyes, his mind was already made up. Chance would be the one who pays for Willy's sins.

"I don't know, but she did," Chance confessed, but he knew he was a dead man when Crystal finds out about him running his mouth. Pitch knew he would have to watch his back from that point on if he were to let Chance go. Every mouth in the room dropped. It could be that they couldn't believe that corny ass Willy was making out with Cat Daddy's main girl, *Mrs. Untouchable* or maybe they had the look of shock on their faces, because Chance went into bitch mode and started singing like a canary. They knew that it wouldn't be long before they got the order to take Willy's entire family out. It would certainly be their next mission.

Pitch then started rubbing Chance's head like he was a pet cat. He was definitely enjoying himself. "Shhhh. It's okay. I believe you. So I'm going to cut you lose so you can take care of these nasty wounds. Take as long as you want. As a matter of fact, you call me when you're ready to go back to work. Doesn't that sound nice?"

Chance nodded. Then Pitch walked over to his tool kit and grabbed a pair of scissors. He started to cut the rope that was cutting at Chance's wrist, but then he stopped and pulled them away.

"Wait a second. I can't do this." He placed the scissors back in his toolbox and pulled the drill back out.

"What…what are you talkin' 'bout?" Chance muttered, with one wide eye and the other one swollen shut.

"You said that you caught them at the Inn of the Dove in Cherry Hill, right?" Pitch quizzed.

"Yeah!" Chance responded as all his hopes and wishes withered away. He knew by Pitch's tone that it was more to it than a simple question.

"My sister, Tima, got her face blown off at the Inn of the Dove in Cherry Hill." There was a long pause. Pitch was fishing and Chance was the bait. At that moment, Pitch's whole demeanor changed. It was like he transformed into a madman, drunk with vengeance.

"Come on, Pitch. Don't go there with this dumb shit," Chance pleaded, but deep down he knew it was a waste of time. Pitch's mind was made up and there was no turning back.

"Either you had somethin' to do wit' it or you know somebody who did," Pitch growled.

"Pitch, chill. Now you really buggin'. How you gon' go there wit' that?" Chance saw there was no reasoning with Pitch. He was determined not to let Chance leave that room alive. No matter what he told him. He was digging deep, making sure that Chance had no way out.

CHAPTER 125

Signing His Own Death Wish

"Fuck all that. You killed my little sister, didn't you?" Pitch pressed the drill through Chance's kneecap. Chance yelled in agony. "Tell me why you did it and I'll make the shit quick." Pitch now had the look of a lunatic.

"I told you already, I ain't do it." Throughout his pain and suffering, images of Oni's beautiful smile popped in his head. He was to leave the game and marry Oni. They were to go far away to start a new life. With Pitch standing over him trying to turn him into grinned meat was nothing more than a reality check. Chance knew at that moment that once he got out of this mess he was getting out of the game completely and never looking back. He was even willing to let Tony go and not pursue the taking of his life. Oni was in her dorm room waiting for his arrival. The thing that bothered Chance the most was that he didn't get to say goodbye. All he wanted was to see those beautiful hazel eyes again and kiss those soft lips.

"Yes, you did." Pitch drilled a hole in his other kneecap.

Chance let out a blood gargling yell. Pitch needed a reason to get rid of Chance while Tuck was gone and what better excuse to come up with. It was a very weak one, but it would have to do. Chance was in the way of his master plan and with him out of the way he could keep things moving.

What seemed like another hour of torture caused Chance to cave in.

"Okay…okay…stop…stop, please!" Chance screamed at the top of his lungs. He couldn't take any more, and knew he just signed his own death wish. It really didn't matter at this point.

Chance needed a relief. He just wanted Pitch to make it quick. Pitch stopped and laid the bloody drill down. The blood caused it to be slippery and hard to control.

"You tell me what I need to hear and I promise you I'll make it quick." Even though they weren't the words he wanted to hear, it still sounded so tempting. He was now ready to accept his fate.

And that's what Chance did. He told Pitch exactly what he wanted to hear. Pitch finally got Chance where he wanted with no way out.

"Yeah, I killed that fat bitch to get to you. I knew you didn't like me, but it was okay. I didn't like you anyway. You's a snake in the grass, doin' grimy shit behind Cat's back. You want the crown. That's why you set him up and got him locked up. You ain't shit, bitch ass nigga. You have no conscience and no soul. You only care 'bout yo'self and fuck everybody else. I'll be waitin' for your greasy ass in hell, pussy."

Chance knew that saying this would plant a seed in everyone's head. Once they believe what he said then their loyalty wouldn't last. He knew that it wouldn't be long before one of these killers would take him out before he gets comfortable with his newfound position. If he did get Cat Daddy locked up for his position then he couldn't be trusted.

Pitch stood there in silence as tears ran down his face. Hate and anger showed in his bloodthirsty eyes. Pitch then grabbed his blood covered, slippery drill and ran it through Chance's temple. He pinned his head down with his free hand while doing so. Chance screamed in agony as it entered his skull. He stopped and held it there as Chance continued to scream in pain. Then Pitch pushed it in deeper as it drilled his brain. A loud scream slowly withered away like a deflating balloon. Pitch, still in a rage started running the drill through Chance's eyeballs. That wasn't enough. He started running it through his nose and skull, yelling like a wild animal. There was no way they would be able to recognize him now and that's what he wanted. Pitch had a deep hatred for Chance because God blessed him with the looks that could attract any woman with no effort. No one said anything nor were they willing to stop him. They just continued to watch a loyal soldier being tortured and abused as his lifeless body shook and convulsed.

"Pitch, chill. The nigga's dead already." Bones was the only one brave enough to yell out.

Pitch snapped out of his blood rage, breathing hard as if he just ran the four hundred meter relay. He inspected the scene to see blood everywhere. The scene was so gruesome, like Chance's body exploded from the inside out. Even Pitch was shocked at the damage he'd done, but he still was able to maintain a hard exterior. Everyone watched in horror. This was the fear he wanted to see. Now they would know what they would face if they ever tried to cross him.

"You ain't pretty no more now, muhfucka," Pitch yelled out as he coughed up phlegm and spat on Chance's corpse.

CHAPTER 126
Looking Out For Your Boy

Mark rushed back to New Jersey to try to hook back up with Yolanda. Rolisha had him make the trip home for nothing. They never got robbed and the cab fare to New Jersey from New York was expensive. Rolisha made it up to get him home. Mark was spending too much time in New Jersey and was neglecting her needs, but her actions were only pushing him further away from her. Mark had a few choice words before leaving her and for the very first time, Rolisha broke down crying. Mark didn't know how to take it. For all he knew, she was faking and this was another weak attempt to get him to stay home. Mark wasn't buying it as he stormed out the house. If she hadn't made that desperate attempt to lure him home, he would have been enjoying the sexual pleasures of Yolanda. Shit, for three thousand seven hundred dollars, he deserved a minimum of two orgasms.

Mark made a few attempts to reach Dave by phone, but he didn't answer so he left a few messages for Dave to hold Yolanda there until he got back. As he got near Dave's home is when he spotted her car. Good, Dave kept her there for him. Mark was glad to have Dave as a true friend. He knew how bad he wanted her and to do him this favor, to hold her there until he got back, let him know the love he got for his boy. Now all he had to do was create another good lie to top the one he told her previously. He had a good one and knew what to tell her after seeing how gullible she was. Mark rushed in the house, but it was empty. She must've been waiting for him in the bedroom.

Good…Then she knows what it is and no need for small talk.

He adjusted his appearance before entering his room, but it was empty. *What the fuck is goin' on 'round here? I know she ain't in Dave's room*, he thought, as worry set in. *I hope she ain't doin' him.* He began to pout as he got to Dave's room. The door was unlocked so he let himself in. Mark wanted to know what was going on behind that door and the art of surprise seemed to be the logical approach. Entering the room caused him to go into shock. Right in front of his own two eyes was Yolanda getting fucked by Dave, hard. Her ass was in the air, taking all dick. Dave was ramming her pussy with force, like he was on a mission to destroy it. His eyes were closed, smiling from ear to ear. He was in total bliss.

Mark was now seeing red. That was supposed to be him smiling from ear to ear with his dick all up in her raw. Out of all the dumb shit Dave did to him in the past, this right here topped them all. Dave might have gotten the pussy first, but Mark was making sure he wasn't going to get a nut off while he was around.

CHAPTER 127
Not Taking His Threats Lightly

Pitch had Bones and a few guys untie Chance's body and wrap it in a big green rug. They tied the ends of the rug and carried it out the room. Pitch approached the Young Hitters and looked them over as if he was having second thoughts on what to do with them. They looked so young and innocent. Pitch could still see the fear in their eyes. This was what he wanted. He pulled out his weapon and let it dangle at his side. There were rules to the game and smoking these young soldiers without justification would surely weaken his crew's loyalty.

"You young muhfuckas gon' either get down or lay down?" He quizzed. This was a test and if failed, there was no possibility of a retake.

The first person he stepped to was Pemont. Pitch knew the young killer was the head of the three-man squad and his decision would affect the rest of the group. Pemont looked up at him with watery eyes. If only he had his glock handy. There would be no hesitation in putting a few rounds in Pitch's body, but he was outnumbered by his goons and defenseless. A good punch in the mouth would be acceptable. The satisfaction would be temporary and to act upon it wouldn't be a wise decision. This was a life or death situation and choosing death was out of the equation. Pemont gave him a head nod.

"Nigga, speak the fuck up!" Pitch roared. "I know yo mouth works, muhfucka." He was still amped up and eager to lay a few more bodies down.

"I'm down," Pemont uttered. The words burned as it left his mouth.

Pitch then stepped to Syphee. He was the youngest of the three and his face was wet with hot tears. "I'm down," he said, never looking up. So young and still bewildered. With death, it came easy. Once it's over, you're done with it, but life in general was hard and so confusing. It felt more like a biology course and class was in session. He couldn't afford to fail this test.

Pitch then stepped to Dundy, who was giving him a hard stare. Pitch saw his future would present a problem if he were to let him live. If he smoked him now, the problem would be much greater. Dundy had pause and that alone could justify Pitch's reason to end his existence.

"What the fuck, you stuck, lil' nigga?" Pitch thundered, while cocking back the hammer. Everyone's eyes widened with anticipation.

"I'm down," Dundy finally spoke up. His anger and hatred toward Pitch was evident. With Dundy choosing to be down, granted him the time to gather his thoughts and think wisely. Pitch would pay for his action. Maybe not today, but in due time.

"Good, that's the shit I want to hear." Pitch chuckled, as if the entire experience was entertaining for him.

All three of them had agreed to be down with Pitch, seeing they had no choice in the matter. After watching the long torture of a captain of his squad let them know they could not take his threats lightly.

CHAPTER 128
The Wake-up Call

That night, the Young Hitters went to Dundy's house and cried their asses off. Dundy lived with his oldest sister, Samore. She was working two jobs and a full time student at Rutgers University in Camden. Only time she was home was to get some sleep. Dundy would purposely drive her crazy and keep her up at night with weed smoke and loud music. She ended up staying with her boyfriend on campus for peace and quiet.

The ringing of his cell phone awakened Pemont. He answered it without checking the caller ID.

"Yo, what it do?" Pemont mumbled, still unaware of which way was up.

"Fuck up and get yo ass out here, now!" The voice boomed.

"Fuck is this?" Pemont roared with anger. He was up now.

"It's Bones, nigga. Don't be tryna flex," he barked.

Images of him wrapping Chance in a rug kept playing in Pemont's head. This only created a newfound hatred toward Bones, as well as for Pitch.

"Yeah, whateva. What's good?" He tried to play it off.

"Pitch want all y'all lil' niggas to take him somewhere."

This didn't feel right. Why did he want the three of them to take him out? What happened last night put a nasty taste in their mouths. This was a direct order and not a request. Nothing more than a test of their loyalty to him.

"Well, let Pitch know that it's too early to be clubin' and we is way under age to get in." Pemont was looking for an excuse not to go.

"It ain't that type of ride. So stop fuckin' around and get yo ass out here," Bones barked.

"A'ight." Pemont pouted.

"Make sure you holla at Dundy and Syphee. I've been callin' them niggas all day and they ain't answerin' they phones."

"They right here sleep. I'll get them up. A'ight…one."

Pemont disconnected the call and got Dundy and Syphee up. It was a long night of mourning, which they cried themselves to sleep.

CHAPTER 129

Plan in Motion

Pitch entered the Camden City Jail, while Pemont, Dundy, and Syphee waited in the car. They weren't sure if he was making them Tuck's and Chance's new replacements. Pitch entered the visiting room to see Cat Daddy seated behind the thick glass.

"Yo, what up, Cat?" He picked up the phone receiver and placed it against his hear.

"Not a damn thing. These fools be tryna keep a nigga here. Every fuckin' day they come at my neck with some more dumb shit that seem to be fallin' from the damn sky and more evidence from some ghost-face snitch. I know someone is settin' me the fuck up." Cat Daddy's eyes were filled with anxiety.

"Don't worry 'bout that. I'll have someone look into it." Pitch was hoping to calm his nerve. Cat Daddy was looking like he was on edge.

"So how's your vacation trip comin' along?" Cat Daddy was talking in code for the great escape he was planning. He knew everything he said was being recorded. He was hoping the judge granted him a bail by tomorrow. If not, then this would be Plan B. From the evidence that led to him receiving more charges made Plan B appear to be the more logical route.

"It's all good. Me and my girl is planning on leavin' this Friday on a four o'clock flight." He was planning to break him out of jail at that time. Only if he was unable to bail out.

"Four o'clock. Isn't that around rush hour traffic?" Cat Daddy muttered with concern.

"Yeah, I know and it's gon' be worse because of everybody leavin' for the weekend. Ain't nobody gon' be able to move in that kind of traffic." He was letting Cat Daddy know the heavy traffic would make it hard for the cops to get around freely. It should slow them up enough so they could get to their destination in time.

"Oh…okay…I hope y'all make it with no problems." He was leery. This was his chance to get out the game and disappear for good. There was no room for fuck ups.

"Did you ever make that appointment with that doctor for your girl?" He was now asking if he set it up with the cosmetic sergeant. Cat Daddy was going to get a complete face-lift before moving out of state.

"Yeah, I took care of that. I made sure I got the best doctor that money could buy."

CHAPTER 130
Who Did It?

Tony raced through the hallways of Cooper Medical Center. The smell of penicillin and peroxide was making him sick to his stomach. Hanging around for an extended period did help him get immune to it, but the smell of it when he first walked in was overwhelming. The pounding of his chest was hard enough to crack ribs. Tony was overly excited and anxious; he was finally going to hear his father's voice. The hospital called to inform him his father's doctor had given clearance to bring him out of his induced coma. Tony wanted to be the first person he saw after spending so much time in total darkness. As he reached the room, the three, armed guards were hanging in the hallway.

Tony entered the room to find his stepmother draped over his father, her arms around him. Frank was going in and out of his coma-like state. While in the hospital bed, he still looked weak and frail. Tony stood by the doorway and waited patiently. A few minutes later, Frank's wife looked up and noticed Tony. Her name was Arleen. She married his father. They had a son together: Frankie Debartello, Jr., Arleen's and Tony's mothers were pregnant by Frank at the same time. Frank wanted to marry Tony's mother, but after finding out he already had a child on the way by another woman, she wanted nothing to do with him. Frank ended up marrying Arleen instead, which she named the child after him. It felt good having a brother. They cherished the few little time spent together, but Frankie's life was cut short by the hand of the hitman, Larry Payne, but Tony was to believe that Willy was the one who killed his brother. Someone mysteriously placed a clear plastic bag on his front doorstep, which contained a bloody hammer and towel. Tony had a detective who was on his payroll check the blood sample, which came back as being his brother's, Frankie's, but the fingerprints on the hammer belonged to Willy Mays. Now Tony was the only child his father had left to carry his legacy. Arleen gave him a fake hug and rushed to the other side of the room. The tension between the two was thick.

"Pop, it's me ,Tony." He pulled up a chair by his bedside.

Frank was still delirious. "Tony," he managed to throw out with hard breaths.

"Yeah, Pop, your son," Tony emphasized.

"My son…Frankie," Frank huffed, his lungs still weak and vision blurred. To him, Frankie and Tony looked and sounded alike.

"No, it's me, Tony, Pop."

"Ah, Tony…my boy." Frank gently touched his face and smiled with recognition. He looked so proudly at his son with watery eyes. Tony could feel the pain he was going through with the loss of his first-born. Arleen stormed out the room. It pained her to look at the result of her husband's dirty deeds.

Tony grabbed his father's hand and held it. "Pop, who did this to you?"

Frank turned his face away, refusing to answer.

"You…shouldn't worry…about this matter. I'll…take care… of this…myself," Frank struggled between each breath in his weakened state, still facing away.

"But, Pop, whoever did this to you could still be out there looking for you. It took a lot of money and hard work to make you disappear. You could at least tell me who did this so I don't get caught off guard if they were to approach me." Frank felt Tony's words as he looked at the armed guards standing outside his door and the alias name, Paul Mininno, written on the marker board next to the words: patient's name. He lost one son who was unaware to his killer and wouldn't be able to live with himself if anything happened to Tony. He looked at Tony. He opened his mouth to speak, but it was a low crackle. Tony leaned forward as Frank whispered the words in his ear.

"It…was…the hitman."

If you enjoyed reading
HOLLOW MINDS,
You will enjoy this sneak peek…

* * * * *

PROLOGUE
Part 4

Chaos and Tuck's plane had landed at Atlantic City International Airport. Unlike Philadelphia International Airport, it was very quiet with fewer people. Vacationers rushed past with luggage on wheels. A female voice made an announcement over the intercom of the next departing flight. The parking lot was very easy to access. Spirit Airlines made it very covenant for their passengers. The cost of flying was cheap for those with a membership.

Exiting the airport, Tuck met up with his young goons, Pemont, Syphee, and Dundy. Not even old enough to drink, they still presented themselves professionally, making them his pride and joy. They wore custom business suits, looking like up-and-coming dons. He knew they did this to impress him. Tuck wasn't used to seeing them dressed this way, but it looked good on them. That only meant business was doing good. The flashy Rolex watches and thick gold chains were a little too much, but they were still young and it was expected. He made a mental note to school them on attracting unwanted attention. Besides the flashy jewelry, the Young Hitters still conducted themselves like true soldiers. This new swagger seemed to come naturally and Tuck was feeling the new look. To Tuck, it was good to get them young and mold them into his own enforcers. Something Cat Daddy did with him. The young gunners had real heart and they wouldn't hesitate to lay a nigga down. They stood proudly with their heads held high, as he approached them.

"Yo, what up, Tuck?" Pemont, his top hitter said, as they all showed him love.

"Yo, what it do?" Tuck looked his goons over. Chaos stood behind him silently. "Where's Chance?" Chance was his right-hand man who never left his side. Tuck thought he stayed behind to keep an eye on things or was up in some pussy like always, but he was supposed to be here to meet Chaos and go over the new business. Something was off and Tuck could feel it in the air. Tuck wasn't slow; he knew something was wrong by the youngin's just being there without Chance. Even worse, the saddened expressions on their faces were enough to alarm him.

Pemont dropped his head. Tuck saw the pain in their eyes. "We need to talk."